ISOLATION

Will she make it out alive?

Jenni Regan

Bella Publishing

Tom

5 November 2018, 6 p.m.

The house was illuminated by flashing lights, turning the quiet driveway into a Vegas Strip of sorts. It was bonfire night, and every so often the sight and sound of colourful explosions would shatter the scene, but in this spot, the lights were provided by the persistent flashing lights of emergency workers, not the flashes of colour in the sky that drew gasps of wonder. It was hard to work out who was doing what, although Tom was sure it was a well-oiled machine. He knew the ambulance was there for the living, but he also guessed that the police's main job at that moment was to deal with the dead.

He had never felt so useless, so impotent, knowing he couldn't take a step into the house that had once been the centre of his universe but which now held many horrors. He longed to take some kind of action, but all he could do was stand with the rest of the bystanders who had turned up to watch this ghoulish spectacle. He looked over at his sister, Rachel; she looked as white as a sheet. He knew she would have similar thoughts, although he now knew the house had been full of terror for her long before any of this happened.

The unkempt look of the house and the garden strewn with rubbish caught on dead plants only added to the appearance of a house of horror.

Suddenly he noticed a flurry of activity as radios alerted various officers to a discovery. He turned to the friendly cop who had been standing with them for most of the afternoon sharing cups of tea and tips for visiting NYC.

'Can you tell me what happened? Have they found something?' he urged.

The cop's whole demeanour had changed. 'Sorry, sir, but someone will come and talk to you as soon as we have more clarity on the incident. I know it's hard, but you need to be patient.'

This was like asking a starving dog to not eat the bowl of food in front of him.

Tom paced while checking online to see if anyone had leaked anything to social media, knowing the journalists standing around probably had contacts in the force. As he paced, he couldn't even meet Rachel's eye. At the moment that they should really pull together, they found themselves wrenched apart again, each caught up in their own private hell of imagining what the search had uncovered and just what on earth had taken place in the home.

Eventually, after what felt like hours, he saw one of the big bosses striding towards them. Considering the way others almost parted to let her through, this woman was obviously high up in the ranks. Instead of a black-and-white uniform, she was wearing a shocking-pink coat, which clashed with her bright-red hair.

Without waiting for her to reach him, Tom rushed straight over. 'What have they found?' he demanded.

She ignored his urgency and put out her hand to introduce herself. 'Mr Carmicheal, I am DCI Kingsley and have been brought in by the CID to lead this investigation. I'm afraid we don't have a full picture yet, but it appears the team has found something of interest: some remains. We will, of course, keep you updated.'

With this, the whole thing stepped up a notch. New cars arrived and people dressed in white suits and hairnets stepped out. Some police officers came out of the house, most looking quite traumatised, and they did a tag team with the men and women in white suits. A young officer put tape near the front gate to show that this was now officially a crime scene. Tom had seen all of this before—not in person but more as a show-and-tell in court where the crime and the victim were just names instead of someone close to him.

Someone produced some hot, sweet tea from somewhere and took Rachel and Tom to sit on the edge of the ambulance.

The presence of this lifesaving vehicle now seemed ironic since whoever they had found was in no need of any medical help.

Eventually another woman came to speak to them. She introduced herself as the family liaison officer and said she was there to bridge the gap between them and the police. Rachel practically jumped on her, asking a hundred questions, most of which the lady couldn't answer yet.

'Let me have a word with the guys over there,' the lady finally said, 'and see what they have found out and what I can tell you. Give me a minute.' She walked away with purpose.

Time felt as though it had slowed almost to a stop. The five minutes that she was gone felt like five hours. She eventually returned with DCI Kingsley who looked almost annoyed that she was being taken away from the real work.

'Listen,' Kingsley said, 'I am going to send you both away soon because we need to excavate what has been found and we don't believe you should see any of that. I know you want to find out more, and I promise that I will do my best to tell you what we have so far.'

She paused and became less business-like. Softer.

'The team has unfortunately found what we believe to be human remains in the basement. They are partly decomposed, meaning it is impossible for us to tell at the moment who they might belong to or how they died.'

'So, how long before you can tell us who it is or what happened?' asked Rachel desperately.

'It could take days, as we will have to run a lot of tests, but we will try to get you some answers as soon as possible. I know this is the last thing you want to hear, and I'm sorry to be the bearer of such news. We will ensure that you get all the support you need in the meantime.'

Tom felt sick. There were so many horrific possibilities flying through his mind. Still, if he kept wishing and praying, even with his hardcore atheism, then maybe, just maybe, the body in there wouldn't belong to Alice.

An image flashed into his mind of Alice being smashed over the head with a hammer or strangled with a rope, and his body could no longer hide its disgust and he was sick all over the withered plants.

Rachel
5 November 2018, 11 a.m. (Earlier that day)

The wakeup call had come early—it had still been dark outside —but Rachel had already been awake. In fact, she hadn't really slept. All night she had felt so helpless. Dark, twisted shadows had crept into the hotel room, snatching her from her dreams and forcing her to wake up as soon as she drifted off even for a minute.

She got dressed quickly and met Tom downstairs. He was knocking back a coffee, and he handed a cup to her. Neither could even think of eating. The smell from the buffet was sickening rather than enticing this time round. The police had called to say they would gain entrance to the house today. That was the last place that Alice's phone had given off a signal—the family house, the home that had once housed Rachel and Tom.

The pair drove over to the house and could almost hear the gossip escaping from every home, school and shop as they drove through the suburbs. Rachel gasped in horror when they arrived. There were at least three police cars, an ambulance and what looked like people in riot gear. What did they expect to find?

The woman they had spoken to on the phone came over to introduce herself. She was cheery but straight-talking. 'Now this might look like an overreaction to a disappearance, but in this day and age, we don't know what to expect.'

Rachel noticed officers were walking around the house, just as she and Tom had, looking for an easy way in. They had already knocked and rung at the door, and they had even tried to shout through the letter box only to find that it had been taped up.

Another officer was looking through the windows and knocking on them. He didn't seem to find anything worth reporting back. The panes of glass looked dusty and smudged.

'Has that piece of shit you have in custody told you anything useful?' Tom asked the woman.

'No, not really. He admits that he and Alice were sexual partners but insists that the last time he saw her was months ago. We are still holding him, though, so please feel reassured that if he has anything to do with this, whatever it is, we will investigate it fully.'

'I don't suppose he told you he abused her on film and shared the film for every pervert around the world to see, did he?'

Rachel gasped; she hadn't known the details.

'Thank you for bringing that to our attention. It is truly horrific. It appears that he has been profiting from a lot of young girls. Thanks to the information you provided, we will be inspecting his growing business empire. You understand it may be hard to prove that these girls haven't consented, but if we find out that any of them are underage, then we will throw the book at him.'

'And what about his fondness for the more extreme ends of the scale? My IT contact told me he had found evidence of snuff movies being made and sold on the dark web. Are you also looking into this?'

'To be honest, we have never discovered a murder carried out in this way in the UK and have every reason to believe those kinds of films are really just an urban myth—at least in this country. But we will, of course, be investigating fully.'

'But how do you know?' Rachel asked. 'There must be plenty of women that go missing every year—prostitutes, drug addicts, women who are sold into modern slavery.' Rachel wondered if this wasn't being considered because this was taking place in the sleepy Dorset countryside rather than a big city.

'We will leave no stone unturned with this young man. Please don't worry.' The female officer appeared to be shutting the conversation down. Rachel guessed they wanted to focus on the here and now and not some hearsay from one of Tom's contacts. She noticed the group of police were regrouping, and the woman was called over.

'Sorry, I have to go. Looks like we will have to resort to Plan B. The house is like Fort Knox. On the plus side, that would have made it very hard for any perpetrator to gain entry.'

Yes, but what good is a security system when evil is invited in rather than breaking in, Rachel thought. She was about to ask what Plan B was when she saw two officers appear with what looked like a battering ram. Upon seeing them, Rachel burst into tears; up to that point, they could all just pretend that it was a wild goose chase, but it was suddenly so real. They don't go smashing down doors unless they are expecting to find something bad inside.

She watched through her hands as a group of officers ran towards the front door. Each time they crashed the battering ram into the door, she could hear a crack that made her wince. Finally, with an almighty bang, the door fell as gracefully as an oak tree. They were in.

Alice

I didn't always post pictures of my food—I wasn't one of those In-stagram wankers who would carefully style every morsel, watching the salad wilt and the eggs go cold while getting the perfect shot—but a well-presented dish could always guarantee a few likes. Likewise, people apparently liked to hear about my dreams and what I thought of last night's TV. This is why I usually found myself eating with one hand, phone in the other.

Of course, I would rarely share what was really on my plate; clean eating was all the rage, after all, unless I had been out the night before and was nursing a hangover. There were so many hashtags involved in hangover-style fry ups, it was too good an opportunity to miss.

This was how I had first met Stan. He had liked and commented on a particularly beautiful eggs benedict I had posted up following a wild all-nighter in a club. I had been wary when I looked at his feed—full of cars he obviously couldn't afford and stupid memes about smoking weed—but he was undoubtedly a looker, and within a few days of him complimenting my every move and look, I was hooked.

He loved the idea of having a girlfriend who was also an airhostess, and I loved to tell him about all the places I visited, tagging him in posts about beaches and bars and privately sending him pictures of my boobs. It was the latter that he was a bit obsessed with, always begging for me to send pictures. Often, I couldn't be bothered, so I picked a few randoms from Google with similar skin tones in a bid to keep him satisfied. He seemed more than happy to show me his; indeed, most messages would involve either a dick pic or a few well-placed aubergine emoticons. My gran had always said that boys were obsessed with their bits, and Stan was a perfect example.

Of course, there were other men who messaged me wanting to hook up, and with the world at your fingertips, there is no need to stick to just the one, but Stan was special somehow. He was so attentive, he made me feel like a princess. In fact, he was the most charming man I knew.

Tom

4 November 2018, 2 p.m. (The day before)

Rachel realised almost immediately that it was her daughter in the film, even though it had been years since she had laid eyes on her.

She turned to her brother. 'It's the same bloody curtains! I mean, they must be rotting by now. It's Alice, isn't it?'

'We don't know for sure,' Tom said, trying to reassure her.

'Well, I know. I know because it was me in that room, staring out night after night, trying to count the number of blue flowers on each curtain or making up little characters for each of the flowers . . . anything to take me away from the horror of the situation.'

'Rach, I will have to watch this, you know. We need to know if it holds any clues.'

Tom turned the screen to face him and punched in his credit card, sickened that he was now apparently supporting this low-life scum financially. His eyes were drawn to some comments below. Some were commenting how bigger was better, but others were abusing the woman in the film and calling her a pig.

He felt even more sick as he pressed play. He could immediately hear *the monster's* voice telling her what she should be doing. Tom realised very early on that this was not something Alice had done before, willingly or not. There was pain and confusion in her eyes, and she was constantly trying to hide her body. Scared of what might be coming next, Tom stopped the film and quickly closed down the site.

He walked off quickly, and Rachel went to the bar for a couple of medicinal brandies. When Tom returned smelling of smoke, he grabbed his drink greedily and drank it down in one shot.

'I haven't had a smoke for about ten years, you know, but it really is that kind of day.'

'So, it's bad then? Do you think I should watch it?' Rachel asked.

'No need, Rach. It is probably what you imagine: girl being taken advantage of and filmed by a disgusting sexual predator.'

'But it doesn't explain what has happened to her. After all, he is obviously making a few quid out of this film, so why would he harm her?'

Tom silently typed a site into his phone and held it up for Rachel. She read it, puzzled.

'What the fuck is this? Some kind of sick joke?'

'No, and I didn't want you to know about this at all, but one of my colleagues in the New York office has been digging for me. I don't know if you are aware of the dark web, but it is the horrid side of the internet. You can get all sorts on there. Guns, drugs, sex.'

Rachel nodded. 'So, what is this? Some kind of sick fantasy porn?'

'Well, no. Sadly, he says there is evidence that some of the women being abused and killed in these videos are *actually* murdered; it is not just some badly directed slasher movie. Apparently, they are a growing thing in other parts of Europe, but more dubious porn peddlers have got into them in this country.'

'So does this Stan have links?'

'Not that I have found yet but look at the stuff he sells.' He flashed her the site. 'It is all disgusting, and look at that car he was driving when we met him. That wasn't bought with the profits of a few soft-focus movies.'

'So, you think this Stan man may have somehow used Mum's house as some kind of studio for his sick film? Shit, Tom, this all sounds so ridiculous.'

'I know, and I hope I am wrong, but why else would Alice have disappeared off the face of the earth? And why the hell was she back in her gran's house when we know that she was living the dream life in Bournemouth?'

Tom left Rachel at the bar and went off to make a phone call to a private detective who had come recommended by one of his more dubious legal clients. In many ways, he hoped the detective wouldn't find what he was dreading to see, but it was clear they needed someone who was more useful than the actual police force.

Alice

I didn't just use my laptop for silliness and sexting. I loved the way I could keep in touch with hundreds of my friends with so little effort. No matter where I was in the world, I could share everything about my trip, down to the hotel view. My gran used to tell me that in her day the best anyone got was a postcard, which wasn't even a selfie but rather some random view highlighting whichever strange foreign country you were in. She used to have a few yellowing cards stuck to her fridge door from various friends. I used to find them fascinating as a child, as it gave a little glimpse of the world outside my sleepy hometown. Maybe it was this that inspired my love of travel. Sadly, I don't think my gran ever made it further than Torquay.

I did feel guilty about that. At the time of her life when so many of her friends were off on cruises or taking up exciting hobbies, my gran was at home looking after me. While her friends were sharing photos and enjoying occasional days out with their grandchildren, she was feeding and clothing me every day, acting as good cop, bad cop, nurse and chef.

The internet also meant you could be whoever you chose to be, and a few times a week I became Tania. Tania was thirty-seven, had three kids and came from Birmingham. She loved karaoke and holidays in Spain. Unlike my actual profile, Tania only had a handful of friends in contrast to the hundreds I had racked up.

Logging on to Tania's profile, I was excited to see that Rachel had been online only three minutes ago. This meant there was bound to be something fresh up there. I was rewarded by finding out that Rachel had to get the car fixed that morning. Pleased to see that no one had commented yet, I quickly liked the status and started thinking of a clever comment. As always, I had to try a few in my head before committing.

Fingers crossed, my old rustbucket cost me an arm and a leg last time I went! LOL

In my head, Tania drove an old clapped-out Ford with a leopard-print steering wheel and some kind of funny sticker in the back window—

something I would never be seen dead in, of course.

I could see that Rachel was online, and I almost held my breath while the minutes ticked away, but it was all worth it when I finally saw her reaction. It was only a simple like, but nonetheless, she had noticed me—well, this version of me.

Rachel was thirty-nine, lived in London, had two young kids and had a boyfriend named Dave. She worked as a teaching assistant and often moaned about her job. Rachel spent a lot of time playing games involving digital prizes on Facebook, which was what Rachel and Tania had bonded over despite living worlds apart. Tania had given Rachel a precious frog for her game, and the two had quickly become online buddies.

Rachel was also my mother.

I had come up with Tania a few months before when I was reading a story about women paid to be people's online girlfriends. This could have been an interesting sideline for me, considering the amount of time I spent with my head in my iPad, but it was what it had sparked in me that was of real interest.

No matter how much my gran had tried to look after me, I had always been curious about my mum—a case of wanting what I couldn't have, I guess. Knowing all contact was banned from either side in real life, the idea of Tania took shape. It was a way to find out all about my mum without upsetting anyone. There had been a few false starts —after all, Rachel had changed her name—and I must admit I had expected to find a monster. My mother had become an evil, dark being in my mind over the years. The vision was fuelled by comments from my gran and half-remembered truths. Instead, I was pleasantly surprised when I'd finally come across the pretty and friendly Rachel. She made me laugh and was a confident and encouraging online presence.

Rachel had two girls aged nine and seven who were obviously the apple of her eye. I sometimes found myself feeling jealous when I saw the new outfits she gave to them or read about their latest scrape, but before going into a downward spiral full of resentment, I would remind myself that these were actually my sisters. Instead of feeling bitter, I would be the big sister by liking every time Rachel posted a family snap. In my lower moments, I would dream about revealing all, hoping for a family reunion where Rachel could proudly boast about my every move, but I knew this would hurt my gran too much. Somehow having access to all their family information made me feel closer to them, and I would content myself with pretending I was the cool older sister and dream daughter.

The fact that Rachel had a new family made me think it was me that was the problem, not her. I had always been told that she had been estranged from me and the rest of the family because she had done some really awful things and was unable to look after me, but when looking at her picture-perfect life now, this didn't appear to be the case. She seemed like a pretty good mum. But I guess I know as much as anyone that a family can look perfect on the outside but corrupt to the bone on the inside.

I was looking through some new pictures that Rachel had posted of a family day out when I noticed my stomach was rumbling. My little inbuilt body clock was telling me it was time for elevenses, another of my gran's little routines I had taken on. I loved the whole routine: filling up the teapot to the line, pouring the milk into the jug with a slight chip in the lip and above all putting all the biscuits on the plate. It always had to be the best cup and saucers. Mugs were for builders.

Stan

4 November 2018, 11.05 a.m.

Well, that's the last time I ask anyone for help, thought Stan as he slammed the phone down. Why had that weird American guy given him his details if he was then just going to shout at him? Maybe he was having a bad day. After the last set of questioning, Stan had decided that he needed a lawyer. He also needed his mum but wasn't sure if he would get laughed out of the station if he asked for her.

After about half an hour, he was led from his cell into the horrible questioning room where they were joined by a worried-looking young man in a cheap, shiny suit. Stan nearly swore when the young man introduced himself as the duty solicitor. He didn't look old enough to buy beer let alone save Stan from prison.

'So, Stan,' the questioning officer said once they were all seated, 'you were telling us about your relationship with Ms Carmichael. Can you give us a few more details like how and when you met?'

Stan couldn't work out who they were talking about for a moment. 'Oh, you mean that girl Alice? I wouldn't really call it a relationship. She booty called me once. But we had got friendly before we met.'

'So, you travelled all the way down from your home in Brixton to see her in Dorset? Are we supposed to believe you did this because she had promised you sex? Surely there are easier ways of getting laid.'

Stan privately agreed with him, especially now, but he didn't want to appear uncaring. 'I guess she is a special girl, so I went the extra mile.'

'So you drove down there and had sex with her. Can you tell us how you then ended up with this stolen bank card? For the purposes of the tape, I am now showing the CCTV inside the Natwest branch in Dorchester Town Centre that appears to show Mr Crane.'

Stan was surprised to see how nervous he looked on the screen as he shuffled into view, head down, eyes darting nervously around. He stuck out like a sore thumb. Jeez, he would have arrested himself!

'That's easy; I was doing her a favour. Alice asked me to go into the bank and move money around for her.'

'Why didn't she go herself? After all, she had only just met you. Don't you think it's strange that she handed over the card to you?'

'Yeah, of course it's strange, but then the whole situation was strange. She gave me some sob story about not feeling well.'

'So, the bank has uncovered a clearly forged document giving you the power to act on Ms Carmichael's behalf. Sadly, a lot of these rural branches tend to trust people.'

'Alice gave me that,' Stan quickly said.

The officer looked at him in total disbelief. 'OK, so if she handed it over to you, I'm guessing you went straight back after visiting the bank and gave it to her, right?'

They had him. Up to that point, everything he had said was true to some degree, but this was the sticking point in his plan.

'Well, no, I was called back to London in an emergency.'

'Right, so I guess you posted the card back or went down to hand it back a few days later?'

This was giving Stan a great get out.

'Yep, I sent it but forgot to do that special delivery thing. You know my generation; we don't know what those post-box things are for.' He looked at the mute teenager to his left who was supposed to be offering legal advice but who had been sitting on his iPhone for most of the interview.

The young man looked up from his phone and said, 'You can always say "No comment" to whatever they ask you.' His suggestion was a bit too little too late.

The officer continued with a sly smile on his face. 'Right, Mr Crane, so why is it we have various CCTV shots of you taking money out of cash machines using this card? All in all, we have worked out that you stole nearly fifty thousand pounds. That is a considerable amount of money.'

Even Stan was shocked; he thought it was just a few quid here and there. 'No comment,' he replied, finally exercising his right to remain silent, seeing as his powers of persuasion hadn't got him anywhere.

'So we are playing it that way, are we? Well, it doesn't really matter. We have more than enough to charge you with fraud and theft. The only other issue is to work out why this Alice girl didn't report you. In fact, at this point, we haven't been able to locate Alice.'

Stan looked at his lawyer for some reassuring words but saw him once again looking intently at his phone, probably checking Twitter. Stan sat back in his chair and cursed the day he had ever set eyes on Alice.

Alice

Alice was always so busy that she didn't know where all the hours in the day went. You could see on her profiles what she was up to. Her Insta was mainly for showing off the beautiful views of her travels in her dream job as an airhostess. Facebook was for sharing gossip and maintaining friendships whereas Twitter was a bit more serious. She was not one for news or even politics, but she did like to keep up to date with what was going on in the world, particularly when it came to celebrities!

Alice loved the freedom the online world gave her and how she could curate the life she shared with the world. After all, everyone did it, right? Social media was more like scripted drama than documentary. If everyone showed what was really happening in their lives, it would all be so depressing. This way she found out about news almost instantly, she knew what the issues were in the world and she could find out what she should be supporting and who she should be voting for.

It was also a welcome distraction. Alice had no chance to dwell on the past; after all, it was all about the here and now. As well as sharing her life, she loved a good inspirational quote and knew that others strived to have a life as full as Alice's.

Thankfully her phone and iPad were always there for her. Even when the darkness threatened to creep back into her mind and overshadow her perfect life, she could just cast it aside by immersing herself in her online world.

Rachel

4 November 2018, 11 a.m.

Rachel was well aware by now of the truth of the saying, 'A watched kettle never boils.' She and Tom had been looking at Tom's phone for what felt like hours, hoping for an update. It didn't really make any difference where they were, but they felt unable to leave their hotel room. Rachel had also spent ages looking at Alice's online presence—all the silly things she had posted about lovers, nice holidays and her love of crap TV, just like her mum.

It felt like this was a chance to see what her daughter had become, and she was thrilled with what she saw. She had been so tempted to look Alice up online a number of times, but she knew it wasn't fair on the girl. After all, she guessed that Alice had been fed years of lies about her from her mother who had made it quite clear what would happen if Rachel ever showed her face again.

Rachel glanced up at Tom as soon as the phone rang, expecting to hear an update from the police. Tom snatched it up on the second ring. She could see him looking puzzled and then asking a few questions. He already had a pen and notepad out, and she could see him scribbling down a few notes. She tried to read them, but they were illegible. Then his face changed completely, twisting in anger.

'Are you fucking kidding me?' he shouted into the phone.

'Oh, yes, that is hilarious. You want *me* to help a lowlife scum like *you*? Wow, they say the world is a small place, but this really takes the biscuit.'

Tom went on to shout more abuse into the phone, but whoever was on the other end hung up.

'Ex-partner or ex-client?' Rachel asked in bewilderment. She was even more disturbed when Tom started laughing. It almost sounded like he was crying at first but soon he was practically hysterical.

'You will never guess who that was,' he said between the hysteria. 'Remember my good-Samaritan act outside the kebab shop the other night?'

Rachel nodded, although her memories of that night were a little fuzzy and tinged with sadness.

'The guy that I helped was calling asking for my help.'

'But you gave him your card and told him to get in touch. I don't understand.'

'He has been arrested. For fraud, burglary and possibly even far worse—all against a Ms Alice Carmichael!'

As the two tried to digest the news, Rachel led them both out to a local pub. This one definitely wasn't a gastropub, and she stuck with beer. She knew that she had been drinking more than usual lately. Her drinking was normally under control these days, but this was a difficult time, and no one could blame her for letting her hair down. She knew she would have to get back to looking after herself better when she got home, particularly knowing what she now knew. It wasn't like she would end up in a crack house after a week on wine.

Tom was now filling her in on the conversation that had taken place. 'I mean, he was terribly polite, saying he was sorry for bothering me, but he said they had suggested a lawyer. He told me it was some crazy girl he only met once, and when I wrote down who the charges involved and what had allegedly happened, boom, he named her.'

Tom had already begun his online search to find out all they could about this Stan bloke. They were pleased that the police were taking this seriously but felt they couldn't sit idly by and wait for a lengthy investigation. The social media profiles threw up the usual: London boy obsessed with his car, smoking grass and pussy, in that order. Looking at his thousands of friends, they finally came across Alice's profile.

'That just means they knew each other, not that she was involved with him,' Rachel said quickly, trying to make herself feel better more so than appeasing Tom.

There was little that was interesting apart from when they clicked on the *About* section, which told them he was educated at the 'school of life,' he was a former worker at 'your mum's pussy' but most interestingly he was director of bbxfilms.com.

'Didn't have him down as a creative media type,' said Tom, clicking on the link.

Suddenly his laptop screen was full of pop-ups and red flashing messages. Rachel shouted at him to turn it off in case it was infecting his computer, but Tom knew what this was. His tastes were much classier than this stuff, but he knew what a porn site looked like. Tom clicked to prove he was over eighteen and got rid of the other annoying pop-ups trying to entice him in.

Rachel had never seen this kind of stuff before. She had obviously seen porn—in fact, her ex-husband had been quite into them watching it together—but that had been ordinary porn, where an ugly man hit on a gorgeous woman with some kind of weak storyline and the odd lesbian sex thrown in. This was a whole different world. The site was for people with deviant tastes. She could see from the screen grabs and descriptions that these women had been penetrated in every way possible. The shots also looked like they were bad quality, likely shot with a handheld phone in poor lighting rather than in a nice, lit studio.

Suddenly something caught Rachel's eye. In the main picture, which represented the film rated number one by all the hungry viewers, were some curtains. Rachel knew those curtains because they were the same curtains that had been hanging in her bedroom when she was a child—the room she had hoped she would never lay eyes on again.

Stan

4 November 2018, 10 a.m.

For once, Stan's charm was getting him nowhere. He had pumped hard at the gym and drove home on a high, and then that high had been completely ruined. The police had been waiting for him when he had walked through his front door; his mother was sitting in the kitchen with them. She looked broken, and he wanted to run over and hug her. He wasn't sure exactly why they were there, but he assured her he would sort everything out and went with them willingly. He felt a bit like a gangster in a movie as he sped through the streets in the back of a police car.

When they arrived at the station, the two officers who had brought him in led him through to the scummy interview room, which had no windows and a stained carpet. He accepted a cup of plastic-tasting tea. Although Stan had always brushed with criminality and had been stopped in his car many times, he had never been questioned in a police station before. He wouldn't admit it to anyone, but this scared him.

He was hoping that the hot female officer who had been at the reception desk would be interviewing him. She couldn't hide her tight little body and sexy mouth behind that drab uniform, and he gave her his most intense look that told her exactly what he wanted to do to her.

His fantasy about her and handcuffs was cut short when a man and a woman without uniforms followed him in. The one behind the counter would have been putty in his hands, but these two looked like they wanted to tell him off, and they were more his parents' age.

The older officer started the interview. It seemed like he carried his world-weariness on his shoulders and was probably counting down to the day when he would retire.

'So, Mr Crane, do you know why we have asked you in for a chat today?'

'No idea, mate. Although I do usually get stopped for being a young black guy in a nice car.' Stan felt uncomfortable using the race card seeing as the woman was much darker than him, but maybe it would bond them.

The young woman spoke, and all hopes of solidarity flew out of the window. 'Funnily enough, this does all relate to the stop and search that took place in Deptford High Street last week. I know that method gets a lot of criticism, but sometimes it throws up the odd treat for us!'

Stan stayed quiet.

'So, after we pulled you over, we did some routine checks. We found nothing wrong until you popped up again yesterday in connection with a robbery, fraud and potential murder case.' The cop held up a picture and described it for the tape.

Stan sighed as he realised why he was here. It wasn't for dealing weed or selling a few knock-off items. They had finally caught up with him. The picture was of Alice.

Alice

There were times when I was caught between sleep and wakefulness and my brain didn't get a chance to block the dark thoughts.

It would always start with the smell. It's amazing how memories have a smell, like a rogue piece of food that had escaped in the oven and burned to a crisp or the metal taste of the dentist trying to save teeth from destruction.

This was what I smelt whenever my brain forced me to re-live the disaster.

When I had opened my eyes, it was dark. It must have only been a matter of seconds that I had been away from the room. I don't know if I had passed out or if my body had forced my window to the world to shut, perhaps to save me from the horror.

The scene had completely changed.

In its place was a dark world full of twisted metal and screams that were different than the screams of the hungry, tired child I had noticed sitting near me before. Those were to gain attention from the mother. These were screams of desperation, pain and shock. There had also been a deathly silence when it first happened, and I wondered, for more than a moment, if this was it—if we had all died and this was now my hell. For this, I almost welcomed the howls.

At first, I hadn't felt a thing, and I wondered how I had escaped this when I could see the twisted bodies and blood all around me, but then the pain started—a throbbing in my leg, a knife between my shoulders, the feel of liquid seeping down my face.

And then I was frozen, stuck to my spot on the floor as people moved around me. I wanted to get up, move away from the death and destruction, find help, give help, even start recording this, but there was no way my body would move. All control was whisked away from me. I was a pawn in a much bigger game.

So I sat and waited, watching the scene in front of me unfold as though it was yet another emergency medical drama or fly-on-the-wall documentary. It followed the formula, and eventually there were people in uniforms amongst the bloody and the broken. People were there to take control, to assess, to help.

Apparently, I didn't speak the entire way to hospital. I knew I was one of the lucky ones. Many hadn't escaped with their lives that day, but somehow this sent me into a prison, in my mind at least, one I almost wish I had escaped from instantly in a body bag rather than being catatonic in an ambulance.

At least at the hospital there was tea.

Tom

3 November 2018, 3 p.m.

Tom was sorting out his already spotless hotel room when he got a phone call from his new copper pal.

'Hello, Mr Carmichael. After I spoke to you last and you told me about your mother being dead, I did more probing, and we have uncovered something a bit strange.'

Tom frowned in concern, although strange was good in his book for now. 'In what way?'

'It appears that someone has been taking money from your mother's account, but it wasn't Alice. Let's just say we have a person of interest we are trying to locate!'

Tom couldn't quite get his head around it all.

'You mean that someone has robbed my mum?' He tried to feel some anger, but in reality, he really didn't care if his mum had been the victim of robbery.

'We don't know for sure yet, but our investigations threw up some unanswered questions, and we would like to question someone. I am liaising with my friends in the Met, and they are sending people to the address in question.'

'That's good news, I guess. Can you tell me anything more about this person?'

'Not yet, unfortunately. We will tell you more if we decide to charge him.'

Tom was about to hang up and relay the conversation to Rachel when the officer asked a final question.

'One other thing, Mr Carmichael. You mentioned that your mother had passed away. Do you have any more details about how and when this happened? We have tried to find her death record but have failed to locate it at this point in time. This isn't unheard of, but it could show something slightly darker than just some fraudulent withdrawals. It could even show that your mother has been harmed intentionally and that the injury or death was unreported. Or, looking on the bright side, it could mean that your mother isn't actually dead, in which case she potentially becomes a missing person.'

'This may sound silly, but we only found out by looking on Alice's Twitter feed where she described the funeral. We couldn't find the death record using the site we paid for.'

'So you were informed of your mother's death through a tweet?' He sounded unbelieving.

'I know it sounds terrible, but the truth is, we haven't been in touch with our mother for years. You could say we are a pretty messed up family. Alice had lived with my mother, and I had kept in touch with Alice but had totally missed this information until it was too late, and then we stopped being able to contact Alice.'

'I guess it would be a strange thing for someone to lie about, so we will keep an open mind. Did you say you have been to the house also? Is the house significant to you?'

'Yes, it is where we grew up—me and Rachel in our hugely flawed unhappy family.'

Rachel glanced at Tom with a warning stare. If he was too negative about their mother, they might find themselves under suspicion.

Tom felt as though this was all the wrong way round and that it should be the police telling him this. The police should be the ones investigating.

'Yes, we have been a couple of times but there is no sign of life. It looks like it has been abandoned for a while.'

'OK, thanks. We will see how we get on with our person of interest, and if he sheds no light on the whereabouts of Alice or her grandmother, then we will send officers over to look inside.'

Tom didn't like how the conversation had gone, going from a

young girl nicking a few quid from her dead grandmother's bank account to what he could only presume was a possible murder scene. Who may have been murdered and who may be the perpetrator were unclear at the moment.

Tom

3 November 2018, Midday

The trouble with the internet was that it was such a huge un-policed site. Moments after he saw the *Just Giving* page set up to honour Alice's apparent demise, the news had spread like wild-fire, with tributes coming in from around the world and even #RIPAlice trending in the area. He called the police immediately, using the direct line he had been given. As soon as he had got through to his contact, he started shouting.

'Why is it we are finding about Alice's death through the god damn internet? Surely you could have had the decency to inform her family first. I have reported her missing on two separate occasions, and you definitely have my contact details.'

'Sir, can you calm down and tell me what this is about?' the officer calmly responded. 'You can probably guess it has been a very busy time for us here.'

'This is Tom Carmichael. I spoke to you days ago about my missing niece Alice, who may have been caught up in the Bourne-mouth attack. In fact, I have been speaking to your officers over the past two months. However, you not only told me that this wasn't the case but further that there was little you could do to help because of her age.'

The penny seemed to drop for the officer, and he could hear her tapping away on a keyboard.

'Then today I find out that not only was she actually killed but that a whole load of really kind strangers have raised over twenty grand to give her a good send-off.'

He could hear more tapping and a deathly silence.

The officer's voice finally returned. 'Sorry, Mr Carmichael, I wanted to double-check a couple of things. We haven't released any more names of people caught up in the attack. We have located everyone now, and I am pleased to say that I can confirm, beyond doubt, that Alice is not amongst them.'

Tom almost collapsed onto the chair behind him, and Rachel immediately thought the news had been confirmed.

The woman continued kindly. 'Look, sadly there are a lot of horrible people out there who will stop at nothing to make a few quid—those who exploit situations like this for their own gain. We will look into this for you and get this page shut down. Is there any reason that Alice would have been targeted in this way?'

'Well, I did put feelers out for her, saying she was missing,' Tom said, suddenly embarrassed that his concern could have triggered this.

'Don't worry, we know of at least ten other cases similar to this from this attack alone. Usually they are people who are not even alive or at least not living anywhere near the attack. The trouble is we often have problems prosecuting people as they are hidden behind their desktop somewhere in a remote part of the world. But we will get it shut down as soon as we can.'

Tom was about to hang up when the officer spoke again. 'You mentioned before that it was Alice and her grandmother you were looking for. Have you had any luck using any of the lines of enquiry I suggested?'

'We found out that my mother had died, but it as if Alice has disappeared off the face of the Earth. If I hadn't had spoken to her a couple of weeks ago, I would have doubted that she had existed.'

'I'm so sorry to hear about your mother and that you have had no success with Alice. Considering the current situation and the page you have found, let me see if there is any more we can do here. Will you leave it with me?'

As soon as Tom got off the phone, another terrible thought crossed his mind. What if Alice was actually behind this terrible fundraising? After all, she had practically begged him for money for her birthday. He hated himself for having these thoughts and not being grateful and relieved that she hadn't been shot in cold blood by a murdering extremist, but he couldn't get away from the fact she had lied to him about his mum.

He quickly turned to hug Rachel, pushing his horrific theories to one side. 'It's OK, Rach, it was a hoax—someone trying to make a few quid. She definitely didn't die in Bournemouth.'

The two were on such a rollercoaster together, they wanted to sit it out and draw breath, but the uncertainty was pushing them forwards. They had no idea where this particular ride would end.

After lunch, they checked into a nicer hotel, one that was faceless and corporate enough for them to feel invisible. They had discussed heading back to London after spending a wasted day getting no further in their search, but they both felt as though they should stick around. Tom had phoned his office and extended his compassionate leave, giving his mum's death as a reason, and Rachel told her ex and current partner that they would have to deal with things without her for a while.

Their first visit of the afternoon was to the bank on the high street where their mother had banked when they were children, and since she was very set in her ways, they hoped she had continued to bank there until her death. They were also hoping that Alice had followed in her footsteps.

Once they arrived, they asked to speak to the manager, hoping they wouldn't have to make an appointment. Luckily, this seemed to still be a bank with a human face, and the manager emerged a few minutes later and ushered them off into a side room. Tom recognised him immediately as the same man who had been behind the counter when he was a child and used to come in to deposit his very rare pocket money. The fact he had only ever saved enough to get one of the deliciously kitsch piggybanks they handed out was testament to how tight his parents had been. Still, in a way, it had driven him, and he was out earning as soon as possible. He actually still had the ugly ceramic pig in his apartment and threw his loose cents in there.

The manager was, of course, a lot older now, with half-moon glasses and a bald head disguised badly with a comb-over, but he still looked like a kind man.

'Good afternoon. I am Mr Williams, the manager of this branch. How can I help you?'

'We are trying to find my daughter who is missing and wondered if we could ask you a few questions,' said Rachel.

'Oh, I am so sorry to hear that. Of course I will help if I can. Did she use this bank?'

'Well, we are not certain,' Rachel admitted. 'She lived with her grandmother, Josie Carmichael, for many years, and we really hope that *she* was still banking here.'

There was a sudden flash of recognition. 'Of course. You are Mrs Carmichaels' kids! I thought I recognised you. I never forget a face! Even though it must be, what, twenty-odd years? Remind me of your names?'

'I'm Tom and this is Rachel,' explained Tom smiling, secretly pleased.

'Oh yes, little Tom and Rachel. I used to see you come in here during the school holidays with your mum and your little books. Tell me, are you still good savers now?'

'I am, but it's all automatic now, so it just gets scooped away each month before I notice it,' said Tom proudly, flashing back to the earnest ten-year-old he had been.

Rachel blushed and Tom guessed that she had little disposable income let alone savings. This was like being back at school.

'Oh yes, everything is automatic now, which makes it a lot easier, I guess, but I still think it meant more when you had to come in and hand it over in person,' Mr Williams said wistfully. 'Anyway, how is Mrs Carmichael? We haven't seen her in ages. One of our best customers, she is; never signed up to any internet or even telephone banking. She was in here like clockwork every

Thursday. Prefers the human touch. We haven't seen her for a few months though. I hope everything is OK?'

Tom and Rachel looked at each other in surprise. 'Actually, she died a few weeks ago,' Tom said. 'We thought you would know this. We actually wondered if Alice Carmichael, my niece and Rachel's daughter, had an account here. It's her we are trying to find.'

'Oh gosh, I am so sorry to hear that. What a shame. She was such a lovely woman—always had the time for a chat. I'm sure the accounts have been closed, but that often happens through some faceless call centre, so we may not have been told directly.'

'And Alice?' Tom prompted.

'I do remember Mrs Carmichael bringing in her granddaughter a few times when she was quite young. How old would she be now?'

'Twenty-one. I mean, twenty-two,' answered Rachel.

'Well, I haven't personally seen her in here for years, but she probably has one of those new-fangled internet accounts. I can check for you if you like.'

'That would be great,' answered Rachel.

The manager left the room, and when his investigation seemed to take hours, Tom and Rachel joked that he must be going through a filing cabinet letter by letter. Finally, he opened the door.

'We can see that Ms Carmichael had a savings account here that, in fact, a Thomas Carmichael had set up. I guess that is you?' He looked towards Tom who had completely forgotten that he had done this and had therefore neglected to pay into it for years. 'However, after taking a quick look, it doesn't look like she has touched it for a good five years. I suppose she must have gone to a rival bank that probably offered free CDs or something!' It was clear from this assumption that poor Mr Williams didn't have much contact with young people.

'OK, thank you so much. I guess there are no clues here then.' Tom collected his belongings.

'No, I'm sorry. I hope you find her. You know what kids are like though; they are in a world of their own. My daughter was forever running away when she was a kid. Now she would love to run away from her own kids!' Tom and Rachel smiled at the joke and immediately felt sorry for his grandkids who probably received yoyos and wooden toys for presents each year.

'There was something strange though. You said your mother passed away in August, but the account is still active and has been used since then. Of course, it is often the last thing people think about when a loved one passes, but legally, on death, the money in the account goes into probate, so it shouldn't really be touched. Anyhow, now that you have told me, I will need you to bring in her death certificate so I can put a stop to the accounts and the card.'

'This has been really useful,' Tom said. 'Thank you so much for your time, Mr Williams, and it was really nice to see you again.' Tom handed him a business card and shook his hand.

They were almost through the front door when he called out to them. 'I forgot to say also that I spoke to Lisa behind the till, and she told me she knew your mum was ill because her nephew came in to do some of her banking a while ago and said she was in hospital. I'm only sorry we forgot to send fruit or a card!'

'Does she mean her niece? That was probably Alice then,' said Tom, thinking this was actually the first sighting they had of her in the real world.

'Oh, yes, that is probably what she means. A bit forgetful, that Lisa. I was taking my wife to the hospital for her hip that day, or I would have remembered. I never forget a face!'

Tom and Rachel thanked him again and set off out the door.

Alice

As well as sharing the shinier side of life, the online world was also an occasional source of support for me—not that this was ever public. As I knew more than most, even people with picture-perfect lives on the surface had their demons.

I had found incredible support groups dealing with all sorts where I could be anonymous. Grief, trauma, abuse, even addiction, although that wasn't really relevant—well, not directly. I was mainly a bystander, watching and quietly supporting as others poured their hearts out. It actually made me feel better, even though I never had to talk about anything. Talking would mean opening many cans of worms. As a family, we liked to keep it all locked away.

That didn't mean I didn't share my feelings with my online friends. They knew when I was happy, sad, annoyed or angry. But this was the sanitised version, presented up with a cool gif and relevant hashtag. No one wanted to know what had really happened over the years. Well, no one had really cared up until now.

Rachel

1 November 2018, 11 a.m.

Rachel had enjoyed the buffet—she was such a sad cow that she still got a thrill out of 'free' food—but as soon as she had wolfed her plate down, she felt an instant wave of nausea. She could no longer put this one off. She had made excuses of tummy bugs, hangovers and even dodgy kebabs in the last few weeks, but she knew what this was.

She wasn't really one for religion, but the guilt side still shone through occasionally, drilled in through draughty churches and serious teachers all those years ago. Was this god trying to punish her? She had lost her firstborn, possibly forever. Her relationship was at a breaking point, and she was worried she may have discovered something terrible about her partner, and it was NOW she was *blessed* with a pregnancy.

For now, she was happy to put her head in the sand. With the others, she hadn't shown until she was at least three months gone. If she could keep her sickness hidden, no one would know at this point, nor did they need to, at least until she knew what she would do. She made the best of rinsing her mouth out in the hotel toilet and headed back out to join her brother with a fixed smile on her face.

Tom was dubious that Rachel's car would make it as far as Dorset. It seemed to have become even more rusty and decrepit since the last trip from the airport. It was a rare warm autumn day, and he opened the window, guessing that air conditioning hadn't been invented yet when the car was made.

'You Americans love your icy cold fake air, don't you?' Rachel joked.

'I hate to make you look stupid, but I was not actually born in America. I'm still British through and through. Although, yes, air con is one of the modern miracles in life.'

As they drove, Tom told her about a couple of road trips he had taken on wide, straight roads where you could switch on the autopilot and watch as mountains turned into desert right outside your window.

Rachel was agitated; she had gone over her usual caffeine allowance already that day, but that wasn't causing the jitters. The last time she had made the journey down towards her family home, she had been driving into the unknown, with the fear that her mother and daughter would reject her, yet again. Now, she knew her little girl needed her more than ever. This time she couldn't wait to get there.

They arrived in Dorchester around lunchtime. Neither of them wanted to eat after the huge breakfasts and nerves, but they didn't really know where to start so they parked up and went in search of a decent café. They ended up in a Costa. They were equally relieved and horrified that such a symbol of globalisation had reached their home town. They both ordered a limp panini and yet more coffee and settled in at a table.

'I guess we should make a plan,' said Rachel, hoping that this was the point where Tom would take over. He duly got his pen and paper out.

'We need to work out where Alice goes and who she speaks to,' he stated.

'I have no idea. Did she not tell you?' Rachel asked.

'No details. She always seemed to be busy and out having fun, but she never mentioned specifics. Let's start with some facts.'

Rachel laughed at him as he drew an awful stick figure with long hair in the middle of a page in his notepad and started some sort of diagram.

'Hang on a minute, Tom. Shall I get you some crayons to colour this in? Are you going to draw your way out of this mess?'

Tom ignored her and continued drawing. 'This is actually a well-researched way of getting the ideas flowing. It's called a mind map. Now what do we know about her?'

'You told me she lives in Bournemouth. Does she live alone or with other young people?'

'She has a little one-bedroom flat, near the town centre. Apparently, she is the one to host the after-party when she and her mates go out drinking.'

'Have you ever been there?'

'No, but she only moved in there a couple of years ago, and I haven't been back from the States for so long—no reason to, really.'

Rachel looked hurt, but then she hadn't exactly been inviting him over with open arms. He hadn't gone to her wedding or met her other children before now.

'Here, she sent me some pictures a while ago.'

Rachel looked at the pictures, which looked amazing if not a bit too perfect, almost like they had been lifted from an *Interiors* magazine.

'I am surprised she can live there alone. I mean, most young people can't afford to leave home these days. It's actually nicer than where I live.'

'Rents are much cheaper down here and apparently she got a really good deal from some old dear who didn't know market rates. Remember, her job probably pays pretty well too.'

'I know, I can't believe she is an air hostess! When I was at school, it was the height of sophistication, although I guess these days it is more serving lots of stag parties overpriced booze and dealing with pensioners trying to get their oversized bags in the lockers.'

'She must work for one of the good ones like Emirates or even BA, as she always seems to be on long haul flights,' said Tom.

'You mean you don't actually know who she works for?' Rachel asked with a frown.

'Do you?'

This shut her up.

'Did she come and visit you in New York a lot then?' she asked.

Tom looked uncomfortable. 'Well, no, I was always inviting her, but she never seemed to come through the States.' He suddenly felt a bit foolish. He had been so caught up in his own life that he had never really pushed Alice on this.

'Let's look through her Facebook again and see if she has any pictures of her in her uniform. I mean, whoever she works for must have realised she is not turning up for work, right?'

Rachel looked through what seemed like hundreds of pictures of Alice's life. There was something strange about it.

'There are literally no pictures with her in them, apart from her profile picture. I thought young people were obsessed with selfies these days.'

'How nice that your daughter is more excited about the world around her than she is about sharing her own face!'

'But that's it. She seems to document literally every second of her life, but it is always her viewpoint and never her. I can't see anything about where she works, or any colleagues. I mean, she mentions a few captains she has apparently woken up with, but no real details.'

'Maybe she doesn't like mixing business with pleasure. Let's have a look through and chart where she has been over the last few months to build up more of a picture.' Tom started another of his mind maps much to Rachel's delight.

It was an odd combination. Mainly Europe, with France seemingly a favourite, but then she would throw in the odd view of a beach in Bali or South America. Rachel noticed that Tom looked upset as Alice seemed to have been in New York at least twice that year without going to visit him.

'Well, it is definitely not Easyjet!' Rachel said.

Tom looked worried.

'Listen, don't be annoyed that she didn't come and see you. She was probably in and out of the country in hours.'

'No, it's not that. It's just that a lot of this doesn't add up. I mean, according to her Facebook, she is all over the place for a few weeks and then nothing for ages. There is no pattern to it. It makes me wonder if this "job" was perhaps a cover-up and that she was actually involved in something dodgy.'

'What do you mean, like she was an international drug smuggler or something? Jeez, Tom, that is quite a leap to make. You have been spending too much time with criminals.'

'I know it is probably stupid, but what if we are worried about the wrong thing? There is nothing to say she couldn't have flown off somewhere after I spoke to her. You never know, maybe she is languishing in some foreign jail or something. I don't suppose they allow Facetime in most.'

Rachel actually brightened at this idea. True, it wasn't really what she hoped for her daughter, but if the choice was between Alice being in some morgue or being in prison, the captivity won out every time.

'Let's go back to your silly drawing. What do we know about her friends or boyfriends?'

'I know she was really popular. I mean, she has nearly 3000 friends, but I can't say I know who she was close to.'

Rachel scanned desperately again through the feed. There were hundreds of entries about her being out in bars, restaurants, the cinema, but she never tagged anyone else, and again, the pictures all seemed to be of Alice's view of the place rather than a view of her group.

'There does seem to be one man who was sniffing around a lot. He looks like a right twat though. Your daughter obviously has no taste, just like her mother!'

Rachel tried to laugh, but after what she had told Tom the other evening, she was reading far too much into everything. Did he think that whatever happened to Alice was all her fault?

He clearly realised what he had said. 'God, I'm sorry, Rach. I didn't mean any harm in that comment. This is all so new to me, and I don't really know what to say most of the time.'

They both looked at the profile Tom had clicked on. It was a man a bit older than Alice, and he stood next to his car, waving a handful of notes while a massive joint hung from his mouth.

'He looks like that bloke you helped the other night, doesn't he?' Rachel noted.

'I imagine there are probably hundreds of men across London who look like that. The car isn't as flashy for this one, so he obviously hasn't robbed enough grannies or sold enough weed!'

'You never know, though; I mean, he is pretty much advertising his love of dope, and you did say you thought she might be flying around the world selling drugs.' Rachel was still clinging to this idea.

'I hope that if she is a drug dealer, then she is at least a bit further up the scale than flogging grass to kids. I would hope that Alice would have better taste!'

They had drawn a blank, and Tom screwed up his pretty map in desperation.

'It is like every bit of her life is on there for us to see and yet we know nothing about her.'

Rachel could see how frustrated Tom was, so she decided to try a different tactic.

'Let's start with Mum, then; she was always a creature of habit. If we can work out where she used to go, then we might find out what happened to Alice. That is, if she wants to be found.'

After their unappetising lunch, the siblings took a trip literally down memory lane. They started at the house, which, as Rachel had reported back, looked very unkempt and abandoned. The rubbish she had seen last time even seemed to have increased and had been joined by a couple of mattresses and a burned-out motorbike. They guessed that it had now become the area's communal dumping ground. They tried all the windows and doors, but it was like Fort Knox. Tom remembered that his mum had been burgled years ago and had therefore paid a small fortune for security. She may have been mean, but people stealing off her annoyed her far more than some silver-tongued salesperson flogging her unnecessary locks. Tom suddenly wondered if the house had been sold or if it was going to be knocked down. Either way, they wouldn't have been told. He mentally added local estate agents to their list.

Next, they drove to the local corner shop, although not local in city terms as it was still a good five-minute drive away. The walk had felt like hours when they were kids. They knew their mum had blessed the day that huge superstores had seduced the British consumers into spending away from the high street, but surely she must have needed the odd pint of milk? The woman behind the counter eyed them wearily. She was primed for the packs of rude, thieving kids that would be invading her soon. While Tom strode straight up to the till, Rachel grabbed him back and moved around the aisles, filling her arms with shopping. She had been in crappy retail jobs before and knew they should offer up something in return for information.

When she finally walked up to the till, Rachel smiled and said, 'Hi, so have you worked here long?' The woman looked unnerved, as if she was not used to polite chit chat and was immediately suspicious of 'outsiders' in case they were trying to sell her something.

'Me and my brother used to live round here; we are just having a good look around our old area.'

With this new information, the woman looked a little more comfortable and even made eye contact as she rang up the random goods.

'We are actually back because our mum sadly passed away.

Don't suppose you knew her? Josie, about five foot one with a big mouth and a permanent fag on the go?'

'Oh yes, dear old Josie! I wondered what had happened to her. She used to pop in every Wednesday and Saturday for the lottery and chocolate. Always had an opinion, your mum!'

Tom and Rachel smiled like the doting children they were pretending to be.

'That's strange because I usually know most of what goes on around here, but I hadn't heard she had died. Was it recent?'

'It was about a month ago,' Tom said solemnly, not giving away the fact they didn't actually know how or when she had gone.

'I don't suppose she ever brought her granddaughter Alice in here or sent her over to buy bits and bobs?' asked Rachel, trying to keep the desperation out of her voice.

'Oh yes, little Alice, she was the little plump one, right? Lovely young lady, always had good manners; she loved her sweets, that one!'

'So, you know her?' Rachel said with relief.

'I used to, but I haven't seen her for years. I presumed she had moved away. Josie never really mentioned her; used to complain about the unfit mother though. Right old junkie apparently!'

Thankfully, the woman hadn't put two and two together, but Rachel still bristled with this former label she would never shed.

'So, you don't know where Alice is then?' said Tom, losing patience.

'No, sorry, like I said, I haven't seen her for years. Funny, she used to come in for her gran's fags, but I haven't seen her since she could legally do that!' Tom thought about reporting this woman to the police for selling tobacco to underage kids but realised he had bigger fish to fry. They made their excuses and left with a cheap plastic bag full of snacks and vile-coloured drinks.

It was much the same story everywhere they went. Most knew Josie and were surprised to hear she had died, and most also remembered Alice but hadn't seen her for many years. That was understandable; after all, Alice had moved out around two years ago, and before then, what teenager wants to be seen with their ageing gran? The sad thing was that Josie herself seemed so forgettable. Those that had known her had a couple of good anecdotes about her, but no one had really missed her. They also had yet to meet anyone who had attended this apparently packed funeral.

They had been to all the estate agents in town and none seemed to be selling the family home, nor had any of the funeral directors conducted the funeral. They still had a couple to visit, where the managers had been away. They had also not made it in time to the bank where they guessed their mum still banked; she was a creature of habit. Both feeling frazzled and emotional, they headed to the B&B where Tom had made a hurried reservation that morning.

'Funny how a lot of my colleagues would queue up to stay in a place like this. They would think it was so quaint,' said Tom as they arrived at his door. Each room had its own character with ornaments and reproduction art on the walls. His room, number five, had a Da Vinci theme, although the Sunflowers definitely looked a bit droopy.

They had been shown the breakfast room on arrival but were certain there would be no buffet in sight. Tom and Rachel had gone their own way for a couple of hours, as both had calls home to make. Rachel found she was nervous as she called her partner Dave. She had only left him that morning and yet it already felt like there were miles between them. She guessed that geographically there was, although the actual distance was not the problem. She knew she felt like this even in the same room.

He answered after a few rings, sounding like he had just woken up.

'Please tell me you are not sleeping at five in the afternoon?' shouted Rachel. She knew he would think she was overreacting. He was always blaming her for nagging him these days, but his whole routine had gone downhill since he lost his job.

'Oh, hello to you too, babe. I was just having a little nap. I must have fallen asleep in front of the TV.'

'I wanted to check that the kids made it to their dad's alright,' she said bluntly, disappointment oozing out of every pore.

'I guess so. I don't know, didn't you arrange for him to pick them up from school?'

'Yes, but I thought you would at least call to make sure they are OK. They do have phones now after all.'

'But you told me to take their phones off them before they went to school.'

Rachel almost screamed at him. 'But I didn't mean today when I knew they would be going to stay with their dad for a few days. How am I supposed to check up on them now and make sure they are safe?'

'I guess by phoning their dad like a normal human and asking to speak to them that way.'

'You will have to go round there and drop off the phones.'

'No bloody way. You have the car and it will take me an hour on the bus.'

'God, you are so selfish. Do you really not care what happens to them?'

'Rachel, I really don't understand you. Most of the time you tell me I am too close, too nice to our children, and yes, how you love reminding me they are not my flesh and blood, and now you have suddenly become the overreactive parent. I don't know what I should do half the time.'

He wasn't angry; he just sounded frustrated. She knew she shouldn't fly off the handle, at least not now while she was so far away. God knows what he might do.

'Listen, why don't you give the kids a call on their dad's phone tonight—you probably won't even have to deal with him—and then I will head over there in the morning. I can get my sister to give me a lift.'

'OK, that would be good.'

'How are things anyway? Have you sorted all the family stuff out or are you going to need a couple of days?'

At this rate, Rachel thought it would take years to sort out this mess, but she told him she hoped to be back in a few days. Maybe, just maybe, she might sit the kids down then and tell them all about their big sister. That was if they could work out what had happened to her.

Although the B&B offered a dinner service, they had made a mutual, unspoken decision that they would eat out when offered this choice. The smell of frying liver permeating the reception area would have swung it even without the claustrophobic tables and their starchy table clothes. They wandered over to a pub they had visited earlier that day, one they remembered from their own childhood. Back then it had been a proper pub with drunk men at the bar, but these days it was far more about the food.

Without asking, Tom ordered a bottle of pinot at the bar when he grabbed menus.

'Actually, I was going to have sparkling water,' said Rachel as he placed it down on the table.

Tom stood up to head back to the bar, but seeing the lovely looking wine changed Rachel's mind, even though she knew she should stick to the water. 'I was only joking!' she said, grabbing him. 'I think we have more than deserved this today'.

She really didn't want to drink, particularly because of what she had found out that morning but hadn't yet shared with anyone. However, she was aware of how fragile and new their relationship was. She hadn't seen Tom for so many years before this, all thanks to the family being torn apart by their secrets—well, by their mother really forcing them apart. It almost felt like they were at a job interview rather than estranged siblings trying to reacquaint themselves. She poured herself a small glass. She started by pretending to sip it, but it tasted so good she convinced herself that a couple wouldn't do any harm.

As she went to order their chosen potato-and-meat combination at the bar, she left Tom checking his emails. Rachel was heading back when she noticed him drop his phone. The blood drained from his face, and she practically ran to him. The last time she had seen her brother look like this was when their very old cat had been run over. She knew this was something serious.

'What happened?'

'Oh jeez, Rach, I can't believe it. I was so sure she was screwing us over.'

Still white as a sheet, he turned the phone round so she could see. It was a Go Fund Me site, and it was attempting to raise money for the funeral of an Alice Carmichael who had apparently been killed in the Bournemouth terrorist attack, which still hadn't left the world's media. The prime picture on the page was one of her daughter—his niece—taken a few years ago with a big smile on her face and a bow in her hair. The face of an angel.

Alice

I always wondered what my In Remembrance *page would be. There was always the worry, of course, that people may not realise I was dead—after all, I knew how elusive I could be—but I was a prolific presence on all platforms, so I was sure people would realise something was wrong quite quickly.*

I guess just like when, in previous generations, people would think about what they wanted for their funeral, I had the same thoughts about my page. I always made sure that the most flattering picture was my profile pic. Of course, no one really looks like their photos, not with so many editing apps.

I hoped that all the people I had been in contact with would leave a thought, a gif or even a good death quote. Dying seemed to raise people to the level of saints or angels. I didn't really think about the death itself; I just thought about the reaction.

In fact, I have to admit there were times—rare times—when I was feeling lonely or morose that I would think about pretending to be dead for a day or two to see what people really thought about me.

Tom

1 November 2018, 9 a.m.

Tom slept poorly despite the sleeping pill and mini-bar brandy he had used to calm himself down. The streets of London were noisy, and they clearly hadn't heard of double glazing in this hotel. For some reason, Halloween over here suddenly meant fireworks being set off at all hours. It hadn't even been a marked event when he was a kid.

He was feeling jittery after dealing with loud explosions all night, especially after what had happened in Bournemouth. He could imagine there were a lot of people feeling shaken.

He had tried to call his boyfriend, Will, before bed, but Will hadn't picked up, which filled him with dread. He was already awake, thoughts whirring, when Rachel called him.

'All set. My lazy lump of a partner has finally shown some balls and agreed to take the kids to school. Then, my lazy lump of an ex-husband will pick them up later. I also told my school that I have conjunctivitis so I can't possibly go near a classroom, so we are good to go!'

Tom felt like he would be kicking a puppy when he told her later what he now knew. He could sense a fire in Rachel, different from the downtrodden woman who had met him at the airport two days ago. Unburdening herself, spending time with her brother and being on a mission to find her estranged daughter had definitely given her a spring in her step. He felt horrible that he would be the one to crush it.

'Oh, and what was it you wanted to tell me?' Rachel asked.

'It can wait until I see you. Do you want to come and join me for breakfast? They do a great buffet here . . . as many greasy sausages as you can eat!'

Tom was a frequent hotel dweller and had long since lost the childish enthusiasm for the breakfast buffet. He was more of an egg-white-omelette man these days, but a full English with all the trimmings wouldn't hurt for once.

He waited until they had sat down with their bulging plates before he broke the news. He had even piled up the glistening food to a grotesque level to make her feel comfortable. In a way, it was timely given the obsession his mother had in sending everyone off in the morning with a cooked breakfast inside them.

'So, I found something out after our meal that might change a few things. I wanted to tell you in person.'

Rachel looked expectantly, and Tom really didn't know how to break the news to her.

'It seems that Mum has indeed passed away.' Even he cringed at his use of language; he thought he sounded like a vicar.

Rachel showed no emotion. 'I guess we always thought that this could be the case. It's not really a surprise given her lifestyle of fags, fried food and sitting on her beloved sofa. What was it that finally got her?'

'Well, I don't actually know yet. I only found this out through looking at Alice's Twitter feed, of all things.'

Rachel didn't have a clue about Twitter; she was a bit obsessed with Facebook but couldn't understand people updating their every move and thought in just a couple of lines.

Rachel's heart immediately went out to Alice. 'Oh my god, my poor girl; she has had to go through all of this by herself—all the hell of finding funeral directors and getting death certificates—with no support!'

'This might sound strange, but it almost seemed like she enjoyed it! She even posted the outfit she wore to the funeral on Instagram and described literally every second of the service.'

Rachel's maternal instinct had fully kicked in. 'I can't imagine that any of Mum's bitchy old friends were much company; no wonder she turned to her real friends. That's what kids do these days.'

'OK, but why did she blatantly lie on her birthday? I asked her how Mum was, and she told me she was fine. According to this, Mum would have been dead and buried for at least three weeks by then. You think she would mention it.'

'Bullshit, Tom. She knows what kind of relationship we both had with her gran. She probably thought you didn't give a shit. Oh, my poor girl, all alone in the world.'

'I am actually worried that the death might have pushed her to do something to herself. The message I got from one of her Twitter followers yesterday kind of suggested something along those lines. This girl was really concerned because apparently Alice posts at least twenty times a day, but there's been nothing since the funeral.'

Rachel gasped. Tom realised he was scaring her and moved into other territory. 'I think it's much more likely that she has raided Mum's piggy bank and gone on holiday. You know, looking at her Twitter feed, it is as though I never really knew her. She seemed like such a quiet little thing, but really she was always out on the town or on a beach, all while dating inappropriate men.'

'You don't really believe she is capable of that, do you?' Rachel asked.

'Who really knows? After all, she was brought up by that evil witch we called *mother,* so some of that must have rubbed off on her.'

'Well, now we at least have some facts. This means that we need to get down there and find out more. Let's set off and get some answers.'

Alice

It was one of those days when not even funny cat videos could cheer me up.

I had no idea how to deal with grief—real grief—and was feeling so empty and alone.

My grandmother was dead, and I had realised that she wasn't coming back. This was something I hadn't yet made public, and this was probably why I hadn't really accepted the news. Nothing was real until it was out there in the online world. Maybe my way of beginning to grieve was to post it up. Rather than my own memorial page, I could start giving Granny the immortalisation she deserved.

I spent ages thinking up what to say, and I eventually decided I would post on all platforms for maximum efficiency. It was difficult to know exactly how to say it; after all, this was probably the most important thing that had happened in my life up until now.

Absolutely devastated that my granny has passed away, words cannot describe how much she meant and how much I will miss her #tragicday

I thought this sounded dramatic enough; after all, one of my online friends had lost a cat a week earlier, and the mourning and sympathy was still going strong—not that I was looking to milk it. As expected, I didn't have to wait long before the messages flowed in, with most posting comments below my update but with some of my closer online friends messaging sympathy directly, which was nice.

I found myself in tears for the first time since her death, so I posted an updated message about how lovely everyone was and how they had made me cry. Of course, I did it with the famous Britney Spears meme.

Then I noticed a message from Stan, who I hadn't heard from for a while. He was always blowing hot and cold. This was, at last, a change from the pornographic content he was so fond of sending through.

'Hey baby girl sorry to hear bout yr nan, mine died a couple of yrs ago and it sucks. Keep smiling babe! X x'

This made me cry even more. I had begun to think he didn't give a shit about me, but this told me different. It showed he really did care, and not just in a sexual way but with real-life feelings. I didn't use my usual five-minute rule, and I wrote back immediately; after all, he had opened his heart to her.

'Soz to hr about yr nan too, I know it sounds a bit stupid but I feel like I lost my best friend! xxx'

'Look after yourself babe xxx'

I told him I was being looked after by all my friends and family and hoped he would write more nice things, but then I saw he had logged off.

I soon realised that sympathy lasted a lot longer than joy in the online world. By day four of my online grief, all I seemed to do was post about the death, and that was even before the funeral. I described a world of death certificates, visits to the registry office and various meetings with the undertakers, often with the manager who I had renamed Mr Necro as I was sure he was sneaking into the chapel at night and having his way with the corpses. My friends really loved the fact I still had my wicked sense of humour, even at a time like this.

Planning the funeral meant spending hours researching readings and poems online and going back through Granny's Spotify list (that I had actually put together for her). I found the best coffin—a simple oak casket with a brass plaque—and chose plain white lilies to sit on top, avoiding the tacky names or objects that were also available. I didn't think Gran would want a religious funeral—after all, I didn't remember her ever going to church—so I found a registrar I liked the look of to carry out the service.

The day arrived a couple of weeks after Granny had died. In a way, I was dreading the day, but I hoped it might bring me closure. I chose my funeral outfit carefully, a black dress with a vibrant turquoise scarf, which had been Gran's favourite colour. I posted a couple of selfies inside the kitchen. Lots of friends sent condolences and kisses, but I was also rewarded with people telling me I was looking too skinny. I almost laughed at the irony; most people lost weight when they were grieving, but for me, it seemed to have increased my appetite tenfold. Still, it didn't matter; you never had to look fat online when you could reduce your weight in half with a few clicks.

I thought about tweeting throughout the little 'service' but thought this may be considered a bit disrespectful. As soon as it was over, I broke my self-imposed social media ban with some relief.

So sad to be saying goodbye to my gran but beautiful service to give her a good send-off.

Later that evening, I signed off with one final update, knowing people would worry about me if I didn't tell them how I was feeling.

All cried out after an emotional day but glad we managed to say goodbye to my gran properly.

I went to bed that night satisfied that I had finally given Granny the send-off she deserved and touched that so many people out there obviously cared about me. However, there was a deep and growing hole inside me, making me feel empty and lost. I had to face the facts that apart from a blossoming relationship with Stan, I was now completely alone in the world, despite all my online friends. I finally dropped off in the early hours of the morning, drained and out of tears.

Rachel

30 October 2018, 11 p.m.

Rachel couldn't sleep that night, so she headed downstairs after everyone was in bed and heated some milk. It had been so strange seeing Tom in her house. She couldn't quite match this slightly distant man with the boy who had been her world for so many years. She had been popular at school, but it was hard to become close to people when you could never invite them to your house. She had become so good at cutting herself off from her family that she had almost believed she was an only child and an orphan. Her current family life had become very important to her, and she had been devastated when her first marriage hadn't worked. All she wanted was love and stability for her kids, but she seriously doubted that this was what she was providing right now.

She hated how Tom now made her feel like he was the one who had made it—the successful one. They had started from the same platform, backgrounds and opportunities, yet he had managed to escape almost unscathed. It didn't seem fair. He even seemed to have met the love of his life in Will, who not only seemed like a good man, but he was also loaded!

Rachel was constantly feeling anxious, and she knew she was taking it out on the kids and on Dave. He may deserve it, but they didn't, and neither did Tom, really. Some people, when they were stressed, lost lots of weight and kept busy. Rachel found herself becoming a wiry insomniac with a churning stomach and bad skin.

Her biggest worry was obviously Alice. Who knew that someone she had not laid eyes on for nearly two decades could rule her thoughts so much? But joining these thoughts and sitting happily alongside all her familiar niggles were a couple of new ones—things that were eating away at her soul and things she couldn't tell anyone. Just like the horrific secret she had been forced to endure all those years ago, this one had the power to destroy every part of her family home.

Tom

30 October 2018, 10 p.m.

After all his research, Tom finally had a proper lead. He had received a direct message from one of Alice's many Twitter followers. Tom had followed almost everyone on her list in a desperate attempt to find out what had happened.

Hi, I saw that you are looking for Alice. I don't actually know her but I do know that her gran died recently, she was really upset about it for a long time. I know that they were really close. I hope she didn't do anything stupid as none of us have heard from her for a while.

Tom didn't tell Rachel that he had been sent this, mainly because he didn't want to upset Rachel's kids, but it had been a ruined meal for him once he saw it. He even decided on their behalf that none of them would have dessert, claiming he was tired and had to get back to his hotel. The girls were understandably upset at having their most important course snatched away, but Rachel had placated them with the promise of something sweet and full of artificial flavours when they got home.

Tom waited until he safely dropped them all off at home before starting his investigations. He felt stupid; he had checked all her social media feeds for the days before and after her disappearance, but he hadn't gone back any further than that. There was so much to plough through. He immediately brought up her Twitter profile and, sure enough, he came across the whole story of his mother's death from a few weeks earlier. Tom was shocked to feel incredibly sad. He had known, of course, that this was a possibility and had felt numb towards the idea, but seeing it written in black and white made it real. He realised that he had, in practice, been mourning his mother for years, at least the mother of his youth—the slightly scary lady who smoked like a chimney, fed him a load of crap but had always been there to patch him up, whether it was a scraped knee or an argument at school. She had also stood at times as a buffer between him and his father. She never condoned or condemned the violence that her husband had unleashed on his kids, but, somehow, if she was in hearing distance, the beating would never be as bad. He wondered if that had been the same for Rachel's situation.

He read on. There were no details posted by Alice about how her gran had died, but she went to town describing how she was feeling and sharing memories. Tom was astonished to note how much of the funeral Alice had shared. It sounded like a wonderful ceremony full of love and remembrance, and he noted with shock that Alice had even held a wake back at the house. He was surprised she hadn't livestreamed it, considering the amount of detail that had gone into it. Tom didn't know what to think. He realised that Alice had been lying to him, as this death definitely preceded the last conversation she had shared with him. Alice had told him that his mother was downstairs at that time. Surely he had a right to know if his mum had died. He had always thought of Alice as being a victim and someone to be pitied, but this showed extreme cruelty. He guessed that she would be the one beneficiary named in the will, but then he found himself wondering if this wasn't the case and if lovely, sensible Alice was somehow keeping quiet for her own gain.

Feeling guilty that he hadn't shared this with Rachel yet, he quickly texted her, hoping that she would be in bed already. He told her that he had found something out. The problem was that these facts had completely thrown what they had originally been looking for out of the window. Would they actually discover Alice living a life of luxury on her dead gran's pension in some penthouse apartment? Maybe his niece wasn't the sweet, popular girl she seemed to be. What else were they going to discover?

Tom

30 October 2018, 5 p.m.

Tom knew he had screwed up as he booked an Uber for his new-found family. He would be the first to admit that he didn't have a clue. He had been throwing expensive gifts at Alice for so many years now instead of any meaningful contact that the line had really blurred between what was affection and what was being grateful for a nice present. At least the children seemed to appreciate it; they had insisted on sitting in the back with him, one on each side. Both now played with their phones rather than talking to him directly, but they were sharing everything they found. He was being introduced to the delights of Snapchat, the hashtag girls, a scary-looking animated Barbie with an accent that would fit in with many of the upmarket boutiques in Manhattan and most bafflingly a game where you had to build a farm.

He could sense Rachel frowning from the front seat. He had tried to pacify her by saying he had already set up accounts that he would pay each month, thinking it was the expense that was the problem, but she was still being cold with him. He was hoping, of course, that with this new start for them all, these handsets might be the gateway to him staying in touch with his nieces, as he had done with Alice. As the silent treatment he had experienced so often as a kid permeated the car, Tom almost wished that Dave had joined them rather than telling them he had a 'prior engagement.' Even banal football talk was better than this.

The kids gasped when the car pulled up outside the restaurant. They didn't actually put the phones down but used them to take selfies which he guessed would then be pinged all over London. Having checked out *Time Out,* which he was amazed to see was now free, he had decided that Planet Hollywood was still quite a pull. He knew it was just an overpriced burger shop with a few pictures on the wall, but the way the kids were snapping away, you would have thought he had taken them to Hollywood itself. Even Rachel looked happier; he remembered that she could never stay angry for long. He could sulk for weeks, but Rachel would often be smiling by the end of the day after an argument. Knowing what he did now, he wondered if she had ever actually been happy or if the smile was painted on, at least after a certain age.

'I've actually always wanted to come here!' Rachel admitted, looking slightly embarrassed. Tom smiled back, enjoying the thaw.

They were seated and given menus by a ridiculously young and perky waitress with a terribly fake American accent. Tom decided that she was probably hoping for a West End role but could guarantee that the only people who would spot her in here would be randy dads. As soon as their drinks were served, Rachel started her grilling, pleased this time that the kids were absorbed by the phones and aged merchandise around them. They didn't even know who Arnold Schwarzenegger was—not as an action film star and definitely not in his later political role.

'So, what did you find out then?' Rachel demanded after sipping her huge coke. Tom had a slightly mean thought. Rachel hadn't so much as asked about her daughter for many years, but now suddenly she was demanding to know every detail.

'I don't really have much more to add to the text updates. I spoke to the police again and luckily got a much nicer copper this time. Maybe news about my intervention last night had spread! They still said they can't actively investigate as we have no proof that Alice is missing, but she has given me some good pointers.'

'But did you tell them I went to the family house and it seemed abandoned?'

'Of course, but again, for all we know, Mum might have become sick and moved out. We know that Alice wasn't even living there, just staying.' He didn't add that this was his much-preferred outcome. 'So PC Barnes suggested that we start with births and deaths. Turns out there is quite the market in people telling you stuff about dead people! I thought it was just the Yanks who desperately wanted to prove that they have some distant relative who has blue blood!'

Rachel didn't laugh this time. 'And?'

'Nothing, nada, no Alice or Josie Carmichael from Dorset have died recently. Although, they couldn't guarantee that their records would have recorded everything in the last few weeks; it takes a while, apparently. I also did a lot of research through the local papers, and apart from the obvious Bournemouth attack, there have been no freak accidents involving grumpy old women or shy young girls.'

Rachel let out a sigh of relief, more because Alice didn't seem to be dead than relief over the far more likely death of her mother.

'I still don't think we can rule out the terror attacks though,' Rachel said. 'She could have been hurt and lost her memory, she could be unidentified or she could even have run away or done something terrible to herself because of the attacks.'

'We can't completely rule it out, but the cops seem pretty certain they know everyone affected. The police also recommended that I try other places such as banks, utility providers and the benefits agency. That will take a few days, as I have had to apply for access in extenuating services. We may be related, but neither of us are named as next of kin on anything. After all, you are not even Alice's legal guardian anymore.'

This comment stung Rachel, but she guessed that he was being factual rather than hurtful. 'The police should do all of this for us. It is ridiculous; they have the power to uncover all this information, but it will probably take us weeks!'

At that point, the food arrived, plates piled high with cheap burgers and glistening chips. Tom knew it wouldn't be anywhere near as good as a proper New York burger, but he bit into it greedily. The girls were overjoyed with their dishes, and Tom wondered if this was a rare treat for them rather than a regular occurrence. He guessed that he and Rachel hadn't eaten out as children, but that might have been because it was not really a viable option in those days.

'Mum, who is this girl you and Uncle Tom are talking about? Is she Uncle Tom's daughter?' said Jess, Rachel's youngest daughter, with a frown. Rachel had forgotten how much kids pick up, despite the distractions in the room. Tom threw her a quizzical look.

'Um, no, she is just a girl I used to look after when she was a baby. I will tell you all about her one day soon.'

Tom was horrified that Rachel hadn't told her kids about their half-sister, but then again, he guessed that admitting this would have opened another difficult situation. He spoke as he ate. 'I know you have been down to the family home once, but I think we should go again. Maybe we can speak to actual people in the bank or the local shops. They might tell us more than the bureaucrats in the call centres. I can go alone, if it's a problem.'

Rachel knew it would be difficult to drop everything and head off on a trip with Tom, particularly because no one in her immediate family knew about her long-lost daughter, but she also felt she needed to be there. This whole situation had awakened so many feelings in her that had been dead for so long, it was as if by opening that door an inch, many years' worth of emotions had flooded through. It wasn't exactly welcomed, but, in a perverse way, it had given her a purpose in life.

'It might be difficult for me to get some time away. I mean, I have my hands full here,' she said, signalling toward the kids.

'Could you let Dave look after them for a few days? After all, you said he is looking for work at the moment, and doesn't his mum help out sometimes?'

Rachel answered back almost too quickly. 'No, that won't work.

I can't leave them alone with him.'

Tom was going to question this but could see her barrier go up, so he left it.

Rachel seemed to ponder things for a few moments. She looked like she was trying to work a few things out in her head and finally answered, 'You know what? There is no reason the kids can't stay with their dad for a few days. He hardly shares parental duties as it is, and they will love spending time with their baby brother.'

Kylie looked up from her fries at this and beamed. 'Oh, can we, Mum? That would be awesome!'

Rachel felt hurt that her kids were so keen to get away from her and worried that their dad would say no to the idea, but she knew he definitely owed her one. She had really let him off the hook as a father, and it was time to stand up for herself again.

'Give me tomorrow to sort everything out; then we can head off the next day. I have promised the kids I will take them trick or treating, so I can't miss that. I will have to call in sick to school, mind you; I can't imagine them giving me time off to go on a wild goose chase!'

Arrangements were made and the subject was closed for now. Because of the prying ears, the rest of the meal was eaten with no further drama; in fact, anyone else looking over at them would have thought they were a normal family, out for a fun night. And actually, they could have been, that is until Tom received a message on his Twitter account that changed the whole situation.

Rachel

30 October 2018, 4 p.m.

Rachel was nervously waiting for Tom to show up. Suddenly everything in her life looked so shabby. The little terraced house she was so proud of suddenly looked like a hovel—the windows were smudged and the carpets were stained. The front of the house, along with others in the street, was decorated for Halloween, and she hoped Tom would think the general disrepair was part of the decoration. She even had real spiderwebs.

She had dressed up again and had put her kids in their best outfits, usually reserved for birthday parties or Sunday lunch at her mother-in-law's house. She was at least proud of her daughters; both girls were clever and well-behaved. She guessed she had overcompensated with them after screwing up so spectacularly the first time round.

On the dot of four, there was a ring at the doorbell. Rachel smoothed herself down, had a quick check in the mirror and strode forward to open the door to her brother. They were uncomfortable around each other again, the easy, drunken comradery from earlier having disappeared. They had so many years to catch up on. Rachel showed him through to the sitting room where her partner, Dave, was slumped in a chair. He did at least stand up and shake Tom's hand.

'Alright, mate, can I get you a beer?'

'Oh god, no, I am still suffering from too much wine the other night. Don't suppose I could get a coffee?'

Dave looked towards Rachel, and she rolled her eyes. It was clear Dave didn't know how to boil a kettle. She stomped off into the kitchen, calling the kids down from their room at the same time.

'So Rachel tells me you're some big hotshot lawyer in America.'

'Hardly *hotshot*, and I do more corporate stuff these days. It's boring but that's where the money is. It's nothing like the TV shows though!' Tom joked.

Dave took the conversation back to where he was comfortable. 'And do they have some weird football over there. Not the real stuff like we do here.'

'Yeah, it is mainly American football and baseball over there, although soccer is becoming more popular. You know, we are getting some big names over these days. But no, the Yanks don't really "get it".'

'So what team do you support then?' Dave asked, posing the male-bonding question accepted all over the UK.

Tom really didn't want to admit that he hated football and that, apart from a brief stint as a Manchester supporter to fit in with his school friends at the time, Tom had never even watched a game. 'I guess when I am here it would be Manchester.'

'United or City?'

Tom felt as though he was doing an exam he had never studied for.

'Um, City?'

He didn't know if this was the right thing or not as Dave then started a rant about the season—who was scoring goals, which manager should be sacked. Luckily, they were interrupted by two girls who walked in looking shy, followed by their mum who had a mug in one hand and a can of beer in the other.

'Hello. Mummy says you are our uncle,' said the oldest one who was the spitting image of what Alice had looked like at that age, with brown hair down to her shoulders and big blue eyes.

'I guess that's right. I'm Tom,' he said, putting out a hand and then realised that shaking a nine-year-old girl's hand—his niece, at that—was probably not the right greeting. She ignored it any-way.

'And who are you?' he said to the smaller one, not to be polite but because he really couldn't remember which was which.

'I'm Jess and I'm five,' she said shyly, showing off a massive gap in her teeth.

Luckily, Tom had come prepared and pulled out two beautifully wrapped boxes. The girls descended on them, all awkwardness gone. Kylie opened hers first and screamed in excitement; it was an iPhone, and it looked like the latest model. Jess sped up and was rewarded with the same phone in a different colour. It seems that money really can buy love as both girls ran over to their uncle and embraced him with a look of pure joy on their faces. Rachel wasn't so happy; in fact, she had a face like thunder.

Tom sipped the coffee, and she noticed him make a face. He probably didn't even know cheap, instant coffee still existed. She guessed that his coffee was probably sourced from a part of the world that had mountains and wars in equal measures, not some factory.

'Thanks, Tom, that is really generous of you, but we had told the girls they weren't getting a proper phone until they are at least 11. I mean, Kylie has one of my old Nokias, but they spend enough time in front of screens already, and I really don't want to make them into targets for muggers.'

Tom's face fell. She guessed he had no idea about kids. Rachel looked towards Dave for back up.

'Well, you can hardly take them back now, can you? Not now that the girls have had their hands on them. Come on, chill out, Rach!'

Rachel wanted to punch them both but knew better than to disagree with Dave in front of the kids. Things were bad enough between them at the moment, and she wanted to make him feel like he had some kind of fatherly input, even if his role was in question at the moment. By now, the kids had turned on the phones and were busy setting them up how only children who rarely use pen and paper can. Rachel sighed; she would have to enforce some strict rules about usage and put some kind of parental lock on there. After all, she knew more than most that there are some really nasty people out there.

Stan

28 October 2018, 11 p.m.

Stan was pleased to have been saved by that weird, middle-aged bloke who sounded like a Yank. The cops had been so close to finding his stash of weed. Probably not enough to get him done for dealing—in fact, he hadn't been selling for a while since he now had a more lucrative side business—but he knew if they had found anything remotely dodgy then they may have asked questions, and god knows what they would have uncovered. It did really annoy him that he was a beacon for being stopped by the police just because he liked to drive in some nice wheels. For all they knew, he could be a respectable member of society.

He pulled up in front of a park. As he rolled a joint and ripped off a bit of the card he had been given as a roach, he pocketed the rest of it, just in case. He fiddled on his phone as he smoked. He had been alerted to some fresh meat on his app. One was a bit ordinary but the other would do nicely. She described herself as 'big and bouncy', and he guessed that she had tried to label herself as the fat, funny one throughout her life. It was her sad eyes staring out from the photo that told him what he needed to know. That and her tight top that was straining to contain her massive breasts. He swiped right and sent her a like; seconds later, he was added as one of her favourites. It was almost too easy. He never went in for the kill straight away and would keep her sweet for a couple of weeks before arranging a meetup.

Funnily enough, the film with Alice was still his bestseller, in spite of how amateur he now saw it was. He had learnt a lot since then about lighting and camera angles. Maybe it was Alice who was the main draw. It's a shame he might have burned his bridges there; he would have to put the work in if he wanted a sequel.

Tom

28 October 2018, 8 p.m.

After the first couple of glasses of mediocre wine, Tom found that he was actually enjoying himself, something he never thought would happen when he had made the snap decision to fly over to his homeland. His partner, Will, had thought he was mad and was upset that Tom would be missing from their social calendar for a few days. He could hold his own in most situations, but he liked the comfort blanket that Tom provided. Unlike lots of Americans, Will had spent time in the UK and had found the small-town mentality a far cry from the quaint English villages that so many dreamed of. Tom would often see his home country through Will's eyes. Of course, he had loved London and picturesque cities such as Cambridge, but he too had seen the horrors of Slough and the greyness of small Northern villages on a cold day. They had never talked about holidays or even living back in the UK, although he did still enjoy a few days in London on business. They had both accepted New York as their adopted home. Well, really, Will had decided, and Tom had agreed—like most things in their life.

Tom knew he was looking down upon everything he had experienced since touching on British soil, from the queues at the airport to the tacky, cheap hotel he had booked into. He had almost checked out immediately in search of a hotel in Central London. He could never understand why people, like his sister, he supposed, chose to live on the scummy outskirts of the city. Surely you were paying for the privilege of the capital with none of the benefits, even with the night tube he had heard about. The high street here was full of betting shops and 99p stores, and it could have been any town in the country, apart from the diversity apparent in Polish shops and West Indian barbers.

He was trying and failing to not judge his sister in the same way. She had really aged before her time, and her cheap highlights and supermarket clothes did her no favours. Maybe he was too used to New York women who wouldn't be seen dead out in public without Pilates-toned arms and threaded eyebrows. Still, when he looked beyond his prejudice, he was beginning to enjoy her company. There was something to be said for being with someone who you didn't have to explain anything to. They were still dancing around so many subjects, but the fact they had once shared everything couldn't be discounted altogether.

As Tom went to get another bottle, he vowed to wake up early the next day to go for a jog, hoping he would find some green amongst all the high-rises. Rachel smiled a genuine smile as he replaced the bottle in the cooler, and he immediately felt guilty for judging her.

'So, little brother, when did you get so suave and sophisticated? Last time I saw you, you had too much *Sun-in* in your hair and your clothes were from *BHS*.'

Tom cringed at the memory. 'I guess that's what New York does to you. That and the fact that gay men really have to keep up appearances to fit all the diabolical stereotypes we are forced to endure.'

'So do you love Judy Garland and do you have a dog the size of a rat then?'

'I'm more of a Marilyn Monroe fan, and sadly our very lovely rent-controlled apartment doesn't allow pets, so no, I fail on both counts.' He chuckled.

'Wow, New York sounds so glamorous! Are you out at lovely restaurants and parties all the time?'

'Actually, yes, which sounds very exciting, but as I get older, I would love a bit more time on the sofa, you know? It can get routine going out every night of the week.'

'I tell you what: let's swap. I will go and live in New York for a week and live your life, and you can stay here in my home, cooking every night, looking after my kids and watching as much TV as you like.'

This actually sounded like bliss to Tom, and he wondered if he should make the effort to come and spend a few days with Rachel and her family. Not that he could ever have her over to his home. She would never fit in his world anymore.

'What about kids?' Rachel asked. 'Do you want them? Lots of gay men are doing this these days, aren't they? Adopting or getting someone else to pop one out?'

Tom thought of his ordered life and felt sad that there was no room in there for a child. 'No, I have always quite liked being the fun, gay uncle, you know? Well, at least to Alice, I mean,' he explained, treading on eggshells.

'I really appreciate that you have looked out for her all these years, you know? I know I was a terrible mother, but it wasn't all my fault, you know,' replied Rachel, opening the can of worms an inch more.

Tom tried to change the subject. 'So, you work in a school now; what's that like? Can't think of anything worse, really!'

'Do you know what? I really love it! I am a teaching assistant. I wanted to retrain as a teacher at one point, but you know money, time and the usual crap put a stop to that. I look after the kids in the school who have special needs, and sometimes it is like herding cats, but every so often a kid will do something that makes it all worthwhile. Anyway, it's better than my last job; I was wiping shitty arses years after my kids had grown out of nappies, and it sucked the life out of me.'

Tom was surprised to see the side of Rachel as a carer; after all, she had shown no care to her firstborn.

Rachel inched open the can again. 'You know, I am not trying to shift the blame, but there were reasons beyond the fact that our mother was a tyrant that I went off the rails. I had a very difficult time with Dad, you know?' Tom realised that Rachel was slurring her words slightly. She obviously hadn't been sipping her water between wine.

'I know, I was there too, you know. He used to beat me to a pulp if I ever stepped out of line.' Tom almost added that this hadn't driven him to seek solace in a needle.

'Yes, but it was different for me as a girl. He didn't just punish me with his fists.' Rachel was staring at him intently as though she wanted him to guess what horrors had gone on.

'What, you mean he took away your pocket money and called you a few nasty names? Get real, most kids go through shit with their parents, and they don't completely screw up their lives because of it. I hate it when people blame the parents; it is so lazy. I am surrounded by gay men in New York who spend half their lives and salary on their shrink because *mummy didn't understand me.*'

Tom was getting angry now. He was usually a mellow drunk, but jetlag was bringing out the worst in him.

'What I don't understand is how you could have fucked up Alice's life so spectacularly as well. I mean, it wasn't her fault you hated your parents so much, and the poor cow ended up with them!'

Rachel spoke quietly, all defiance having left her. 'Tom, he raped me.'

Tom wasn't following. 'Who, Alice's dad?' He immediately lost the attitude. 'Oh god, Rach, that is terrible. No wonder you lost it!'

'You don't understand. When I say *he*, I mean Dad. He abused me —had been doing so for years.' With this, she sobbed openly, oblivious to the onlookers enjoying the show.

Tom felt his blood turn to ice. He didn't know if he could believe her or if this was just another of Rachel's excuses. How could this have gone on under his roof without him having a clue?

She spoke, still quietly sobbing but with determination in her voice. 'It started when I was about nine. Do you remember when they finally got us into our own rooms? He used to come in and "tuck me in". I was lucky that he broke his "little girl" in gently, so he didn't actually rape me for a couple more years.'

'But why didn't you stop him or tell someone?' Tom really didn't want to hear any details, and he still wanted her to be making it up for attention.

'I always knew what he did was wrong—we had those awful sex education lessons at school, after all—but he told me it would destroy the family, you would have no dad and that no one would believe me, which actually was true. When I finally told Mum, she called me an attention-seeking whore.'

Sadly, Tom could picture this being said and remembered how Rachel had gone from the girl who could do no wrong to something that his mother wanted to scrape off her shoe. This was around the time that Rachel had started staying out 'til all hours and rebelling against the suffocating family.

'But why didn't you go to the police, anyone?'

'I know it sounds ridiculous, Tom, and I really, really hate him for what he did. He was a monster. It's only now that I have girls of my own that I realise how wrong it was, but he was also my dad. I have some incredible memories of when we were kids, and I guess I really didn't want to be the one that tore that apart. Plus, if you are a young girl whose self-esteem is through the floor and you are told enough times that nobody will believe you, then you think that way yourself. Kind of a self-fulfilling prophecy.'

Tom was fighting back tears. 'I should have known. I should have done something. I could have stopped it.'

'No, Tom, you could never have stopped it, and it is nobody's fault but his. He was a paedophile and an abuser, and Mum turned a blind eye. They were the adults that were meant to be looking after us. And you didn't exactly get off lightly, either; I know how handy he was with his fists if you ever crossed the line.'

He moved around the table and hugged his big sister. It was the first real hug they had shared as adults. They hugged for the childhoods they had lost, for the time they had spent apart and for the girl who had bought them together again.

The siblings spent the rest of the evening being 'normal'. They caught up on years of their lives, both in wonder of how the other one lived. Rachel spoke a lot about her kids, and they made a plan for him to meet them the next day. He would spend the next day as a man on a mission trying to uncover what had happened to his niece. He wasn't sure he knew where to start but felt a lot more confident now that he was physically in the country.

They were both a bit worse for wear as they left the wine bar, holding onto each other for support. He had a stain on his beautifully expensive shirt and could see that most of Rachel's makeup had long since been wiped away. Tom insisted on getting an Uber for Rachel, despite her suspicion over getting into a stranger's car. He was just opening the app when he spotted the kebab shop on the other side of the road. 'You know what? Despite all my years of fine dining in New York's best restaurants, I still get a craving for a good old kebab.'

Rachel practically squealed. 'Oh, now you are talking! I haven't had a donair in years. Do you want to share some chips too?'

'No way, get your own.' Tom laughed as they headed across the road.

They were inside the hot kebab takeaway, littered with other drunk people like them, and waiting for the pile of food they had finally ordered when they noticed a commotion outside. They could see that a man had been stopped by the police and was being forced to stand with his hands in the air by the side of the road.

'You know that he wouldn't have been stopped just because he is in a nice car if he was white,' Tom commented.

They could see that the police were pulling the car apart. They probably didn't even know what they were searching for.

'I thought Asian-looking men with rucksacks were the new target, but it seems black men with shiny cars are still flavour of the month!' Rachel said.

'Look at him. He is probably a lawyer or doctor, and sadly he probably gets stopped numerous times every week just because of what he looks like. This has happened to so many of my colleagues in the States. It's not so bad in New York—I mean, people don't drive in Manhattan anyway—but as soon as they cross the county lines, bam, they are suddenly a person of interest.'

The scene now had the eyes of the whole kebab shop on it, not that this was a rare occurrence in this area but more because one of the officers was being particularly unpleasant.

'I will go out there and see if I can help,' Tom eventually said, after he had heard the officer call the poor man a thieving bastard, despite the fact they had found nothing out of the ordinary.

'Are you sure that's a good idea? After all, I'm not sure if you could walk in a straight line at the moment if asked!'

'You wait here and keep an ear out for our food. This won't take long.'

Tom stepped out of the door, the cold air in contrast to the greasy fug.

'Hello, officer, is there a problem here?'

The mouthy officer looked at the crumpled, pissed Yank with surprise and disgust.

'Nothing for you to worry about, sir. This man is just helping with our enquiries,' said the other cop, the slightly nicer one.

'Well, OK, I just wanted to check in with this young man. After all, I am a lawyer, and it didn't look as though you were treating him that well. Did you have any particular reason to stop and search him?'

The nasty copper looked even more annoyed, but the nice copper looked worried. 'We stopped him because we had reason to believe he was in possession of something he shouldn't have had.'

'Oh right, and not because he a young, mixed-race man driving a nice car then? And tell me, have you found anything to incriminate him?'

'No, not yet,' admitted the nasty copper.

'In that case, I would suggest that you let him get on his way. You wouldn't want to be accused of harassment or racism, now, would you?'

The nasty cop looked resigned; he couldn't be bothered to deal with the paperwork that would accompany any complaint. If he left it now, then it would only be a couple of forms and it might mean he could catch last orders at his local. He let it stew for a few more minutes, writing up some basic notes alongside the name and registration he had already noted.

'OK, so we have completed our investigation and you are free to go for now, but next time you might not be so lucky.'

The police drove off, and the young man thanked Tom.

'Man, that was amazing. Those twats are always trying to pin something on me, but you totally blew it out of the water. I owe you big time!' He high-fived Tom.

Tom was high on the little encounter. 'You owe me nothing. I hate to see injustice. Here, let me give you my card, and if you get treated badly again, I can advise you on how to complain.'

'Amazing! You are a top bloke. Thanks so much.' The man took the card. 'At least let me pay for your dinner,' he said, pointing at the kebab shop.

'OK, mate, that would be great.' Tom smiled and let the young man inside. He high-fived Rachel as well when he was introduced and slapped a fifty-pound note on the counter. After they had said their goodbyes, Tom and Rachel grabbed their hot parcels and headed off down the road to find a suitable bench.

Rachel

28 October 2018, 9 a.m.

Rachel was speeding down the motorway again but this time not towards the coast but to the airport to pick up her brother. She had been so shocked when Tom had called her to say he was flying out to London that night. She had known he had kept in touch with Alice, a fact that she had once resented deeply but now, knowing he was putting his life on hold to try and find her, she felt pleased that Alice had always had a Guardian Angel of sorts.

Rachel hated airports—not that she was in them often. She had only ever managed a couple of cheap weeks in Spain over her lifetime. There was something about watching the emotional hellos and goodbyes between families, friends and lovers that made her feel so alone. If she had flown off alone at any stage in her life, she wasn't sure that anyone would have waved her off, let alone turned up to welcome her home.

As she finally saw her brother walking through arrivals being swept along by the crowds, she had to hold herself back from running up and hugging him. Gone was the awkward teenager she had last seen, replaced by a grown man in an expensive suit and greying hair. She looked to see if he had anyone with him; he had mentioned a partner over the years but was relieved to see that, apart from his expensive luggage, he was travelling alone. He reached her, and they stood awkwardly not knowing how to greet each other, every year of their separation pushing them apart. She offered him coffee, but he was keen to get on the road. He hadn't said how long he was planning to stay, but she guessed he would make it as short as possible.

Conversation was stilted in the car; they were like strangers with little in common. She asked him politely about work, and he asked about her kids. She was surprised and impressed that he knew their names and their ages. When the initial pleasantries had died off, Rachel switched on the radio, tuning it to a talk radio station to fill the silence. The presenter was taking calls about immigration in the wake of the Bournemouth bombing. Rachel bet it didn't take much for the conversation to turn to immigration on this station, and so a bonafide situation where people had died as the direct result of the child of immigrants was like all their Christmases had come at once. The callers all generally had the same view—although it was presented in various ways—that all those who were non-white should be stopped at the border, and those that had slipped through should be sent back to where they came from.

'Wow, I thought the States was bad for this type of nonsense, but this is like a segment from Fox News!' joked Tom.

Rachel was instantly relieved. She had no idea of her brother's political persuasion; after all, their parents had been bigots, and the apple doesn't fall far from the tree, so they say.

'Has Trump made things worse?' asked Rachel cautiously, turning down the radio.

'Oh yes, well, he has legitimised hate speech. All that crap about banning Muslims and building walls. One of my colleagues is working on a case at the moment where a man is locked up because he dared to travel to Syria to visit his dying grandmother. He is a proper, upstanding member of the community, has a well-established business, is a philanthropist, and is even married to a white American, but he is being punished just because he happens to be brown.'

'A kid in the school I work in had his house burned down recently after some scum put burning rags through the door, apparently because his family is Polish. It is not just the non-whites that are suffering over here. Since the Brexit vote—a bit like Trump, I guess—it gives everyone legitimate reason to hate and blame.'

'Wow, what do you think Dad would think if he found out his poofter son and druggie daughter had become such bleeding-heart liberals?' Tom joked, and they both burst into laughter, instantly exchanging stories of his views. He hadn't discriminated against any particular group of people; he seemed to hate everyone. Bonded again by the one thing they truly had in common, they spent the rest of the journey reliving their childhood and skirting widely around anything too controversial.

Rachel was relieved when Tom told her he was staying in a hotel. She had shoved a few things under the bed in her youngest daughter's room, but somehow it was too intimate letting him into her house. He had booked a chain hotel just ten minutes' drive away from her. She was surprised; she presumed he would be in The Ritz or somewhere fancy but was impressed that he was prepared to slum it for a few days.

She dropped him off to freshen up, and they arranged to meet for dinner. She had been forced to tell her boyfriend that her brother was on the way yesterday. Tom was the only living relative he knew about, but she guessed she would have to sit him down and tell him about Alice soon. Having a surprise visit from her long-lost brother had probably ignited his curiosity.

Rachel felt like she needed to impress that night, as she blow-dried her hair and chose her favourite outfit. Despite the fact she was meeting her brother, they were much more like strangers than family these days. Her outfit was really a summer dress, and although it was threatening to rain, she teamed it with a big coat and hoped for the best. Tom was looking a lot more relaxed when she met him in a chain wine bar across the road from the hotel. Funny how these wine bars with their wooden floors and mammoth glasses had seemed so glamorous when they first arrived in UK towns and cities but looked a bit dated now. The fashionable thing now, according to the teachers she worked with, were funny little microbreweries and street food. She had even heard that the massive brewery that had churned out mass-produced beer in her hometown now had its own trendy range.

Tom got up when she arrived in, and they hugged awkwardly. He went in for a kiss on the cheek; she guessed that's what Americans did, but she wasn't ready, and he got her ear.

'What would you like to drink?' he offered with a smile.

'A glass of pinot, please, large.'

'Oh, I didn't realise that you still . . .' His voice petered out, and Rachel suddenly felt like she was being judged. Even more so when she noticed that he had a coke in front of him.

'That was a long time ago, Tom, and it was never really booze that was the problem,' she explained with a sigh.

'I tell you what, I will join you. If we get a bottle, then it will work out cheaper. Did you say pinot?'

She smiled her thanks, relieved that he would not sit and lecture her all evening.

They were both nervous, and the first bottle went down quickly. Rachel was pleased that she had hopped on the bus rather than driving as she guessed that she was already over the limit, but the warmth of the wine seeping through her body and the sight of her little brother sitting in front of her with a smile on his face finally gave her a feeling of peace and happiness.

Tom

21 October 2018, 5 p.m.

The wasted trip that Rachel had taken down to Dorset had at least one positive effect: it had lessened the canyon between siblings, a distance that would be naked to the visible eye but was a seismic shift for Tom and Rachel.

Rachel had reported everything back to her brother. Tom had at first thought she was lying about the whole thing, but then she mentioned the tributes in Bournemouth and her reaction, and the iceberg in his heart melted a little. Tom hadn't seen a human side to Rachel for so many years, and this show of emotion completely threw him. He was someone who saw things in black and white. His mum was evil but misguided and ignorant. Rachel was a selfish bitch who had abandoned her family and dumped her child when the allure of drugs and partying had been too much. He didn't really want to see this human side to her, as it would upset the balance. It was much easier living on the other side of the Atlantic and not having to worry about other people —apart from Alice, that is.

The news that Rachel had found a clearly abandoned house worried and infuriated Tom in equal measures. On one hand, he wondered if his mother's propaganda had finally swayed Alice, resulting in her cutting him out of her life. But then, it wasn't just him. Every time he looked on her social media platforms, searching for life, he was met with silence. There was nothing since the Bournemouth terror attack; in contrast, her pages the week before the attack had possibly hundreds of posts.

The idea that she had been caught up in the gunfire or chaos was still a niggling worry for him. It wasn't a completely stupid proposition. His mother wouldn't be in touch if something had happened; they hadn't released all the names of the dead and injured yet. For all he knew, she could have been injured and not realised how bad she was until it was too late. He knew he was probably overreacting and that she was just being a normal teenager living her life, but he couldn't shake the dread he felt.

It was hard to ignore the situation, particularly with all the crap that was being spouted on social media at the moment. Not a day went by without some kind of false news, whether it was someone making up a loved one who had been in the attack, bomb scares being blown way out of proportion or even reports that Korea was about to launch a nuclear weapon. He had found that sticking to the BBC generally kept his news fairly impartial, but he did still find himself switching to Twitter when something broke.

He knew everyone else would be far too self-absorbed to see that Alice wasn't engaging with the world. Obsessed as they were with their selfies and keeping up with the Joneses, he wondered—and not for the first time—if he should put the cat among the pigeons by alerting her friends to her lack of activity.

A half a bottle of superb merlot later, his mind was made up. He started small, just a tweet about Alice, tagging her with just the merest hint he hadn't heard from her. His first response was not as subtle.

Wat is @Alicetrollydolly MISSING???? #findalice #missingperson #anuthavictim

Tom quickly tried to backtrack, but within minutes the media had become very social and people were sharing and re-tweeting all over the place. He left them to it, thinking it couldn't do any harm apart from embarrassing Alice if she was simply taking a break from the monotony of sharing her life online. He answered a few 'concerned' friends who were asking him when he had last heard from her.

He could guarantee that few of the people responding had ever even met Alice, but he noticed that he gathered followers at an alarming rate. He had only ever used his Twitter account to keep up with work news, so suddenly becoming the centre of attention was disturbing. He noticed quite a few people mentioning the Bournemouth attack and placing Alice near the scene.

This was done almost in glee as though knowing someone that had been caught up in the attack could somehow add to kudos. People were by now sharing pictures of Alice. This was not a girl he recognised; he hadn't seen his niece in the flesh since she was a chubby-faced child, but this scary clone with her duck face and inflated lips looked nothing like her.

By the evening, Tom had made a decision. The Twitter storm he had caused was still rumbling on but was already running out of steam. He needed to actually go to the UK and do something more than sending a few messages. He hated Halloween here anyway, with all those snotty kids knocking at the door looking for candy. This would give him a good excuse to get away. At least now he knew it wasn't just him that was being ignored. Alice had definitely disappeared from public life, and he needed to find out why. He hoped it wasn't for sinister reasons.

Alice

I had been posting pictures of my birthday day out when I first realised something was happening. I had tried to group the shots into beach, cocktails and shopping, but I wasn't happy with the filters.

The first indication of a problem was a sudden avalanche of posts unlike those I was used to; none of these were fluffy and there was not a cat or meme in sight. People were sharing pictures, their shock confusing. It was a never-ending stream, telling a story which felt so disjointed at the moment that it was more like a horror film.

Each notification jolted me further into a completely frightening version of reality. The massive bang, the desperation on people's faces all around me as they dropped to the ground. The racing heart, the sweats, the snatching away of my breath. Sirens, chaos and death, all in the space of a few moments. Suddenly, my entire body was on red alert. I could hear everything as though it was being fed through a loud speaker. The smells all around me grew overbearing and made me retch. I could feel pain all over my body, and my mind could not process where the actual injury was, if any. Most of all, I could hear the desperate screams.

Rachel
21 October 2018, 10.30 a.m.

Rachel usually loved a road trip. It was a chance to sit in her rustbucket of a car by herself and listen to her own music, without constantly being asked to put on *Frozen* or *The Jungle Book*. But today, her body and mind were awash with increasing dread with every mile that brought her nearer to the coastal county of her childhood. She had told Dave that she was visiting a great aunt she had never mentioned before. He had barely looked up from daytime TV when she had left that morning, and she knew she would have to call to remind him to pick up the kids from after school club.

She stopped at Fleet services, noticing the rebuilding that had taken place after a fire almost destroyed the building. It was a vast improvement on the memories of stinking toilets and overpriced greasy food of her youth. It even had a Waitrose now! Maybe that's what she should do when she got to the house of horrors: burn it down and start again. She took her time drinking the ridiculously big coffee she had bought, sleep having escaped her recently. She knew she was putting off the inevitable and so eventually drained her cup, did another wee 'just in case' and climbed back in the car.

She put on her favourite radio station to try to lift her mood, but the jolly demeanour of the DJ and the occasional song of her youth didn't have the desired effect. Her brain was still flooded with thoughts and memories. There were some good memories, of course, like her mum making her sandwiches with the crusts cut off (sometimes even without grumbling) and summer days with her parents and Tom, spent on local beaches where dips in the freezing cold sea were rewarded with ice cream. That was before the darkness had descended.

There were memories, too, of her life as a young mother and her surprise at the instant flood of love for this thing she had carried for so long. For the first few weeks of motherhood, Rachel had barely slept, worried that the baby would stop breathing. Rachel would have never won mother of the year back then, but she had always ensured that Alice was clean, warm and loved. She had some support, like the dreaded visits from the frosty health visitors who she felt were judging her. She even made a few friends taking Alice for long walks in her pram along the seafront. Other mothers seemed to be such naturals, bouncing babies on their hips with glossy hair and made-up faces. She got invited into people's homes to drink cups of tea and moan about lack of sleep, but she knew she could never invite people back to her hovel.

Then she had her neighbours, the lost boys and girls who had ended up in crappy bedsits like her. She wasn't the only mother amongst them, and she would hear rows between mother and child at all hours of the day. Mostly everyone kept to themselves, but there was a community of sorts. She had hung around with a few of them, out of boredom more than anything. As time went by, her mood dipped so low, everything felt like a struggle. She stopped taking Alice for walks, and the invitations from the other mums had also halted.

No one ever sets out to become an addict, and for Rachel, it was a long and slow process. It started with a shared bottle of strong cider to punctuate the weekend, a joint in the evening to send her to sleep and finally the poison in her veins to block out the black memories and long, endless poverty-filled days. Rachel only ever indulged when Alice was in bed and when there were others around, as she would never have put her daughter in danger. By the time Alice was two and a difficult toddler, Rachel had a new label: unemployed, single mother and addict.

Alice had barely been talking when social services got involved with them. She still had no idea who had alerted them—one of her more responsible neighbours, the GP surgery who kept trying to get her to visit for various check-ups and jabs, or even her mother, who Rachel suspected in her darker moments. Given the evident drug use in her flat, Alice was considered high risk and taken into care. Rachel was given support and chances to spend time with her daughter, but it was all done in such horrific circumstances in airless rooms being watched by social workers who clearly showed what they thought of this young mum.

And they were right, she had no idea how to actually be a parent. She was barely out of school; she would have struggled to keep a pet or house plant alive. There was so much to worry about, and trying to do it all with no money and no support felt impossible. It seemed easier just to stop trying. In her heart, she knew she didn't deserve Alice; some other family would be able to give her a much better life.

As Rachel finally passed the town sign that informed her she was back in her home town, she was panicking both about what would happen if her mother and daughter were at home and what she would do if she couldn't find them. The town which had seemed so massive when she was a child seemed like a toy town now. She noticed the gentrification that had crept in with the new cafés and pedestrianised shopping areas. Her home was outside the town centre, and it had seemed like they had lived in the middle of nowhere when she was a kid, but she realised now it was less than a ten-minute walk and the neighbours were still within shouting distance. Indeed, she noticed curtains twitching as she turned off from the main road onto the bumpy track. It was also so much prettier than she remembered. After years of living in urban sprawls, it was surprisingly nice to come to a proper country town.

The sight that greeted her was horrific. The house had always been pretty ramshackle—it was built over a century ago, after all—but this was a clearly unloved home. Ironically, although the town had seemed smaller, the house seemed to have grown in stature. Its grim, grey stone looked down upon her in disgust as its inhabitants had done for years. As she parked up and got out of her car, the stench of rotting food hit her, and she noticed bags of rubbish strewn across the overgrown lawn that her father had spent so many hours proudly maintaining. She had often thought he loved his garden more than his family. The roses were definitely given more care than his kids.

Her parents had always been one for appearances and took great delight in telling anyone who listened that neither were born into money. This house and all that was in it was bought through hard work. Her father had worked on the railways all his life, had invested well and had spent little, so she presumed her mother was left very comfortable by his death, even if he wasn't actually living with her at the time. She was a mean woman, though, and rather than retire in luxury, Rachel presumed she had probably hidden all the money under the mattress, leaving just enough to keep her in her beloved B&H and ready meals. She and Tom had certainly never enjoyed a penny, and while she knew her parents would have been horrified to have a daughter on benefits, they had never attempted to support her, even when Alice was in her care.

Rachel inched gingerly up the path, the same one that had been both her escape route and salvation out of her home for many years. The stones had been engulfed by weeds. She tried the doorbell, but when she didn't hear the usual chiming, she knocked. A few moments later, she was relieved to head back down the path and jump in her car. The house showed absolutely no signs of life. Even the letter box looked like it had been sealed. She guessed that maybe the house had been home to squatters at some point, judging by the filthy litter that had been thrown carelessly on the lawn. Rachel didn't know what to think or how to feel as she drove away. She had been building herself up for a confrontation with her mother all day, and she even had a distant dream in the back of her head that this would be the day of reconciliation for her and her daughter.

She had thought about trying to contact Alice over the years, even sending birthday and Christmas cards, although she wasn't sure if they were ever passed on. She was so saddened by the way she had treated Alice, giving up on her as she did. When she eventually became a mother again, she was so ashamed by what she had done and who she had been that she didn't really try. Instead, she had simply given up and locked Alice away in that box labelled 'don't touch'.

Rachel had even hoped that her mum may have mellowed in old age—she may have even wanted to get to know her other grandchildren—but with the house empty, she had hit a brick wall, and she deserved nothing less. She hoped that this meant Alice was living it up somewhere with people her own age while her mum was shrivelling away in some cheap care home.

Rachel changed her route on the way back to London away from the picturesque country roads, stopping in Bournemouth. The town had an air of sadness to it; everyone she walked past was either walking with their head down or eyes twitching all around, as though they feared another terrorist attack was imminent. The beach, usually packed to the rafters even on a coolish September day like today, was empty, bar a few dog walkers and armed police chatting with the ice-cream and fish-and-chip vendors that would be shutting up early after a disappointing day. She walked through the Winter Gardens and was suddenly faced with the public outpouring of grief that was so openly on display: mounds of withering, dead flowers with candles and photos. Rachel couldn't help it and joined the handful of people in the square who were paying their respects and sobbing gently. Rachel took herself to a nearby bench and cried for the first time in years—for all the innocent people who had died here when a young person with a warped view of the world had decided to end their lives, for her lost childhood and for the child she herself had lost.

Stan

20 October 2018, 3 p.m.

Stan loved the smell of a new car, probably even more than he loved the smell of a hot woman. Both got him feeling aroused, so the current situation of a blow job in his new car was driving him over the edge. She wasn't much to look at, really—scrawny with too much makeup—but the feel of his hands against the soft leather interior in between pushing her head down harder was enough to keep him feeling it.

Stan's life had improved considerably since he had hooked up with Alice. At first, he had been jittery, looking over his shoulder when he went to the cashpoint. Each time he fully expected an alarm to go off, be surrounded by police or at the very least for the card to stop working. But it had never happened; it really was the gift that kept giving. After a week of being cautious, Stan became more daring. Some new clothes, trainers and a few nice bits for his mum led up to this, his dream car. It wasn't new, but it was in good nick. This was what he had been building up to his whole life, buying second-hand cars that were falling apart and spending weeks trying to transform them with blacked-out windows and huge speaker systems. He didn't need to do that with this, as this car needed no embellishment.

He felt like he had gone up in the ranks of the estate overnight with people presuming he was mixing with the big boys. Women almost flagged him down begging him to let them suck his dick. His mum was the only slight issue. She had given him a cold stare when he had first pulled up outside the flat, knowing most of the motors around them were bought with dirty money. However, he smiled sweetly and told her he had won a big contract. She had asked a lot of questions but eventually believed him; he knew she was loving having one over on her mate Karen from across the road as he dropped her off at her weekly Zumba class.

Stan had soon realised that he couldn't survive on stolen funds forever. The bank card with its seemingly unlimited magic money that he had taken from Alice was delivering so far, but he knew it might run out eventually, or she might even be clever enough to close the account. He had invested some of his 'earnings' in his latest business venture. He reckoned in a few months' time he would probably have enough money to move out of the depressing high-rise building he had always called home. However, he knew he couldn't leave his mum, not just because she provided him with all his food and washing, but also because it didn't feel right leaving her here. He knew that the only thing to spur him into moving out was if he found himself a surrogate mum in the shape of a girlfriend, but he wasn't ready to settle down yet and both needs were currently being met. His other dream was making some serious cash, enough to move his mum to somewhere nicer, but he knew despite her moaning what a dump their flat was, she was still a part of the community, and those ties would be hard to break.

Still, business was good—fantastic, in fact. The film he had taken with Alice had really moved him to the big league, and his audience wanted more. With the help of a mate who had actually finished school and the cash injection he had been blessed with from his trip down south to visit Alice, he now had his own pay-per-view website. He figured that he should be the one making the money from his creative genius.

Admittedly, his market was pretty niche. He couldn't really understand it, but there were men out there prepared to pay big for films of fat women—the bigger the better. For the first couple after Alice, he had taken a starring role, but he now used a few of the kids who he used to sell a bit of weed to. He also had an editor and a web designer—in reality, brothers of mates—who knew their way around a computer. He told his mum that they were all sitting in his room playing X-box, but he knew that he might have to look at getting an office soon as she kept bursting in with cans of beer and food offerings. He always knew he had what it took to be an entrepreneur, but he had no idea that this would be his business and the one he would be so successful at.

He had little problem finding the right women. Dating apps meant that there was fresh meat on tap. He knew how to approach women, make them feel good and then go in for the kill. Some were surprised when instead of him turning up it had been one of his crew, but they had a 100% success rate so far. They had sex on camera with a variety of women whose need for attention and love was obviously more than their need for privacy. Deep down, he was a bit ashamed of what he was doing; after all, if someone had done that to his mum, he would be angry and distraught. But he guessed that his mum wouldn't be a slut like the women on here, meeting strange men for sex at the drop of a hat. One of the ingenious ideas he had put on the site was for people to rate each girl on looks and performance. The comments were cruel, but the punters kept paying. They couldn't get enough.

As Stan came, making sure it was the girl rather than the seats that bore the brunt, he thought to himself that meeting Alice was really the best thing that had happened to him in a long time.

Rachel

12 October 2018, 3 p.m.

Rachel had been shaken by the attack in Bournemouth. She had lived for a while in a squalid flat in one of the less salubrious areas of Bournemouth near a crescent nicknamed junkie town because of the residents that had cared more for little packs of brown stuff than fittings and fixtures. It was here that Rachel had given birth to Alice after she had run away from the darkness in her parent's home.

In this flat, after Alice was taken away shortly after her second birthday, Rachel spent a couple more years welcoming the oblivion. In many ways, it was a relief to not have another person to think of or worry about. It meant that she only had to worry about where she was getting her next hit. It had taken the death of a friend and not the loss of her own child for her to hit rock bottom.

Cara hadn't even been a real addict; she just liked to party at weekends. She even had a job and her own lovely flat near the seafront. The rumour was that she would party hard for nine months of the year and then her medical insurance would pay up for a month's retreat into the nearby Priory for a detox, while she told her work she was on some exotic holiday. Cara was found dead on a sofa on a bank holiday Monday, after the party had spilled into the next week and then ended abruptly.

After this, Rachel had fled from the town to be reborn in London. To her surprise, it wasn't too difficult to stop taking drugs with the support from workers in a hostel she stayed in for a while. It was the horrific step back into reality that was harder to deal with. She had found a community in South East London, slowly built up a friendship group and eventually got married and had kids with no one finding out about her shady past. If asked, she told people that her parents were dead. They were to her anyway.

These days, she still mourned for Alice, of course, in the same way she still mourned oblivion, but the memories were so vague and so full of horror that she could almost forget that she had another child. She knew Alice had returned to Rachel's childhood home, which filled her with dread, but at that stage in her life, Rachel had so little to give a child that even that option was better than what was on offer.

Her thought when seeing the horror emerge from Bournemouth was fear for Alice. As far as she knew, Alice still lived a twenty-minute train journey from the seaside town. In the days that followed the attack, she had kept an almost obsessive watch on the news, thinking she had spied Alice's hair or leg in the footage. In reality, she had no idea what Alice looked like or what she was doing. She knew her brother was in touch, but when they spoke infrequently, she never asked.

It was her punishment to be out of her daughter's life, which was why she was surprised and horrified when Tom had texted her out of the blue that day to ask if she had heard from Alice or their mother. She wondered if her motherly instinct when it came to her eldest daughter had finally kicked in, albeit twenty years late. The siblings had been close growing up, but she had shielded him from most of what was happening at home, and so, when she fell from grace so spectacularly, Tom had turned his back on her too.

Rachel was instantly worried; it was hard to be concerned about people who she hadn't seen or spoken to for years, but something that had been pushed deep inside her had been roused. She texted him back telling him that of course she hadn't heard from them (she was the last person they would get in touch with!) and the texting went back and forth for a good twenty minutes with her gleaning that Tom was worried that something had happened to Alice. Eventually, her phone rang, and she saw his name flash up.

He didn't bother with any niceties. 'You see, the thing is, the police think I am being overdramatic because Alice is now a twenty-two-year-old woman and there is no sign that anything bad has happened. But I know Alice, and I know how obsessed she is with her computer, and she has disappeared without a trace. The last time I spoke to her, she was back staying at Mum's house for her birthday.'

'Oh, did she move out then?' Rachel asked, her body flooding with relief.

'She got her own place in Bournemouth a couple of years ago, around the same time she got the job as an airhostess, but I guess you wouldn't know any of that.'

'Have you tried calling her?'

'Of course, but her mobile isn't working and even the home phone at Mum's is no longer available,' he explained angrily as if she thought he was an imbecile.

'Maybe she has changed her number or maybe Mum has finally moved out.'

'It doesn't add up, though. When I spoke to Alice on her birthday, she didn't mention a new phone, and don't you remember Mum always said the only way she would leave that house was in a coffin?'

Rachel felt wounded when he mentioned the birthday. She had remembered, of course. After all, it was her who had brought her daughter kicking and screaming into this world over two decades ago—although Alice wasn't actually a child anymore and Rachel was officially the mother of an adult.

'Is there no one else you can ask to check on her, like any of Mum's friends?'

'I wouldn't know where to start. She wasn't exactly the most popular of women, and I have a feeling she led a hermit's existence over the last few years. I think the only thing to do is for one of us to check on her, and as I am currently walking through Central Park instead of Regent's Park, I guess this one falls to you.'

Rachel felt fear and dread grip her. She hadn't been back to that house since the fateful day her mother had found out about the pregnancy. Any previous expression of motherly love had been wiped out in just a few seconds. But she knew she owed this to Alice. She had been the one that screwed up, and she now had a chance to redeem herself. She promised Tom that she would head down the following week, already thinking of an excuse for her partner. He rang off abruptly, and she reasoned that was his way of showing how little he thought of her.

Alice

It wasn't long before people were sharing what was happening. It felt like I was right in the middle of it all, and I could imagine people holding up their phones, more concerned about getting the right video than saving their lives.

Suddenly, I could hear a series of bangs like fireworks or a car backfiring. I watched in horror as people ran through crowds as the camera finally dropped to capture feet rather than the action.

Screams punctuated the air as shots were fired again and people fell to the pavements, like skittles being knocked to the ground.

Abandoning their shopping bags, people looked dazed and bloody.

And then my whole world went dark.

Tom

9 October 2018, 8 a.m.

Tom had sat up all night and watched the coverage of the Bournemouth attack in horror and fascination. It was a town that had been witness to his coming of age as a gay man. Dorchester had no scene, so after some teenage fumbles where a couple of his mates had allowed some drunken groping as long as he didn't tell a soul, the discovery of a community that was loud and proud was so refreshing. There had been no such thing as Grindr when he was a teen, and the only gay person he had known was one of his teachers (who probably wasn't actually gay but who had been tagged and therefore branded as a pervert by his school mates). So creeping into a bar at sixteen with an understanding female friend hadn't just been an eyeopener, it had completely blown his little mind.

Here there were men everywhere, with every flavour imaginable: cute youngsters like him with tight t-shirts on their soon-to-be muscly frames, scary men with moustaches in leather and beautiful women who were really men strutting like peacocks in their resplendent dresses and glittery eyeshadow. This was where he had his first kiss, his first real grope and, after spectating for several months, the place where he lost his virginity high on ecstasy with a man known as Rog. There had been some very hedonistic years, which made him all misty-eyed when he looked around his stunning yet sterile New York flat.

He had been living in London on 7/7 and came to New York only a few years after 9/11, but for some reason it was Bournemouth that really got to him. It was his real hometown, and it had a name, not just a date. His first thought had been to check on Alice. He knew she had been planning a day out and hoped she had encouraged her friends to meet her in sleepy old Dorchester, rather than dragging her out to Bournemouth.

As soon as he had seen the news, he tried to call, but her mobile seemed to be down. He remembered this happening after other attacks as people jammed the networks with calls to loved ones. It was quite normal for them not to speak for a few weeks, but at times like this, he really felt like he needed to be looking out for her. After all, no one else seemed to be.

It was now three days later, and Alice still hadn't answered either his phone calls or emails. He had even sneaked a look at all her social media profiles, and they all had been left untouched. This was unheard of for Alice who was as addicted to the online world as her mother had been to hard drugs. He still felt a bit silly calling the police and wondered if he could do a social media appeal instead, but deciding to take the grown-up approach, he found the number for the Dorset police and dialled. The phone rang out and he was about to put it down when it was answered with a brusque, 'Hello?'

Tom was thrown for a moment. 'Um, hi, yes, I am a bit worried about my niece,' he told the woman, suddenly very conscious of his mid-Atlantic twang and how it must make him sound like a bit of a twat.

The voice softened slightly. 'Is she missing?'

'That's the thing. I don't know. I am worried she might have been caught up in the Bournemouth attack as I haven't heard from her.'

'Was she in the vicinity of the area when the attack happened?'

'I don't know. I don't think so, but she hasn't been in touch and hasn't used social media since then either.'

The voice immediately hardened again. 'Sir, as you can imagine, we have been inundated by calls. Can you not contact a friend or family member or pop round there?'

'That's the thing, though. She lives alone but had been staying with my mother, and we don't exactly see eye to eye, and I live in New York, so I can't really pop over.'

Tom could tell by the sound of her voice that she thought he was wasting her time.

'Sir, I would suggest that a teenage girl taking a break from social media, particularly after recent events, is not really something to worry about. If I could get my kid to take a digital detox or whatever they call it these days, then I would be a very happy parent. However, if you leave me her name and a few details, then I will keep them on file in case something comes up.' This was said without conviction.

Tom reeled off Alice's description, knowing this was likely to be shoved in a filing cabinet under 'overreacting uncle'.

She stopped him mid-flow. 'You mean she is twenty-two?' she exclaimed. 'I thought you were talking about a child here! Considering that information, there is little we can do. If an adult chooses to not converse with you, then I think it really is up to them, don't you, sir?'

Knowing he was defeated and feeling as though he really was wasting precious police time, Tom thanked the woman and hung up.

Alice

At first, I thought maybe a big bomb had gone off, like the nuclear ones I had learnt about in history. I wondered for the second time in my life if I was dead as my eyes got used to the gloom. The first thing I noticed was how silent it was. I had never known silence, really, but it enveloped me, thick in the air. Not even a distant buzz or beep permeated my world. My immediate thought was that this must be part of the war I had been reading about. The only wars I had ever heard about were fought thousands of miles away by people I neither knew or cared about, but Gran had talked about the war her mother had lived in where people would find shelter in their basements to protect themselves from bombs and would constantly listen out for aeroplanes in the sky.

I sat in the dark and listened but could hear nothing. This made me feel calmer, but then I remembered once watching a film at school about that war and hearing that silence was actually scarier than the sound of engines because it meant the bomb had been dropped. It was a bit like how the whoosh had been worse than the bang all those years ago. I was petrified and once again found myself frozen to the spot. As my eyes adjusted to the darkness, I kept getting flashes of twisted limbs and the pungent scent I now knew signified death.

PART 2

Alice

6 October 2018, 11 a.m.

I woke with a start; the light was streaming in through the windows and my whole body ached from sleeping sitting up. I hadn't meant to fall asleep, and the adrenaline had kept me going for a long time until I had finally collapsed. Again, it was the silence that unnerved me at first. I went upstairs to look out of the window to see if the rest of the world had been destroyed, but everything still looked the same. The trees I could see from my windows still stood and the birds still sang.

Maybe they, whoever they were, were uninterested in sleepy, small suburbs. I wasn't sure if the war had actually reached Dorchester at all, but the news story had said it was spreading across the UK, and with Bournemouth being hit so recently, I presumed that even if they were not yet in control of the whole county, they soon would be. I heard a helicopter fly overhead and wondered if this was the army rule and martial law I had read about yesterday or if it was the enemy. I wasn't sure if helicopters could drop bombs or if it was just aeroplanes, and I felt myself duck involuntarily.

I dragged myself to the kitchen. Everything looked the same, but there was a new smell. I opened the fridge to see that the light was off and the little remnants of food I had in there were not looking too healthy. I realised that nothing in the kitchen was working, not even the kettle, and that a big pool of water told of a freezer that had warmed and spat its unfrozen water to the lino floor. I realised I was starving and couldn't remember the last time I had eaten. I wondered if the army would be sending food or aid parcels out like I had seen in other countries when there was a war on.

I picked up a pot noodle and went to switch on the kettle but then remembered that the house had lost its electricity. That was what had caused the darkness and the silence. I ran the hot tap, and after an age, I got a few seconds of warm water to drench my noodles before it went cold again. I sat on the sofa with my meal, and it was as if I had a phantom limb as I kept grasping for my phone, but it was lying with no power and was about as useful as a chocolate teapot. The truth was, I had never just sat. My entire world was lived in front of an audience who in turn amused me. I never even remembered being bored before as I always had the world literally at my fingertips. Now I wondered if that world had indeed ended. If the electricity had gone, then I guessed there would be no way of people getting online. It was the end of the world as I knew it.

I sat and waited all day. I didn't know what I was waiting for, rescue or the end of the actual world. Without the distraction of food or fun, the day was long. I had no idea what the time was as all the clocks in the house had been digital. I was almost relieved when dusk arrived. With no lights in the house, I was forced to go to bed.

Alice

5 October 2018, 4 p.m.

Seeing what was happening and knowing I had been in that exact place suddenly made it real for me, even if I was just watching this all online without actually being there. My mind didn't seem to know the difference. In my head, I felt like I was there, right there, in the carnage from the attack.

The familiar fear crept over my body as my ears rang with a loud bang. The smell of acrid smoke and burning and the sight of bloodied limbs and twisted metal were everywhere. I felt again as though I was rooted to the spot as I had been on that day, the day of the train crash, years ago, which now leaped into my mind as though I was replaying a graphic video, one I didn't have the off button for. I could feel pain all over my body, and my mind could not process where the actual injury was.

I moved between each social media account, each dishing up descriptions and images that were worse than the last. Joining the horror were pictures of girls like me, mothers like I imagined Rachel to be and old ladies like my gran, all now missing after evil had landed in the once sunny seaside town. People were describing tattoos, clothes and any last known movements of loved ones who were feared caught up in the moment a lone gunman had unleashed terror on the streets of the town.

I stayed up all night glued to my laptop. I watched the same footage over and over, shared the appeals and joined my online world in its collective shock and grief. For once, I clicked on the news stories being shared, desperate to glean any information, and I found out that the attacker was a young man born in the town who had shot himself at the scene. Neighbours, friends and teachers were quick to go on air to say he had been a strange boy but that no one could believe he would do this. Experts were called in to diagnose a range of mental health problems for the boy, although he had shown no signs of any. The only way for many to comprehend evil was to stick a label on it. The attack now had an official 'brand' and a hashtag. The various news channels were offering up coverage with snazzy graphics. Fluffy morning interviews on the sofa were replaced by hard-hitting journalists on location and in black tie.

I slept occasionally and fitfully between refreshing the pages. The shadowy images in my brain while asleep were far worse than what I was seeing on my screen. By lunchtime, the coverage had moved from breaking news to memorials, and pictures were being shared of the mound of flowers, photos and teddies left in the town square. Crowdfunding pages had been set up to fund funerals, accommodation and even shop fronts. I found it hard to work out who was posting what on my feeds as everyone had changed their profile picture to the official #PrayforBournemouth image. Stories were emerging of heroic acts, lives cut short too soon and speculation on how and why the young man had decided to pick up a gun that sunny day.

Nightfall surprised me that day. I had barely moved from the sofa apart from using the toilet and making the occasional cup of black tea. I had even forgotten to eat, which was unheard of for me. I was set up with my laptop, phone and iPad all in front of the giant TV which was churning out Sky News. My thirst to find out new information was currently greater than any other need, and I felt as though I belonged now to this great online world, more than I ever had before. For once, I had no words. I didn't know how to respond, so I just sat and observed.

The story of the gunman had by now run its natural course, and much of what I was seeing was commentary and remembrance alongside the regurgitated videos and interviews I had seen perhaps hundreds of times that day. A tweet suddenly caught my eye with its *Breaking News* strapline. Within seconds, it had been retweeted hundreds of times over. I clicked through, and the headline screamed at me:

Beginning of World War Three, Fanatics with Bombs and Guns Have Invaded Every Town Centre

Accompanying the story was a picture of men with beards brandishing guns in the middle of an unnamed shopping centre. The news hadn't reached the television yet, and I watched for the breaking news to flash across the screen. Yet still people were sharing, commenting and panicking en masse. I turned down the television and could hear sirens wailing outside. Usually this would have made me panic, but the noise meant that at least the good guys were out there. I cursed as my phone ran out of battery. I usually had it plugged in most of the day.

It was sudden when my world went dark. I had known the electricity to go off in the past when a fuse had blown or a storm had knocked out some power line, but not like this as an aggressive form of attack. My silence was broken by a loud ping coming from the living room, and I crawled back in there, thinking if people were watching the house, waiting to attack, then at least they might not see me.

My heart rose as I realised my iPad was glowing its familiar blue colour. Making my way over to the sofa, I almost cried in relief when I realised that my link to the outside world was not completely gone as my iPad still had a dribble of power in it. My laptop, though, wouldn't switch on, as it too was out of power. The ping had been from an email from Tom checking that I hadn't been caught up in the Bournemouth shooting. He obviously hadn't heard about the all-out war yet. I guessed that America wouldn't carry every news story from the UK, and maybe that hadn't reached overseas yet with all the electricity problems.

I quickly switched back to Twitter, hating feeling out of the loop, and noticed the hashtag #worldwar3. I looked in horror at the tweets flowing quickly of people talking about hearing bangs and sirens, the army on the streets and generally all-out panic. The original story had been retweeted millions of times by now and shared on Facebook with thousands of comments of people sharing their worries and similar sightings. I was refreshing the page when the screen went black and I was all on my own again.

Alice
5 October 2018, 1 p.m.

On the day of my birthday, I was feeling almost cheerful. First of all, the kudos that comes from having a birthday online is so much greater than in real life. My memories of birthdays when I was still a member of the outside world were pretty miserable. We never really held parties as such—apart from one year when I turned eleven, but this had never been repeated. Uncle Tom had, of course, made an effort to visit every year, until Gran had disowned him. Then, by the time I was old enough to go out by myself, he had moved an entire ocean away. Gran had made a real effort each year, as if to make up for the lack of a mother, but although Gran usually spoiled me and allowed me to eat what I wanted, it was just like another day.

Not so these days, as everyone knew it was my birthday, without me having to even drop hints. They would have been alerted via Facebook or email that morning. Before I was even out of bed, I had eighty-six birthday messages. I was really touched that some of them included a cake or funny picture; these were my cards, and if I had printed out each one, the room would have looked like Clinton's.

I had eventually blocked and deleted all the horrible Twitter messages I had received and felt safe opening my profile again. I had messaged Stan asking if he had been hacked, but although the ticks told me he had seen it, he hadn't answered back.

I was now in a dilemma as he still had the cash card which was my only access to money. I was already halfway through the tins of food in the cupboard. What he also had was a film of us having sex. I didn't want to annoy him in case it got into the wrong hands. Just a screenshot had sent my whole world into disarray, and I don't know how that had leaked. There was also still a part of me that hoped he still cared. I was so worried that I had put him off by not doing sex in the right way. I had thought he had enjoyed it even if I definitely hadn't, but it may not have been enough.

A couple of hours later, I noticed that something out there was taking the attention away from my birthday. One by one I started noticing people changing their profile pictures to include a British Flag, a picture of a beach and a #prayforBournemouth hashtag.

I then heard my mobile ringing in the kitchen. Despite being glued to my phone, I rarely used it as a phone, so I was always surprised when it rang. I picked it up before it went to voicemail. A familiar voice sang at me.

'Happy Birthday, my beautiful, wonderful niece, and how are you today?'

I tried to sound happy, to not allow my voice to give away the horror of the last few weeks. 'Amazing! It is so lovely to hear from you.'

'So, what are you up to today? Will you be celebrating with the old bag or escaping into town with your reprobate friends to cause havoc in the dusty department store?'

I really didn't like Tom speaking about Granny like that. It wasn't good to speak ill of the dead, although I guessed he didn't know that.

'Gran has made me a special birthday breakfast and then I am off to do some shopping and have a few cocktails with my friends.' The lie rolled off my tongue as easily as it had done for the last few years.

The reality was I had no food in the house, and although there were cocktails if I really wanted them, the thought made me feel ill.

'And how is my lovely mother?' asked Tom, throwing me slightly. He never usually asked after her, and I hated lying a real lie—not a little white lie—to my favourite person.

'Um, fine. She is actually in the cellar right now,' I told him, thinking that it was the truth, albeit with a slight twist.

'Oh, yes, she is probably adding to her panic room down there! We always used to laugh at her stockpiling, but actually, the way things are in the world, particularly with my fantastic, trigger-happy president, dear old Mum will probably be the only one that survives a nuclear war!'

I didn't really know what he was talking about. I took no notice of real news, but I vowed to have a read before I spoke to Tom next.

'I actually tried phoning you on the home phone but there was just a tone. Has the old bat left it off the hook or something?'

'Oh, maybe that was me,' I jumped in, wanting to defend my dead gran so that Tom wouldn't be too horrible about her.

We chatted for a while longer about Tom and his exciting life in New York. As always, he invited me over to visit him, and as always, I told him I would love to, knowing I would have at least a month to make up a good excuse why I couldn't come. I always made sure I only posted about my New York trips on my Instagram in case he wondered why I never visited, despite looking like I was constantly at 30,000 feet.

We ended the phone call, which left me feeling sadder than usual. Usually a message or email was enough to keep me happy for a while, but I found that I was physically craving having someone near me. I hadn't seen or spoken to another person since Stan, and I was feeling very lonely, despite my happy day full of lovely messages.

After I had spoken to Tom, I went to pick up the home telephone in the corner of the room and found that it was dead. I wondered if it was a fault but figured that I never really used it so I could ignore that particular problem for now. I remembered that Granny used to moan about paying the phone bill. She moaned about paying a lot of the bills, but the phone was a particular bugbear. I had never paid any bills before and realised that I had no idea how it all happened.

I returned to my iPad. By now, a lot of my 'local' friends were marking themselves as 'safe' and sharing news stories. I clicked on one with trepidation as the page told me that there had been some kind of incident in the centre of Bournemouth, a town not far away, where I had been shopping with Gran on a couple of occasions. It was the shiny grown-up sister to the sleepy town I lived in, and in fact, this was where most people thought I lived. After all, an air hostess wouldn't still be living with her granny. This was the trouble with reinventing yourself online. You start with one little lie and soon you were having to make up a whole new world for yourself. In fact, the last time I had been there was the time my world had literally crashed in around me when I had been involved in a terrible train crash. I had left the home since then but never returned to that place.

I quickly switched to Instagram where my feed was still full of lovely pictures of sunny holidays and cute pets. I lost myself for a while in the joys of pretty sunsets. After a few minutes, I went back to my social media and was surprised to see that the incident was still dominating my feeds.

I retweeted a few of the links, adding the pre-requisite hashtag as well as suitable emojis.

By now people had shared footage of what had happened. In the grainy videos, I could see confusion. One showed the familiar town square filled with shoppers where one girl was filming her friends. Suddenly a series of bangs could be heard like fireworks, and moments later, the film followed whoever was holding the phone, obviously running through a crowd of people.

Another that was taken straight after whatever had happened saw abandoned shopping bags with people looking dazed and bloody. The most shared was taken from a little way up a hill and had caught the moment that the carnage had been unleashed. Screams punctuated the air as you could hear the sound of shots again as people fell to the pavements like skittles being knocked to the ground. You could hear the person holding the camera swear and scream, but I noted that the filming didn't waver.

Actually seeing what was happening and knowing I had been in that exact same place suddenly made it real. The familiar fear started to creep over my body and I was back there, again.

Alice

30 September 2018, 12.30 p.m.

When I woke, I was shocked that it was already the afternoon. I wasn't feeling hungry but had no energy, and thinking this was down to lack of food, I took myself into the kitchen to make my morning meal. Scrabbling around the cupboard, I managed to find some instant noodles. It wasn't the most appetising of foods, but I was surprised to note that even the smell of the juices failed to arouse my appetite. This was a new feeling to me and the first time I could ever remember not wolfing down the food that was in front of me. Half-heartedly, I grabbed my phone to scroll through as I picked my noodles. I had amassed hundreds of notifications overnight, which would usually keep me busy and happy for at least an hour, but it failed to excite in its usual way. I couldn't even bother posting a picture of my current meal, particularly as the idea of styling my sad snack into food porn made me feel exhausted.

I made the first of many cups of tea and went to sit in the living room thinking that maybe the lovely, new sofa would cheer me up, but it made me think more about how my gran should be sitting on it or how Stan should be watching something silly with me. Switching on the TV, I channel hopped for a while before finally settling on some quiz show, not knowing any of the answers and actually not even trying to answer them. My phone continued to bleep next to me, and after a while, I did something I hadn't done for a while: I switched it off. As I made endless cups of black tea, I considered fetching the box of fags that Gran always kept in her handbag. I could see now why Gran had smoked, as it gave you something to do.

It was as I was heading to put the kettle on again that I noticed Gran's drinks cabinet in the corner of my eye. Gran had always liked to keep a well-stocked drinks cabinet, in case of guests. I wasn't sure why, as no one ever came over, and I only ever saw Gran drink a glass or two of sherry on special occasions. I had never tried alcohol, as the stories of my mother stumbling around had been quite the deterrent. I knew lots of the groups at school had gathered to drink at the local park, but I had never been popular enough to be involved.

For some reason, the cabinet was calling me today. My usual way of cheering myself up—which was food—wasn't really an option, and besides, it didn't seem to be helping anyway. I didn't know which one to pick so I picked up the vodka as I knew it was a popular choice. After cleaning one of the crystal glasses on my clothes, I poured myself a big glass. It looked so much like water that I was incredibly surprised that the taste was so strong and disgusting. The liquid burned the back of my throat and made my eyes water, and I spit out the part of the mouthful I hadn't swallowed. I wondered why on earth anyone would choose to do this to themselves. I had always been a bit jealous of my friends when they were out drinking, having a good time, but if that fun was dependent on drinking something that repulsive, then their smiles must have all been fake.

I wondered if I needed to mix the vodka to make it taste better. There was a bottle full of pink stuff called Schnapps, so I glugged a big measure into the glass alongside the vodka. It now looked nice, like my favourite berry squash, but I knew now that the look of a drink was not a great sign of how it would taste. I took a small sip. This was better now that it had a certain sweetness, and as it went down my throat, it felt like the warmth from an open fire rather than a flaming inferno. I managed a few sips and tried to work out if it was having an effect. I didn't really feel different but maybe it took a while to kick in. I finished my whole glass before sitting back on the sofa.

Twenty minutes later, the room was spinning. I felt as though I couldn't think straight and certainly couldn't concentrate, but I found that actually this was quite a nice state to be in at this point of time. My day had been stretched out in front of me as long and lonely, and yet the addition of this little glass of poison (my gran's words) meant that I felt I could cope a little better. I turned up the TV that was now on some show where people cooked for each other.

With the cocktail heightening my senses, I joined in with the action, describing what each contestant was wearing. I personally thought I was actually funnier than the man with the funny voice who was being sarcastic. One of the women got an Irish band into her garden to wow her guests, and I found myself hauling myself from the sofa and jumping around, before landing very puffed out, yet laughing a few minutes later. I realised that this was too good not to share, and so I switched on my phone to tell the world an edited version of what I was doing. Realising that five o'clock was a bit early for a raucous dinner party, I made it into lunch that had spilled over into the evening, swapping the Irish music for a cheesy impromptu '80's disco in the home of one of my best friends and making up a name for the cocktail I had created with a shot of the drink in a martini glass I had found. Somehow the fact that I had that pink liquid swilling around in me made it all feel more fun and authentic than usual, and I swayed across the room to pour myself another glass, tweeting as I sipped.

My friends couldn't get enough of this 'fun Alice' and were liking and commenting on all my new posts about the people at the party and my wild antics. It was actually easier describing partygoers when they were on the screen in front of me, and I went to town. I felt as though I could be in the room with all of them at this time and wondered if this wonder liquid could ever get me out of the house and into the situation for real.

Then, in amongst all the lovely feedback from my adoring fans, I noticed an enemy. It was a Twitter user, @blackgun, who had a pistol as his avatar. I didn't follow him and I had never seen him before.

@blackgun **Such a FAKEE Fat bitch**

I froze as my heart beat fast and I felt sick. I dropped my phone as though whoever it was could see me. Before I responded, he posted again.

@blackgun **All you hos are the same fuckin cunts pretendin u r so much better than us**

I noticed that some of my followers were leaping to my defence with plenty of smiley faces but also realised with dread that others liked and retweeted his vile words.

@blackgun **I no for a fact that u r just a fat bitch who fucs men 4 money**

Despite the alcohol swishing around my body, dulling my senses, I could feel a sense of dread overwhelm me as I started to gasp for breath. My heart thrashed around in my chest and I clutched it, scared it would burst with the sharp pain and the effort of my breathing. Then there was the blackness which started around me in the room but soon crept inside my brain until I felt as though I was drowning in the blackness, falling with no one to save me.

It could have been seconds or hours before I began to feel conscious of my surroundings again. Now the alcohol was making me feel sick and dizzy, but I knew how good it was at dulling the senses, so I poured myself another glass, with more pink stuff and less vodka this time. My usual way of dealing with these 'funny turns' was to remove myself from the situation. But how could I do that here? My whole life was online, and without that, I had nothing.

I glanced at my phone and could see that my whole feed was filled with the hatred and vitriol being spouted by my nemesis. The usual heart emojis, celeb gossip and cute kittens were replaced with ugly words and accusations. Trying not to read them, I blocked him and again turned off my phone, this time not because I didn't want to take part in life but because I feared the power it held, scared that the perfect life I had spent so long creating was being ripped to shreds by one little person.

After a few minutes of silence, I could no longer bear not knowing, so I turned my phone back on. The original poster was joined by a few others, all calling me horrific names. I felt sick when I realised that one of them was sharing a screenshot from my night with Stan. Luckily it was pretty blurred so no one could really see what I looked like or how I looked nothing like any of my profiles—well, I did, just several stone heavier. Thinking straight away that Stan must have been hacked, I felt relieved. This may have been why he hadn't responded for so long if he had been locked out of his accounts.

The posts had turned even more sinister, with people telling me that girls like me were only good for one thing and that was being raped and killed. One faceless poster in particular was describing exactly how he would shove sharp objects inside me and then strangle me slowly. Every time I tried blocking them, someone else would turn up and start abusing me. It was like that game of hungry hippos, although in this case, I was trying to starve rather than feed my attackers.

Suddenly, I felt sick again, but unlike my panic attack, I knew this wasn't just in my mind. I launched myself into the kitchen but didn't quite reach it as I vomited all over the floor, feeling as though my dreams and hopes lay stinking all over the lino alongside my stomach contents. I couldn't face the mammoth task of cleaning this up, so I stumbled off to bed and passed out into a dark, dreamless sleep.

Stan

28 September 2018, 4 p.m.

Stan had almost closed the door and run when he had first turned up on Alice's doorstep. He knew most girls would air-brush pictures to make themselves look better, but the differ-ence between the girl he had been flirting with online and the obese monster in the flesh were so marked that they may as well have been two different people. In fact, Stan wondered if she had picked out a random fit girl and stolen her identity. She also looked far younger than the twenty-something he had been chatting with—she still had boyband posters in her room, for god's sake! Still, Stan had driven all the way down from London and had spent money on petrol for his precious car and lunch for his 'date', although it didn't look like she needed any more McDonald's. It was ironic, really, that he had chosen the salad for her. So Stan didn't want a wasted trip.

He knew there was a market for BBW—or Big Beautiful Women. It wasn't exactly his cup of tea, but he had heard that some men would even pay to be squashed by fat girls. Never one to miss a business opportunity, and he had to admit curiosity himself, Stan had decided he would at least screw her before he left. Her size obviously left her grateful for any attention. There had been something else really strange about the house. She clearly wasn't house-proud, as there was rubbish all over the lawn, but it was fairly tidy inside. She smelt good, but the house had a really strange whiff in it—there was the smell of air freshener but also something really nasty. He couldn't put his finger on it.

Now he was leaving her house to carry out some stupid errand like some kind of pussy. He blamed his mum; she had always instilled manners in him. Still, at least he could get his petrol money back, and that, along with the money he was hoping to make from his little film, should mean that he was quids in after this little trip down south. Stan even wondered if Alice had any other ugly, fat friends he could meet to make it even more worthwhile.

Despite the letter in his pocket, Stan felt dodgy just walking into the bank. He had been directed towards the type of high street that probably hadn't changed since the eighties with a yellowing department store and run-down shops. He had also noticed that he stood out like a sore thumb with his dark skin, and he could swear people were clutching their bags that bit closer as he walked near. He almost chickened out but then thought of his petrol money and pushed the door to enter. He was accosted almost immediately by a smiley woman with far too much makeup on.

'Good morning and welcome! How can we help you this morning?' she said without breaking her smile.

'I need to transfer some money on behalf of my great aunty,' Stan mumbled, and the smiley lady practically frogmarched him to the counter. He seemed to be the only customer in the building, which made him feel even more nervous. He could hear the clock ticking and was sure it was being drowned out by the sound of his heart beating.

Stan got to the counter and handed over the letter and explained the situation. He told the lady behind the counter that his great aunty was in hospital after a fall, so she had asked him to move money around for her. The woman behind the counter was silently looking at the letter. Her lack of communication was making Stan more nervous, so he gabbled. 'Yes, she had a terrible fall in her house. Lucky I was visiting her that day, really; otherwise, who knows what kind of state she would have been in. You know you have to watch out for older relatives, especially when it gets colder.'

Eventually the woman looked straight up at Stan. 'I was wondering where Mrs Carmichael had got to, as she is usually in here every Thursday, regular as clockwork. Is she in the general, then?'

Stan guessed she meant a hospital and nodded.

'She never mentioned that she had a grandson; of course, she always talked about her Alice.'

Stan almost added the 'black' before the grandson as he knew the clerk had wanted to. 'I am actually her great-nephew; my granny is her sister.'

'Oh yes, is that Rose? She moved off abroad somewhere, didn't she?'

Stan nodded hoping that this might explain the colour of his skin to the nosy clerk.

'Unfortunately we can't go around accessing bank accounts without the proper checks.'

Stan was almost relieved as he put his hand out to get the letter back.

'I will need to see some form of ID, young man, so you can prove you are who you say you are.'

Stan almost choked as he got his driving licence out and showed it to the woman.

'Now, how much did she want to move over to her current account?'

'She said £5000, please. She was not sure how long she was going to be in hospital,' he said as a way of explaining such a high amount.

'Yes, she usually only moves a couple of hundred pounds a week.'

Stan wondered if he should revise down the number, but the clerk was busy typing something into the computer in front of him.

'You know, to be honest, the interest rates are so low at the moment, your granny—I mean, great aunty would be better off keeping her money under the mattress. I shouldn't really say that, working in a bank and all, but if she is going to be in the hospital for a while, you may as well move a lot more over.

Doesn't really make much difference where it's kept.'

'OK, shall we move over £50,000 then? Just so I don't have to come back and do this again in a couple of months?' A plan was forming in Stan's head that went well beyond covering his petrol money. He still expected them to catch him out, so he smiled his most charming smile.

She clicked a few buttons and it was done. 'Now, would you like a printout of the balances for your great aunty, as well as a receipt?'

Stan nodded and then added a quick, 'Yes, please', just to sound polite. He took the papers handed to him and began to walk away. He was almost at the door when he heard the clerk call out.

'Young man, can you come back here for a minute, please?'

Stan thought he had been rumbled and thought about ignoring the woman and walking away, but that would only look even more suspicious, so he turned back and smiled politely.

'I wonder if you would mind filling in a survey to say how we did today? It is all electronic on the terminal over there. I don't see the need, but head office loves it.'

'Oh, yes, of course. You have been very helpful.' Stan now sounded like an Eton graduate, which was just as out of place in this West Country town as his London twang was. He was able to leave without any other interruption and went straight to the cash machine and took out £200. Again, there were no sirens, no police waiting to pounce.

It wasn't until he reached the safety of his car that he felt he could breathe normally again. He looked at the pieces of paper in his hand and gasped out loud when he realised what one balance said. It was sitting there in black and white, all £117,000 of it. Lucky Granny was sitting on one hell of a nest egg. Stan wondered cruelly why her granddaughter was going around looking like a tattered streetwalker when Granny was clearly not broke.

Stan then looked down at the cash card he had along with the letter, and the idea that had started in the bank became real. Alice and her granny clearly didn't appreciate the money—that was obvious from the ramshackle old home. Stan also guessed that if this was the amount that Granny had in the bank, then she would have a stash around at home somewhere too. Alice apparently had a good job as an air hostess (although Stan was doubting this after meeting her.) Stan knew he could do so much with that money, and it seemed a shame to waste it all on a lady that would probably die any minute and her obese grand-daughter. So, he may even be doing Alice a favour; after all, she might eat her way through a few thousand. He didn't owe her anything; she had lied to him.

All the excuses seemed to him perfectly plausible, but Stan was still hesitating. He had only ever dabbled in minor criminal activity, whereas this was grand theft and fraud. Stan wondered how he could get away with it. Would he need to carry on being nice to Alice or was it best to cut her off altogether? Stan decided he would leave it for a day or two to see what happens; after all, she had given him the letter and he hadn't yet taken any money out, apart from the £200 that she had more or less promised him. Feeling equally scared and exhilarated, Stan started the car and headed home to London.

Alice

28 September 2018, 1 p.m.

When the front doorbell rang early that afternoon, I could feel the stirrings of a panic attack, both at the thought of having to open the door again and also, of course, knowing who was standing behind it. I eventually controlled my breathing and checked myself in the hallway mirror by the front door. I tried to open it casually as though inviting men into my home was something I did all the time, but I was sure he could hear my heart hammering. There on the other side was Stan.

He was a lot shorter and skinnier than I had imagined, but I guess I, more than anyone, knew how to project an image online. Trying to act like the sophisticated woman he thought I was, I smiled and invited him in. He looked unsure to begin with, and I wondered if this was new for him too.

'Um, Alice?' he asked, looking uncomfortable.

'Hi,' I replied wondering whether I should kiss him on the cheek or shake his hand.

'I bought us some lunch,' he explained, shoving some McDonald's bags into my hands. I breathed in the heavenly scent of oil and carbs gratefully and quickly shut the door so he couldn't change his mind.

I was glad now I hadn't laid the table, as that was far too formal for this type of date, but I stupidly felt almost too shy to eat in front of him. Maybe this was the answer to my diet dilemma. If Stan was sitting in front of me for every meal, then I may just eat like a normal person. As I unwrapped the bags, it became clear that there was one portion of chips and one salad, which I presumed was for me to accompany my quarter pounder. I almost asked him if I could share his chips but then realised that the girls Stan usually went for probably didn't eat chips. In fact, nor did Online Alice, apart from at the end of an all-day bender. The conversation didn't flow as I hoped it would, and we sat to eat our lunch in silence. I almost suggested that we both get on our phones to message each other since we had never had a problem communicating that way.

When we'd finished, I cleared up the rubbish and then had no idea what we could do; after all, I hadn't had a visitor of my own in the house for many years. I suggested that we go to the living room to watch some TV, thankful for the new sofa.

'You mean Netflix and Chill?' said Stan with a smile.

I knew what he meant, but I ignored this, trying to buy time. 'My gran doesn't have any streaming, sadly. You know what old people are like!' He looked like he wanted to tell me what he really meant but let me lead him through.

I let him flick through the channels. I figured he was the type of man who liked to take control. Finally he landed on some MTV show about people who did up their cars. He seemed engrossed, so I asked him about his car. It was as though a light had switched on as his excitement levels jumped, almost as if he was talking about his own child. He told me he had an old school Mercedes that he had 'pimped out' and asked if I wanted to come and see it in the driveway. I hated to disappoint him but knew I would never make it outside and didn't want to shame myself by having a panic attack in front of my potential new boyfriend.

'Let's watch the rest of this show first and maybe you can show me some pictures,' I said, buying myself some time.

'So where is your gran then? You said you were visiting her, but I thought she had died?'

I thought quickly. 'Oh, yes, that was my other gran; this is where my nanny, my mum's mum, lives.' I crossed my fingers knowing it was a white lie. Of course, Stan had seen my posts of the death; he had even comforted me.

'Oh sweet, she clearly likes her TV,' he said, pointing at the massive box on the wall. It was actually quite old fashioned. It definitely wasn't a flat screen, but what it lacked in technology it made up for in size.

'She's had to go into hospital, unfortunately, so I am house-sitting for her.'

'And you said you were ill too? Better not be something catching,' he said moving away on the sofa slightly.

'No, don't worry, it is just a migraine type thing. I get them all the time. It means I can't really go outside.' I thought this sounded like a very sophisticated illness to have.

Stan looked more comfortable and moved closer again, his hand inching over my leg. I thought it was as good a time as any to try to get his help.

'I was wondering if you could do me a favour while you were here,' I dropped in casually. 'You see, I would usually do it, but my car seems to have packed up and is in the garage, and with this headache, I am probably best not going out. I was wondering if you wouldn't mind going to the bank for me. It's for my grandma, really, as she needs some money moved from her savings account into her current account. Can you believe she hasn't yet embraced online banking?'

Stan looked horrified at the idea of having to run an errand. Not wanting to lose him, I quickly tried to sweeten the pill.

'I can pay you. If you take along her card, then you can take £100 or so for yourself.' I hoped this wasn't a tiny sum for Stan as it still seemed like a fortune to me.

Stan looked like he was thinking about it. 'The money is all very well, but you know what I really want and you know why I am really here, so how about we come to some other kind of arrangement and then I think I would be happy to go out and help your granny. After all, my mum always said you should respect your elders.'

I tried to look alluring as my heart sank. I guess I had always known what was on the cards if I invited Stan into my home;

after all, I had been leading him on for some time. I knew the payment and I knew what men really wanted.

'Yes, of course, I can give you what you want too, since you have come all this way. It really is nice of you to visit me.' I put on a smile for him.

Taking this as some kind of green light, Stan lunged at me, grabbing my boob and clamping his mouth over mine. It wasn't the gentle probing kiss I had been hoping for. The curtains in the room were open, and I immediately felt exposed to the outside world.

'Let's go upstairs to my room instead,' I suggested, taking his hand and leading the way. I hoped I was being seductive, but it felt more like I was walking towards the slaughterhouse. My hands were shaking so much.

I felt even more anxious in my room with all the One Direction paraphernalia smiling back at us. Luckily the fairy lighting in the room was soft, and I hoped the overall effect was sexy rather than dark. He did look a bit taken aback at the duvet cover, but he was too busy trying to take my cardigan off to worry for long. I noticed that he then reached for his phone, and he put it on one of the bookshelves on a mini tripod thing; he spent a while adjusting the phone to get the right angle before he turned his attention back to me.

'I like to have a record of whenever I shag beautiful women,' he explained.

I knew this was the 'thing' these days. Entire relationships were documented and posted online. It was probably unusual for people to do it without some kind of evidence.

I tried to hide the fact that my dress didn't do up—it was far too small for me and I hadn't managed to pull up the zip—by taking it off really quickly. I then tried to get under my duvet cover, but Stan stopped me and turned on the bedside lamp.

'It's better to have more light for the camera and so I can see you better,' he explained.

I hated being seen in so much light. I even got dressed in the dark, so this was brutal. I could immediately see all my rolls of fat and skin, which was pasty and covered in stretch marks. The breasts I had hoped would attract him now spilled out of my too-small greying bra, and my stomach sank heavily over the tight waistband of my knickers. I quickly adjusted myself and lay backwards; at least that way some of my curves would be flattened.

Stan picked up the phone and held it in front of me, the camera taking in everything. 'Take off your bra,' he ordered.

This was tricky to do from my lying down position, so I sat up again and tried to do it one-handed but struggled and had to resort to tugging with two hands pretty quickly.

'Now stay sitting up and squeeze your nipples between your fingers,' he said as much to the phone as to me.

This felt wrong, but I did as I was told, feeling stupid and suddenly scared. Stan then leaned in to touch me. He was a bit hard on me, almost as though he was tinkering with his car, and I wished he was touching me as softly as I had imagined so many times before. I tried making the right noises to pretend that I was enjoying it. As I did this, Stan moved his phone to my face. This threw me and made me feel even more self-conscious, so I closed my eyes and pretended it wasn't there. He stopped touching my breasts and told me to take my pants off. This was quite a struggle, and I got out of breath, but soon enough I was sitting naked in my bed with a man in front of me. It was the moment I had dreamed of.

At last he took his own clothes off, which made me feel more comfortable with the whole situation. Some teacher at school had once told me to imagine everyone naked as I was doing a presentation in front of the school. I guess it was because everyone is a bit ridiculous with no clothes on, even Stan with his little skinny legs. I noticed that he didn't turn the camera on himself; in fact, he put it back on the shelf so that it could capture the full scene.

With no warning, he was suddenly on top of me pushing himself into me. The only thing I could feel was excruciating pain, and I called out for him to stop, but he carried on. This suddenly felt so wrong. Why had I ever thought I would enjoy this, even with a man I was attracted to? He was a dead weight, and I felt as though I would split in half. I couldn't help it and started to cry softly as I tried to push him off me, but the pain carried on. Finally, he pulled out of me, seemingly ignoring my discomfort, but rather than stopping, he told me to turn over. I thought this was the end of it, but I was soon in agony as he pushed himself inside there, holding my arms down.

This time I couldn't hide my crying and wailed openly in pain, begging him to stop. It felt as though a red-hot needle was being pushed into me. If anything, my cries seemed to make him push harder and faster.

Suddenly, I was no longer in the room, and it was no longer my body that was being pummelled. It was as though I was watching a film and my brain was floating up above my body. The pain was gone, and I felt calmer. This is what used to happen back then. This was why the whole horrible situation was a blur. I had magical powers and could take myself away.

Eventually I found myself back in the room as I heard him cry out as though in pain. His whole body shuddered before he flopped onto me. He rested there for a few minutes before rolling off me and freeing himself from the condom he had somehow rolled on. I moved away from the wetness in the middle of the bed and curled up on the side.

Even after all that had happened, I wanted Stan to hug me and tell me everything would be alright, but he had already jumped out of bed to clean up in the bathroom. I guess I was naïve, but I had always imagined that my first time—well, my *real* first time, not what had happened before—would be something really special and wonderful, and I felt horribly let down. Still, I hoped that now that I had given Stan what he wanted that he would do what I had asked.

I got dressed quickly and waited for Stan. He came back in the room, seemingly not bothered by his nakedness, and continued to get dressed. He was so casual, it was as though the sex had never happened. We walked downstairs together.

'So, what are the instructions to help out your granny then?' he asked while getting his coat on. There was instant relief, but even after everything he had done to me, I was a bit annoyed he was leaving already as I had planned an afternoon with him. But then nothing about today had turned out as planned.

I had it all prepared; there was a form signed by Granny (well, forged by me, with lots of practice over the years staying off PE at school). The form stated that Stan Crane had permission to instruct the bank on Granny's behalf. I also gave him the cash card and the pin that Granny had helpfully written in her wallet. I wrote the instructions to move £5000 from the savings account to the current account along with the address of the bank. I knew I was putting my trust in him, but at this stage, I had little choice. I had run out of money and needed to eat. I also knew now that I had given him such a big part of myself that he owed me. Just like when he had arrived, I didn't know how to say goodbye. Were we now lovers? Was he my boyfriend or a friend with benefits? I went to kiss him goodbye as he walked out the door but missed his cheek and got his ear instead.

I sat waiting for Stan's return for hours. My seduction outfit was feeling tight and uncomfortable, but I didn't want him coming back to find me in my usual bedtime gear. Although I didn't want to look too desperate, I messaged him a few times, but although he was online, he wasn't answering. I panicked in case he had been stopped trying to move the money or that he had been in an accident. It seemed that I lost everyone I cared about, and although I was not sure how much I still cared about him, he was now even more important to me, after what I had given him. Thoughts of Stan lying in a police cell or hospital kept flashing through my mind, and knowing I may have caused something bad to happen to him was making me increasingly guilty.

I had Googled to see if there had been any incidents in the area and set up a Twitter alert, but my sleepy hometown only had its usual misdemeanours: cows on the road, a shoplifter being caught and accusations of local council corruption. I had even pulled together a nice meal for both of us using the last bits from the freezer; it looked a bit like Tapas, only my version had onion rings, scampi and wedges in place of more exotic offer-ings. I had put each section on a different saucer, only I had man-aged to work my way through most of it and the rest sat cold and congealed on the kitchen table.

Eventually my phone pinged with an update and I could see that Stan had posted on Facebook. Hoping that he was talking about his visit here, or even updating his relationship status, I was disappointed to see that he was moaning about being stuck in London traffic. In my relief, I commented on his status straight away.

Glad you got back to London safely babe, so good to see you xxx

Then I waited.

Two hours later with still no answer, I went to bed. I tossed and turned for a while, as the room smelt and felt different. I actu-ally couldn't sleep in there, so I eventually went to lie down in Granny's room. This felt strange, but I eventually dropped off.

Alice
27 September 2018, 2 p.m.

I knew ideally I should leave a few days between my phone encounter with Stan and contacting him again, to keep him interested, but as I could see the freezer contents dwindling, I knew I would have to throw usual rules out of the window, so I contacted him the next day. I almost rang him—after all, we had shared such an intimate time online, I felt like I knew him so much better—but then I decided that it was easier with the aid of a computer screen. Unlike Stan, I wasn't good at persuasion and didn't really know how to pitch it as though this would be a good thing for him rather than just helping me out. In reality, I wanted to beg him to come and save me, needing someone else to take over and be in control once more. I had tasted independence, and look where it had got me: possible starvation.

Finally, I messaged him, trying to sound casual and alluring. It took me at least twenty minutes.

'Hey Stan, I really enjoyed our time on the phone yesterday and I wonder if you want to make things more real? Let me know if you fancy visiting?'

I knew I was risking a lot sending this message; after all, he thought of me as a hot, sleek air hostess. He may well be shocked when he realised my true identity as an overweight, ugly homebody, but he did really seem to care and I had excited him over the phone. I was also prepared to do the same in the flesh if it meant that he would help me. Besides, there was something in his voice that really made me want to trust him. He was a real man unlike all those horrible little boys at school who had called me names.

I could see that he was typing and waited expectantly.

'Yeah baby, you are so hot of course I would like to see you in the flesh, wot time & wot postcode r u?'

I suddenly remembered that he probably presumed I lived in London. I tried to break it to him gently. 'Thing is I am staying at my gran's house at the moment so you would need to come down to Dorset! I can pay your petrol money. I have been a bit ill lately so resting down here.'

There was more of a delay this time, and I guessed he was weighing up how much he wanted to see me against a long car journey. Luckily, I guessed his urges won out.

'Guess it might do me some good to get some fresh air, hows about I come 2moro and take you for lunch?'

This sounded so grown up, and I had never been asked out on a date before, but I knew I wouldn't be able to leave the house, even because of this.

'Still feeling poorly so how about you bring lunch here?'

'OK cool ping me your address and I will see you tomorrow, I hope u will be wearing sumthing suitably hot for my visit?'

'Of course! See you tomorrow, can't wait.'

I panicked as soon as I finished my last message. I knew I would need a seduction outfit but had nothing sexy I could wear for him. In reality, I had nothing I could wear at all. I went straight up to my bedroom. Suddenly hating the décor, I wondered if I could take him into my gran's room, if indeed a visit to a bedroom was on the cards, but then I thought it would be far too strange doing such a thing in my dead granny's bed. I decided that if I drew the curtains and switched on the fairy lights in my room, I might get away with it.

I carried on the search for a decent outfit. Eventually I found a dress at the back of my wardrobe that my granny had bought me for my school prom a few years earlier. I hadn't gone, of course, due to the fear of humiliation and also the overriding panic that had started to envelop me when I tried to leave the house. I tried to pull it on. I had gone up a few dress sizes since then and the size eighteen wouldn't do up at the back, but I looked in the mirror and thought I looked quite pretty in the pink silky dress with the lacy arms. It was prettier than my usual pyjamas or tracksuit anyway. I put a cardigan on to cover up the gaping back; it ruined the dress a little bit, but at least it covered my flesh.

Then I started my beautifying routine. I decided for a treat to run myself a bath, using all the expensive stuff my gran had always saved. What a waste it had been to keep stuff for 'special' occasions; my gran should have just enjoyed the lavender soak and rose body cream every day while she was alive. I enjoyed the feeling of the water engulf me even though my bulk meant that I wasn't quite covered. With my new-found freedom, I examined my body as I washed. I knew I had large breasts and that this was something that boys seemed to like online, so I vowed to make the most of them. I was tempted to try and touch myself 'down there' for real this time, so I could get practice in before the visit, but I felt self-conscious doing this. Finally, I washed my hair, which now reached halfway down my back. I used Granny's special shampoo with honey, which made me hungry again, and then stepped out of the bath, slathering every inch of flesh with lotion.

I went to bed early that night, although it wasn't much help as I found I couldn't sleep with thoughts of Stan filling my head. I found that I was feeling a mixture of excitement and fear— excitement that by this time tomorrow I might have a real-life boyfriend to brag about on Facebook and that Stan would help me sort out my financial problems but also fear of being rejected once again. No matter how much I had been able to reinvent myself to the world, the slightest thing could take me straight back to that playground where people would surround me and call me names or to the men who had seemed to want me with a very strange way of showing their affection. I don't know which was worse. When I finally dropped off, my dreams were full of falling.

Stan
26 September 2018, 8 p.m.

As pussy shots went, they were pretty bad; in fact, Stan almost laughed when he first got the grainy image through from Alice. It was unexpected; he had presumed that she would have a sleek, sexy pussy to go along with the whole glam lifestyle she seemed to live, but this was like something out of a museum. He didn't think he had seen so much hair on one since stumbling across his dad's eighties-style porn mag when he was a kid. Still, there was something rather endearing about the amateur image, something that made him think she wasn't as experienced as she made out, and this was a turn-on for Stan who didn't think he had been near a real virgin for years. This wasn't a shot he could sell, as there was no market for bad-quality, hairy-growler shots, but it would do to add variety to his personal collection.

The phone sex had been an ingenious idea to break her in gently as soon as he had realised that she was less experienced than she made out. She kept giving him bullshit about her webcam being out of use, but he knew for a fact she had an iPhone and an iPad, both of which could give him what he wanted. He knew he had to tread carefully with this one. Despite appearances, she clearly wasn't his usual slut, and he enjoyed the challenge. It actually made him horny knowing he might be one of the first to get there, after which he would share his conquest with the thousands of men he sold his images and films to online, of course. He reckoned a few more days of flattery and flirting could bring the results needed.

Stan's mother calling him for lunch broke into his thoughts about Alice. He washed his hands in the bathroom, as he was never one to eat with wank-stained hands. He offered to lay the table for his mum, knowing this would please her far more than the effort it required.

'It's no good you being stuck up there in your room all day. It's bad for the mind, Stan. You should get out and about more.'

'Mum, you know I am really busy with my online business. You want me to be successful so I can care for my beautiful mother in her old age, don't you?'

She smiled. 'Of course, honey, I just don't want you working too hard. Here, take this and go to the cinema or something this afternoon, or maybe you can go bowling with some of your friends.'

Stan took the £20 that was being offered. His mum still thought of him as a young teenager. He could always slope off to the pub for a couple of hours. Stan's mum, of course, didn't know the true nature of her son's business, only that it paid enough for him to buy nice clothes and maintain his car. To anyone that listened, his mum would boast of how her son was an internet entrepreneur. She vaguely knew it had something to do with art and buying and selling. She had occasionally mentioned surprise that she never saw any actual products in the house, but he told her that someone else did that for him.

Stan smiled at his mum gratefully as she brought him the sandwiches she had so lovingly prepared. She still cut the crusts off for him and served him peanut butter and cheese alongside the more traditional ham and cheese. Stan ate up hungrily before returning to his room to oversee his empire once more.

Alice
26 September 2018, 5 p.m.

I was panicking. Despite attempts to ration, I had found that I had eaten my way through most of the last food shop quickly and now, with no access to money, had no way of replacing it. I had never had to worry about how things worked—how shopping was done, bills were paid. I guess I was still in many ways like a child. But this was how Granny had always liked me to be. She had never once questioned why I didn't create my own life, choosing to stay and be looked after. I guess it was a mutual dependency.

I had cut down my meals and been stricter with just eating three times a day, but this had left me hungry and miserable. I realised that I needed help. I sat in front of my Facebook page and read through a list of my hundreds of friends wondering if any of them could be the one to help me. Occasionally I would come across someone who I remembered being friends with at primary school, but then I would remember the constant bullying I received at the hands of so many of my school friends and that avenue would close for good.

I was halfway down the list when I came across Stan. He had been quiet for a while, and I was worried that he was annoyed at me for some reason, but I also knew he was the one person who had been kind and seemed to care. I knew I would need to give him something to regain his attention; after all that had been happening with my granny and the funeral and then running out of money, I had been neglecting his needs recently.

Feeling brave, I went to my room, sat on my bed and pulled down my pyjamas. Sitting on the edge of the bed I took pictures of myself 'down there'. I sneaked a look at the results between shots, as I had no idea what I looked like. I was horrified at the red squidgy mess I could see, nothing like the symmetrical hair-free vaginas I had seen online. I needed to improve things a little, so I got a razor from the bathroom. The only one I could find looked ancient and rusty; I guessed it was my granddad's from many years ago. I wet the razor and scraped away down there trying to get as many hairs as possible. After a few minutes, I took another picture and looked. I was dismayed to see that the razor had only cut a few of the hairs, which meant that as well as my lips being different sizes, my hair was also different lengths. The razor had also left me with a nasty rash. I shoved on some aftershave that stung horribly and went back to my room where the light was softer and took another shot.

Before I could change my mind, I filtered it and sent this to Stan, texting him that 'here is mine finally.' I knew this is what he wanted from me and guessed that if I wanted his help then I needed to compromise. I hoped that I didn't look too different or strange from other girls. Stan didn't reply straight away, which made me feel exposed and worried that I was being rejected. I passed my time by making a list of all the food in the freezer and working out how long it would last me. Worryingly, I only reached four days before I would officially be destitute. I really needed Stan's help.

He finally replied when I was deep in the middle of watching a programme on the iPlayer about fat pets.

'Liked the self portrait sexy u sure know how 2 turn a man on. Hope there will be more where that came from?!'

I immediately switched into Online Alice mode thinking that this would be a conversation I would have had many times over.

'Sure thing just tell me what you want to see next?'

'I want to c u touch yourself. Is webcam working yet?'

'No but if u wait 5 mins I will send picture'

'How about u fone me while u r taking it? That would be really sexy.'

I didn't want to tell him that I had many ways of making a video call on my various computers and decided a phone call would be less painful than filming.

'OK I will call you in 5 mins'

My heart was beating in my chest as I headed upstairs to my bedroom. Even though I knew he wouldn't be able to see me, I still felt exposed as I sat on my bed. I finally plucked up the courage to call him, and he picked up almost immediately. His voice sounded deep and rich with a slight twang that I guessed showed his London roots. He took control of the conversation immediately, telling me where to touch myself and what to do.

I played along giving him a running commentary of what I was apparently doing while actually flicking through my Insta account looking at beautiful travel shots and pets. I found it quite inspiring, and my sexy 'chat' was probably greatly enhanced by what I was looking at.

He asked me to talk dirty to him and so I used all the rude words I knew to tell him about my pussy. I realised that I sounded more like Julie Andrews in *The Sound of Music* than some kind of porn star, but it seemed to work. As I spoke about his hard cock, his breath was coming harder and faster.

'Oh my god, baby, I'm gonna come. Are you coming too?'

I didn't want to let him down, so I racked my brains for what the women had done on the porn I had seen. I seemed to recall them making groaning noises, so I tried a few of my own as well as throwing in a few yeses!

Stan cried out as if he was in pain, and then the phone went silent. I was worried I had done something wrong, but thankfully he spoke.

'Wow, baby, that was really good. You know how to turn a man on. Did you come?'

I lied and told him that, yes, of course I had. I was relieved that I could now stop the pretence, and I wondered if I could find some kind of script or even cobble together some kind of video I could play out next time. I hoped that by doing this I had given him enough to be able to ask for some help in return. As I put the phone down, I sent him one more shot for luck.

Alice
19 September 2018, 3 p.m.

After the whole death and funeral storyline had run its natural course (I found that sympathy waned about a week after the funeral), I felt a bit lost. I was almost excited when I got a text to tell me that my sofa would be delivered that afternoon. I really had to replace the ruined sofa; I was not frivolously purchasing it as this was a necessity. Apart from the Tesco delivery men, I hadn't set eyes on a real person since Granny had died.

I had really got the hang of the online shop now and wondered why anyone would bother going out, pushing a trolley around and returning home with masses of bags when it was so easy to do it online. I still wasn't over the thrill of being able to order whatever I wanted, and so my virtual trolley was usually loaded with sweet and sugary treats of every description. I worried what the delivery men thought of me when they delivered such an excessive order, but I always tipped them and talked about my big family, and I figured they probably saw it all in their jobs. There were bound to be people who were worse than me.

In honour of the imminent delivery, I got dressed. This was something that had slipped in the last few weeks. This was partly because there seemed to be no real reason to get clothes on when I would only have to change back into my pyjamas when I went to bed but it was also because a lot of my clothes were feeling tight on me now and the oversized bedclothes I wore covered up my body with little strain. Still, I found a pair of leggings and a t-shirt that didn't split in protest at my size.

By the time I was ready, it was lunchtime, so I made myself a microwaved lasagne and chips. I still hadn't really got the hang of the washing up in the kitchen and had worked out I could save on plates by eating straight out of the dish. I had also bought disposable forks in my previous shop. There was still waste, and I was becoming concerned about the bin bags that were being flung into my garden from the front door that didn't seem to be getting picked up, but I was sure some kindly bin man would do so, eventually.

Finished with lunch, I sat and waited, filling my time by using an online app where you could re-decorate your home. I didn't really have a clue about decoration but had a go at pinning up a few different wallpapers to go with my new sofa. Eventually, the doorbell went, and I shot up to answer it. Two men in high vis jackets grunted a hello as they pushed past me into the hall.

'Right, love, so where is the old one?' the smaller one asked me. I could smell cheese and onion crisps on his breath, which sickened me and yet made me crave a packet in equal measures. I almost asked if he had any left.

'It's through here in the living room. Can I get you both a nice cuppa or some biscuits?' I offered, thinking this was what grown-ups did with tradesman and finding I was craving company.

'Oh no, you're alright, love. We've got plenty more sofas to deliver this afternoon, so we can't sit around putting our feet up, unfortunately.' The small one answered again, presumably the spokesperson for both.

I was disappointed. I had even prepared a tray with mugs and some chunky chocolate cookies I had bought. Instead of heading to the kitchen, I showed them through to the living room and pointed out the sofa.

'Blimey, love, looks like someone died on there; no wonder you are getting rid of it!'

I almost blurted out the truth that someone *had* died on there but then panicked that these men would have a duty to tell the police or the social workers what they had seen. I thought quickly.

'Actually, it was my poor sick granny, who is now in hospital. She had a terrible bug and was sick all over it and you know what else. My mum is visiting her now.' This last bit was added in case either man thought I was home alone. I knew that I looked a lot younger than my twenty-one years.

Neither man seemed bothered at this story or even wished my gran a speedy recovery, which annoyed me slightly. They huffed and puffed their way out of the room and then out of the house with the old sofa. I suddenly felt bereft; after all, that was the sofa I had grown up with, where I had spent many happy hours relaxing, playing or watching TV with Gran. But it was also the scene of some of my worst memories. Seeing it going onto the truck no doubt headed for some dump, I almost felt as sad as when my gran had died, but then I pulled myself together. It was only a sofa, and really, Granny should have replaced it years ago.

I was excited when I saw the two men unloading my new sofa. Granny would have hated it. She was a lifelong fan of chintz, but the new eggshell-blue creation was just right for me. I hadn't really thought about the practicalities of having a light-coloured seat just sitting there and welcoming stains from plates of food and cups of tea. After a lot of toing and froing, they got the new sofa in the house and safely installed in the living room. The carpet and the rest of the décor looked immediately old and dated compared to the shiny new sofa. I wondered about getting online and ordering up a whole new room immediately, but I could hear Granny's voice in my head calling me a spend-thrift, so I gave up on the idea almost immediately. Once the men had gone, I jumped onto the sofa and lay on the whole length of it, enjoying the feel of the crisp new fabric and soft cushions. Finally, this room felt like a room I could sit in again and not just some place my granny had died.

I was on the new sofa doing my new bi-weekly shop when I hit a new problem. My little trolley was full, and I had put the card details in when an error message came up telling me that my card was declined and advising me to contact my bank. I couldn't do this as it wasn't actually my bank card, and I couldn't well ask Gran to do it as she was no longer here.

This didn't make sense; I knew Gran had lots of money as Grand-dad had left her well provided for, so I decided to investigate. Heading to the room that had always been called the study but was in fact just a room with a table and a filing cabinet, I felt like a detective. There was a familiar smell in here of Grandad's pipe. I had once loved that smell but now it made me feel sick.

I wasn't sure what I was looking for as I rifled through the files, but I hit the jackpot when I came across the files marked *Bank*. This contained what seemed to be hundreds of pieces of paper with lots of funny codes and amounts written down. I guessed these must be bank statements. I had one bank account of my own that Uncle Tom had started when I was young, but I knew it only had a couple of hundred pounds in it and I had only ever looked at this money online; I didn't even have a card for this account. My gran had always provided for me knowing I couldn't sort things out for myself. It wasn't as if I wanted for much anyway; I didn't really have much use for money until now.

Eventually, I worked out that Granny had these statements in date order. There were two different types, one called a current account and one a savings account. In the current account, there seemed to be a few hundred pounds moving around each month, and I could see things like bills and shopping going out regularly. I guessed that this was the account that was related to the card I had been using. Much more impressive was the savings account, which had a grand total of £117,692 in it in the latest statement. The only things marked on these statements were monthly interest and a monthly payment out into Gran's current account. I then remembered that Gran went to the bank and the post office once every couple of weeks. I hadn't been with her for years but guessed that this was when she picked up her pension and moved money from her savings account. Gran had been such a technophobe, she would never have set up online or even telephone banking. I realised with a heavy heart that I had access to a whole heap of money but annoyingly couldn't touch it unless I ventured out to the bank myself.

I knew after my last attempt at leaving the house that this was highly unlikely to happen.

I felt like giving up, I was more than happy to carry on my life exactly how I was living it. All my needs were met in this house. There was no longer any danger, and it was just my thoughts that scared me these days. Ironic that it was this house that held some bad memories and yet it was the world outside the door that sent me into a panic. I knew the sensible thing to do would be to tell someone—I could work out who—but I also knew this would mean being thrust back out there. It would mean authority and questioning, and after what had happened before, I couldn't bear to go through that again. I had done nothing wrong and wasn't harming anyone by living this way, but I needed to think of a way to make this a long-term plan.

I put all the papers back and sat and had a think. I probably had enough food in the house to last me a few weeks, and in the meantime, I could try and figure out a way of getting my hands on the savings. I was tough; I could live with black tea for a few weeks, and something was bound to come up!

Alice
13 September 2018, 2 p.m.

By day three of life without Gran, I was almost getting used to things. It was amazing how quickly you could adjust to situations. The new became the normal. I was quite enjoying the freedom of being able to do and eat what I wanted when I wanted. I had unfortunately run out of a few things like milk and bread, but I had stopped making my gran cups of tea and had switched to cans of coke myself. I kept the TV on all day and had totally immersed myself in the online world, holding as many conversations as possible to distract myself from the growing problem in the living room.

The growing problem was my gran. I could no longer pretend that she was just sitting there asleep. Her face was almost unrecognisable, her body was decomposing despite me keeping the heat off, and the smell was overpowering, far stronger than the shake and vac I had sprinkled around and the growing number of Glade plug-ins I had dotted around the place. I knew I had to do something but didn't know what it was.

Feeling strong after a breakfast of crumpets, ice cream and bacon, I turned online for some advice. Feeling like a criminal, I typed in, 'What to do with a dead body?' hoping that no one was spying on me from the government or even Google. My choices seemed endless, from the sensible (call a doctor) to the ridiculous (set it on fire in the middle of a river, according to some religions). Then I came across a site that had the 'Top ten TV body disposals.' I knew quite a few of them, including the acid bath that had failed so spectacularly in Breaking Bad, but most options seemed to need a car or lots of equipment. Then my eye landed on something that could work for me, the classic 'body in the freezer.' Admittedly, this talked about sawing the body up, and in the TV series they were talking about, it was a walk-in freezer at a mobster-run restaurant. Nonetheless, I still thought that this was the most sensible option in my situation.

I headed down to the basement, opening the chest freezer and mentally working out how I could fit my gran in there. I reckoned that if I took out about half the food, then the body would fit in. I transported food from the basement to the kitchen. Some would fit in the freezer upstairs, but I soon ran out of space. I put the rest in the fridge, knowing I would have to eat it up pretty quickly.

Next came the mammoth task of moving my gran down to the basement. Thankfully, my granny was quite a small lady, as she was a feeder instead of a glutton like her granddaughter. I hoped she would be as light as a feather. Firstly, I went into the kitchen and pulled on the rubber gloves that had a comedy fur trim and big diamond ring on them, a gift I had found online for my granny last year. I also put on the apron. I couldn't reach the tie around my waist, so I left it hanging loosely. Grabbing the roll of bin liners, I was armed and ready.

However prepared I felt, the reality was very different when I came face to face with the problem. Sitting in the room with my smelly, decomposing grandma, I burst into tears. I had always had my gran to tell me what to do, and now I longed for someone else to step in and take over. I thought again about my options. Number one, I could contact a family member, like Uncle Tom or even at a push Rachel, my mother, but that would need a lot more explaining. Option two, I could call 999 and pretend that I had just found my gran. The third choice, and the one I had previously decided on, was to hide Granny and pretend that nothing had happened.

This could be my chance to stand on my own two feet rather than being probed and manipulated by the authorities as I had all those years before. I also had to consider that neither my mother nor my uncle had ever had any kind of relationship with Granny, so why would they care now? I also couldn't shake off the idea that either may reject me again; after all, my mum had never tried to get in contact with me and Tom had moved to the other side of the Atlantic. Neither offered hope that they would love and support me through this. After weighing all the pros and cons, I felt there was only one option.

I could barely bring myself to touch my gran, and I kept gagging at the sight. I wrapped bin liners around my arms to offer more protection against the decaying corpse. I wondered if I should wrap my gran in the bags before or after I moved her. For my peace of mind and so I didn't have to look at the horrible sunken face of Granny, I covered her head with a bin bag. I then decided it would make more sense if the whole body was covered, so I grabbed the parcel tape from the kitchen and set about mummifying Granny. I imagined it was like dressing a baby in a Babygro, only a lot bigger—and possibly easier since Granny was not wriggling around. With the black, faceless shape in front of me, it was a lot easier to imagine that this was an inanimate object rather than a body, and in my head, I decided that I was moving a roll of carpet.

I soon realised that I could not lift Granny all the way. I tried several different options, but she was still too heavy to move far. I pulled her from the sofa to the floor, the bin bags stretching but sliding across the carpet. I noticed with disgust the full extent of the mess on the sofa, stained a kaleidoscope of colours. The closest I had come to physical exertion in many years was helping my granny put the shopping away, so I soon found myself red and breathless.

Then I remembered the shopping bag on wheels my granny always took out with her, returning with it filled to the brim with goodies. I went to get it from under the stairs, and then I lifted my gran into it headfirst. It didn't make life much easier, but it meant I could kind of drag and pull her along, stopping every couple of minutes to get my breath back. I was doing really well until I reached the stairs down to the basement. I wondered if I could lower the bag down gently, but when I tried, the weight was too much for me. Figuring that my gran was dead and wouldn't feel anything anyway, I took her out of the bag and pushed her down a step at a time, a little like one of those Slinky toys I had seen as a kid.

Eventually, I reached the freezer. Opening the lid, I managed to haul her up against it and eventually topple her into the ice. At first, I couldn't close the lid, but after shifting a few things around and taking a few more bits out, I finally closed Granny in.

It was at this moment that the room swam and a pain in my chest started to hurt so badly that I worried I would follow my gran to the grave. I knew I was unfit; despite posting various #nopainnogain selfies, the last time I had actually exercised was not in some swanky yoga studio but in a draughty school gym. Suddenly I was gasping for breath and my body was freezing yet sweating at the same time. I found I couldn't move and even felt like I was looking down upon myself rather than in the room. After what felt like an hour—but could have easily been only two minutes—I felt better. I was ashamed to see the puddle at my feet that betrayed the fact I had wet myself.

I was frozen to the spot and couldn't quite believe what I had done. I had good reason, but the reality was the only person I had truly loved was dead, and I had now made a decision to hide this. There was no turning back now; I knew I wouldn't be able to explain what had happened here. I longed for someone to come and take all the decisions away from me.

I had tried to keep my emotions out of this. I knew it was a strange and not very nice way to treat a dead person, but I also thought at this stage that it was for the best. I couldn't help it; the fact Granny was now resting in a freezer rather than in a coffin was a horrible thought, and I thought again about phoning for help. In the end, I was too scared. I had no idea what would happen to me, as I had no real experience of the outside world. As long as I could carry on and pretend, to myself as much as anyone, that everything was OK, then I was sure somehow it would be.

After my exertion and funny spell, I was starving and thirsty, so I headed back to the kitchen to see what I could cook up. I removed my gloves and protective clothing, keeping them to one side for when I had to tackle the living room later. Thankfully, defrosting away in the fridge were some Aunt Bessie Yorkshire puddings and prawn balls, so I started up the oven and the deep fat fryer. There was a part of me that really wanted to update my Facebook with 'Wow who knew a little old lady could weigh so much #deadgrannyinfreezer' even as a joke, but I didn't want to attract any attention to myself. Instead I told the world I was having friends over for dinner later and was wondering what to cook, knowing there were lots who would be oh so eager to share with me.

After eating and stacking the plate up in the sink with the rest of the three-day washing up, I tackled the living room. The smell made me gag, and I nearly bought back up my lovely prawn balls, so I fashioned myself a mask out of a dishcloth and an old Glade refill that sat under my nose. I had grabbed many sprays from the cupboard under the sink, and I sprayed them randomly. I soon realised that this would not be enough to shift the mess and then discovered that there was a zip on the side of the cushion. Taking the covers off, I sprayed the cushions underneath until they were soaked with bleach. Then I took the covers through to the kitchen. One slight hurdle was that I had no idea how to use the washing machine. Granny had always taken care of the domestic arrangements. Switching on my tablet, I Youtubed my make of washing machine and was rewarded with step-by-step instructions on how to do a wash.

I then felt the overwhelming need to feel normal, so I broke my own rules by messaging Stan. It was nothing heavy, just me asking how he was and telling him I had a very busy week ahead. I filled my time waiting for a message back by watching an episode of *Friends* on my tablet. I was halfway through when he responded.

'You know what I want from you babe, I already showed you mine now I want to see some pussy on my phone, cmon don't be a tease.'

I wasn't sure I liked this new side of Stan. The old Stan had always made me feel wanted and desirable, but my gran would say that this Stan was only after one thing. At least I guessed that's what she would have said if she were still alive. Then again, I, more than most, knew men had needs.

I was still working out what to say when I got another message from Stan.

'Babe I hope you know how bootiful I tink you are, I just can't get you out of my head and I hate reading about you with any

other man, sorry if I come across as a bit jealous at times but you drive me wild!'

I smiled to myself. This was the Stan I knew and loved, the one who made me feel like a princess, the one who made me feel lucky that I had ever responded to his friend request on Facebook feeling flattered that someone like him would even look at someone like me.

I figured that giving him what he wanted was the only way to keep him interested, especially now that I knew he was jealous of my other apparent 'online' hook-ups. I wasn't quite ready to bare all just yet, but I thought a boob would be doable. I knew I could go on the internet and download hundreds of pictures, but I wanted to show Stan the real me. Escaping to the privacy of my bedroom, I drew the curtains and took off my top and bra —my granny had always joked that I could fit my head into one cup. Pushing my sizeable breasts together, I took a shot with my iPhone. The first couple of shots were pretty blurred and unrecognisable, but after a few tries, the results were impressive. My breasts looked big and perky, almost exactly like ones I had seen online, and from that angle, you couldn't see the rest of my body where the fat dispersal wasn't so impressive.

I sent off my favourite shot to Stan with a note telling him that this was for starters. I was sure this would buy me a couple more weeks without having to do much more. He replied almost immediately.

'Wow, you are so hot babe, wish I could get my hands on your titties I would squeeze them and suck them hard.'

I guessed I needed to respond to this, so I Googled 'talking dirty.' I copied and pasted a few lines about how Stan was making me horny and sent this off.

After a few hours of playing my favourite online game where I had to collect animals for my zoo, I was feeling out of sorts. My day was usually punctuated by the little rituals and cups of tea that my gran had insisted on including in our lives. Now I was eating what I wanted when I wanted, and my day seemed to have no routine. It was strange as we had lived separate lives in many ways, but it was amazing how knowing someone was in the next room could keep you from feeling lonely. I wondered how else my granny filled my days apart from TV and remembered she used to do a fair bit of housework. Now, this was something I could learn.

I looked around the kitchen and realised that I needed to start there as it already looked like a mess. I had dumped the gloves and bin bags I had used in my clean-up mission earlier in the corner, so I started with that, using a second pair of rubber gloves to protect me while I picked up the pile and put it in the bin which was already overflowing. I pulled the liner out and tied it, gagging again from the smell which seemed to be a mixture of rotten food, shit and something surprisingly pungent that I couldn't put my finger on but guessed was related to my granny.

Then I walked to the front door, determined to make it to the end of the path where the wheelie bin sat. My heart was already pounding as I reached for the handle, the cool air hit me and was a relief after the stuffiness and smells of my home, but it was also terrifying as it signified the outside world. I tried to take a step outside and finally got one foot out the door. After a while, I ventured with the other foot, but this was too much for my poor nervous system. I suddenly found that I couldn't breathe. I felt sweaty and dizzy, as though the world was closing in on me. I threw the bin bag as far as I could down the garden path, hoping that the binmen would take pity on me, and rushed back into my sanctuary, trying and failing to catch my breath. The panic lasted at least twenty minutes, and when it finally subsided, I felt tearful and shaky.

I comforted myself with a slice of black forest Gateaux and a drink of black sweet tea that was surprisingly nice. I felt I could probably get used to being without milk. After all that, I didn't feel well enough to carry on with my cleaning, so I gave up for the day and instead watched almost an entire series of my favourite box set through my laptop, still not able to be in the living room with its strange smell and fragile memories.

Rachel
13 September 2018, Midday

Rachel was having a bad week. Not only had she had to fork out a fortune for her old rustbucket of a car, but she also had a terrible day at work. To top it all, she had gotten into a huge argument with her boyfriend, Dave, about his inability to find a job. She had come home tired from a full day at work to find him sitting on the sofa in the same spot she had left him, beer in hand and two hungry kids sitting by his feet. Her friends always told her she was lucky he had stuck around, particularly for kids that weren't even his, but at that moment, she didn't feel lucky, just annoyed.

When she had first met him down at her local pub on a rare night out, he hadn't exactly swept her off her feet, but it had been a long time since anyone had paid her any attention, so she had lapped it up. She knew she wasn't a bad catch in spite of the obvious baggage. She was in her thirties but could pass for twenty-five, her body was in good nick despite the three kids, and her best asset was her hair, which was long and brown. She probably spent more on her hair than she did her car. It currently had chestnut extensions, which weren't real because it would freak her out having some person's actual hair attached to her head, but they still looked real enough. At the time, Dave had been working at the nearby car plant and had been generous with the drinks that night. He had ended up staying the night and they had kind of stuck together ever since.

Rachel was no angel these days, but she was a hard worker and a good mum. Sometimes when she was having a bad week, she remembered her dark days, vague recollections of week-long benders with her taking whatever she could get her hands on. Rachel had to admit that sometimes she felt like reaching for a glass of vodka well before lunchtime, but she was much stronger than that these days. She hadn't touched a drug stronger than wine, caffeine or tobacco for over ten years. She knew Dave and her friends would be shocked if they knew about her past. That was the good thing about London; you could re-invent yourself.

Rachel still kept in contact with Kylie and Jessica's dad, Rob, much to Dave's disgust. The two men would grunt at each other territorially when Rob occasionally came to pick them up for the weekend, although it was generally her dropping them off. He wasn't the most hands-on of fathers. As much as Rachel loved having time to herself, when this happened (albeit in-frequently), she also missed her kids horribly. She would try to fill her day with online bingo or games. She loved being a mother so much. It made dealing with all the rude kids at the school where she worked worthwhile when she could buy Jess the exact coat she wanted or Kylie the latest scooter she was after.

Knowing her time was running out, Rachel was craving another baby. There was something so amazing about the smell and touch of a baby, something so magical. Rachel had mourned each time her babies had stopped breastfeeding as this was the start of a downward slope of them not needing her as much. She was proud when Jess had started school earlier that year, but she had gone home and cried her eyes out at the knowledge that before she knew it Jess would be staying out late and hating her mum. Rachel also knew no matter how many kids she had, she could never replace the one she had lost, but it could at least fill the gap for a while.

Tom
12 September 2018, 8 p.m.

Tom was more shocked than upset; after all, he and Will had stopped having regular sex early in the relationship. The realisation that Will was having plenty of sex—only it wasn't with him, it was with his personal trainer—was not only a slap in the face, it was also such a cliché. Sure, Tom had sought sex outside the relationship on occasions, but he thought what he and Will had was stronger than a quick fumble. Tom, of course, had been the last to know, only being informed by one of their bitchier friends who had taken quite the delight in telling Tom how he had spotted his partner and the fit young instructor holding hands over a latte.

Tom lay in wait for Will that night. They were supposed to be going to an opening on Broadway, but Tom had been firm and assertive in telling Will to come home that evening. He was nursing a large glass of Riesling when the front door went.

'So why all the drama, my darling? Don't tell me you think we need to start acting like the middle-aged bores we are and staying home every evening?'

Personally, Tom thought a few evenings in a week sounded like a joy, but he refused to get sidetracked.

'I thought it was important we had a chat; after all, I feel like we never sit down and talk anymore. I feel like I always have to share you.' Tom poured Will a glass, wincing as his boyfriend leant in to give him a dry kiss.

'OK, then, what shall we talk about? How is work for you, dear?' Will said sarcastically, mincing round like a 1950's housewife.

Tom remembered that when they had first met, they would stay up into the early hours some nights, talking and sharing their secrets and dreams. This had been Tom's first real, grownup relationship. There had been plenty of flings, even a couple of women along the way, but finding someone who he had connected with on such an intellectual level had been a huge aphrodisiac. In terms of their hopes and dreams, they had both surpassed what they had wanted back then, at least on a superficial level. However, somewhere along the line, they had lost the thing that had pulled them together. Tom tried to keep it light.

'I wanted to check in, you know, see how you were feeling? How is work?'

'Jeez, I thought it was us Yanks who were supposed to be over-sharers. I know, how about I share my Google calendar with you? Then you can see what I'm up to at all times. Then maybe rather than sitting here talking about shit, we could catch late dinner with Danny and Rob and hear all about the play we should be at right now.'

Tom was getting angry. He didn't know if Will was feeling guilty or if he really didn't care about them as a couple.

'That would be great, and maybe you could share the details of your personal trainer with me. I have heard he is great at working you up into a sweat.' Tom saw something flash across Will's eyes, but to his surprise, it wasn't guilt, it was annoyance.

'So what if Alex is giving me a few extras? When you are a fat, balding fifty-something in New York, you take what you can get. Don't tell me you have never done the dirty. I mean, we never do it anymore, and I know you can't live like a complete monk.'

'Yes, there have been a few over the years, but they have always been hook-ups from bars or Grindr. From what I hear about you and this Alex bloke, it is all romance and hotel rooms.'

Will stepped towards him. 'Hon, you know it means nothing. Alex is young and hot but incredibly stupid. His only topic of conversation is around muscle groups, and eating out with him is about as much fun as eating out with Hitler, but it is hugely good for my ego to have him chase me. It is so different to what we have, though. It need not get in the way.'

'So, are you saying you don't want to stop seeing him?'

'Not really, no. I'm sure he will get bored and move on to his next paying customer soon, so what is the point? Variety is the spice of life. Remember, we used to enjoy involving others in our sex life.'

Tom thought back to the men they had bought into their bed at the beginning of the relationship with fondness but not long-ing. The day they had decided to become serious and move in together had been one of the best days of his life.

'What if I say it is me or him? Surely you are not going to chuck away what we have, our solid decade-long relationship, for something so meaningless?'

'You would be the stupid one, Tom! You know I bring the most to the table in this relationship—the rent on this place as a start —and would you really want to end up with just your boring old lawyer friends to socialise with? Just be cool and let this run its course. You know I don't like being told what to do.'

This was said softly with a smile, but Tom knew he was serious. Will really hated anyone trying to control his life. Tom felt like he was being rejected but knew what Will was saying made sense. This was his whole life now. He had invested so much into this relationship, this perfect gay New York existence, that to throw it all away would be stupid. He hated backing down, but he knew Will had won, like he always did.

'OK, but I really don't want my nose rubbed in it. Please be more subtle, and if Alex starts turning up to our social scene, then I will think again.'

'Of course, darling, anything to make you happy. Now, let's fin-ish off this bottle and then head out. After all, what is the point of living slap bang in the middle of the city that never sleeps if we are the ones sitting at home and waiting to die?'

Tom finished his glass and went to get changed but then sud-denly changed his mind. He was torn knowing letting Will off the leash could be sending him into the arms of his younger rival, but the idea of having to go and sit with their so-called friends and pretend that they were the perfect couple was too tiring.

'You know what? I am actually going to hang out here and get an early night. I might even make myself a bowl of pasta or something.'

Will looked surprised. The kitchen was more for show than function, but he let it drop as he headed off into the night, leaving Tom settled on the sofa yet feeling increasingly unsettled in his own life.

Alice
11 September 2018, 7 a.m.

I awoke feeling fearful. There were a few minutes between sleeping and waking when I couldn't remember why I was feeling this way and wondered if it was my nightmares. Then suddenly it hit me, chilling my blood and causing panic to rise in my chest. Something had happened to Granny, the woman who had been my entire universe for the last fifteen years. I still couldn't really comprehend the enormity of what this might mean, so I decided the best thing to do was to carry on as though nothing had happened.

I picked up my phone and told everyone I was back in the UK today. It was hard work having a public persona as an air hostess.

Yuck can't believe I have flown into all this rain DISLIKE!;(

I then headed downstairs and ventured into the kitchen, walking around and gathering everything needed for my daily fry up. The quietness was scaring me, so I switched on the radio, letting my nerves be soothed by the inane chatter of some morning presenter that my gran loved. I ate my breakfast in the kitchen while checking my phone for any updates that needed feedback, wondering what kind of reaction I would get if I posted up the real situation going on in my home right now.

Eventually, I could put it off no longer. I boiled the kettle and made two cups of tea, taking them to the living room. The first thing I did was open the curtains, and I was horrified to see the state of my gran. She was still sitting up rigidly and had turned a horrible purple colour. I noticed by the stain on the sofa and the smell I hadn't noticed last night that Gran had obviously messed herself. I knew she would be mortified by this and vowed to clean this up as soon as I had the courage.

I sat on the other end of the sofa and put Gran's cup of tea down on the table in front of her, trying to pretend that everything was normal. If I didn't acknowledge the situation, then perhaps it would go away.

'Here you go, Gran. I've bought you a cuppa for you to enjoy in front of Lorraine. Shall I put it on?'

I reached over and grabbed the remote, feeling a sense of relief as the room filled with the dulcet Scottish tones of Gran's favourite morning presenter.

'Oh, look, she is talking to that woman with the amazing dog who rescued the group of children. Remember we saw something about this on the breakfast show last week? Isn't he cute?' I turned the TV up a bit. 'I used to always want a dog when I was a little girl, remember? But you always told me it was far too much work. You were probably right.'

Lorraine moved onto the paper review, which was something I had no interest in, so I took my tea back into the kitchen and fired up my laptop. I was annoyed that I had received no more messages from Stan even though I could clearly see that he was online. I changed my status and tweeted out about unpacking, and then I went onto Stan's profile page. I could see he had shared a funny video a few minutes ago, so I liked this. I knew not to be too keen, so I stopped myself from messaging him directly. I saw that he had updated his status.

So got myself some quality pussy last night #soredick

I felt sick with jealousy. I knew we were not officially in a relationship, but I had thought he cared about me enough not to go after other girls. I thought about texting him to let him know I was upset, but I knew men didn't like to have women angry with them, so I left it, knowing I would have to think up a new plan to win him back.

I then got drawn into a debate on Twitter all about some pop star's new haircut. I personally thought the bleached crop looked good on the starlet, but I was apparently in a minority with many calling for her to hide herself away in a paper bag or calling her an 'ugly, lesbo bitch.' Seeing that there was such a strong feeling against the new look, I changed my viewpoint, switching to the haters' side. I never liked to go against the majority viewpoint. It could make you unpopular.

At five to eleven, I boiled the kettle again and put tea and biscuits onto a tray, shoving a few into my mouth as I walked into the living room. After setting it down on the coffee table, I removed the cold cup of tea that was not touched, which wasn't surprising as there was no sign of life.

'Here you go, Gran, a fresh pot with your favourite biscuits.' I had even given up my favourite chocolate digestives in favour of the slightly odd garibaldis that my gran loved so much but which reminded me of dead insects. It was even more off-putting today as I noticed flies circling around Gran.

After elevenses and a bit of Jeremy Kyle, it was almost time for me to start on lunch. Realising I could eat whatever I wanted, I went into the kitchen and Googled 'lunch ideas'. Overwhelmed by the pictures, recipes and blogs that came my way, I got lost in food porn heaven for a while. A lot wasn't necessarily to my taste—lots of foreign foods and vegetables, neither of which Gran or I were keen on—but some pictures included mountains of chips or juicy sausages stuck artfully in buttery mash. I then went to the freezer to pick out my meal. It was like I was a kid in a sweetshop. There was so much choice, and I had never been very good at making decisions. I went for a mixture and pulled out a lasagne, chicken nuggets, chips and potato wedges, dividing the food up between microwave and deep fat fryer.

As I was waiting for my feast to cook, my phone buzzed to let me know I had a new message. I hoped that it would be Stan back to tell me how beautiful he thought I was or how he wanted to whisk me away and marry me, but I was disappointed when it was Uncle Tom. Then I felt bad because Tom was my second favourite person in the world. A message from him was undoubtedly a high point of my day. However, I felt instantly paranoid that somehow he knew what had happened, what I was trying to cover up. The message from Tom was short and told me about his week, described what meals out he had enjoyed with Will and asked me how his favourite niece was.

I felt thrown by the niceness in his email and immediately thought about telling him the truth about the current situation. He wasn't authority, and he had always looked out for me, but then I decided that I really didn't want to worry him as he was so far away. There was nothing he could do. He might want to get professionals involved. I wondered how he would feel considering that Gran was his mother, but hadn't he been the one who had vowed never to speak to her again after she had disowned him? Not to say he would be pleased that something bad had happened to her, but he might not be that upset either.

After lunch, loneliness hit me like a tonne of bricks. For once, the familiar sounds of daytime TV and the comradery of my on-line friends wasn't enough, so I signed on to Facebook as Tania, needing warmth and reassurance from Rachel. Sometimes the comments and likes from my online friends didn't fill the gap, and I really craved what most other people had: a family, a mum and contact with people who really knew me and cared—not about what I looked like or what I was apparently doing but because I was me.

It was days like this that I was tempted to tell Rachel exactly who I was, hopeful that she would be as motherly towards me as she was to her two other kids, but I knew I was only inviting pain and rejection if I told the truth. Instead, I posted a funny picture about mothers and daughters to my wall. Rachel liked this and added a comment and three kisses below which left me satisfied for now.

I wondered what kind of comment she would have left if she could see how bad her own mother looked right now. I was beginning to realise that this wasn't some made-up news or some unbelievable soap story. My gran had died, and I had no idea what I should do.

Alice
10 September 2018, 6.15 p.m.

It was nearly teatime when I left my room. As I was walking down the stairs, something felt wrong. The TV was blaring out the *Six O'Clock News*, something my gran never watched. She was only a fan of real life when it came packaged up as a reality or talk show. I presumed Granny had fallen asleep in front of the box, as this was becoming a more frequent occurrence these days. Still, this gave me a chance to help my gran out by cooking dinner.

It was a Friday, and I knew my gran always liked to have fish and chips on a Friday, often from the local chippy, but I thought I could cook it as well myself. The fridge freezer in the kitchen had no chips, so I headed down into the slightly spooky basement and opened the chest freezer that was filled to the brim with all the special offers Gran had picked up on her shopping trips over the months. After a quick rustle about, I found chips and a fish pie. Finishing my haul with some onion rings and peas, I felt pleased with myself.

Once back in the kitchen, the fish pie went in the microwave and the chips and onion rings went in the deep fat fryer. I noticed that the fat in the fryer was looking old and had a few bits in it. Secretly, I enjoyed finding random bits of fried food in my meals, but I knew this wasn't for everyone. As I cooked, I spread marg and ketchup on thick white bread, initially to serve with the meal, but I was so starving I shovelled it into my mouth, grabbing a couple more bits to butter as the meal accompaniment. After a few minutes, the microwave pinged to tell me all was ready, and I piled the food onto the plates, knowing my gran would only want about half of what I did. Shoving the ketchup under my arm, I grabbed both plates and cutlery and trudged into the living room, all smiles.

As I had suspected, Gran had fallen asleep. I stifled a laugh as I could see my gran's eyes half open and a fag that had burned down to the filter still in hand. I knew my gran would hate me staring at her.

'Gran, I have made dinner for both of us!' I shouted, putting the food down on the coffee table. My gran didn't stir. I shook my gran gently, but this still got no reaction, so I shouted louder and touched my gran on the cheek. This was when I noticed that my granny was slightly cold to the touch. Feeling out of my depth, I grabbed my iPad from the kitchen and Googled 'cold to the touch'. Alongside lots of silly videos and articles, one stood out from the rest. It looked official and was in bold at the top of the page. I clicked on the link and it took me to the NHS website. To my surprise, the article was about what to do in an emergency. The website told me to check and see if the person was breathing, so I leant in close to my gran's face, worrying she would wake up and shout at me for being so close. I couldn't hear any breathing. I read on. It told me to check for a pulse, so I took the fag out of my gran's hand and felt her papery dry wrist, but I wasn't rewarded with a rhythm.

I looked at what to do next. The website told me to phone 999. This was something that had been drummed into me as a young child at school, but I had also had bad experiences of the authorities. When I had been taken into care at a young age, it had been the worst time of my life. It was only when my gran rescued me and took me into her home that things improved.

I knew what happened when outsiders got involved; we would be separated. She would be sent off to some home and I would have to go god knows where. I couldn't decide between the two outcomes, so I settled on skipping that step for now and moving on to the next one.

Paying full attention to the YouTube video that showed me what to do, I pressed down forcefully on my gran's chest, willing her to wake up. I carried on chatting, hoping that this might help things along.

'You are going to be so gutted that you are missing *Hollyoaks*.'

'Come on, Gran, the food is getting cold.'

'If you keep this up for much longer, you are going to miss all your evening viewing!'

I didn't know how long I had kept this up, but my action didn't seem to make any difference, so I took a break. Sitting back on the sofa, I sat my gran back up again.

'OK, I guess I will have to watch what *I* want on TV for a change,' I said loudly, wondering if I could goad my granny back to consciousness. I turned over to the Channel 4 News, something my gran would definitely never watch. I had no idea what to do next, so I distracted myself with news about politicians I had never heard of and countries I was unlikely to visit. Every so often, I would check my gran, but there was still no sign of life. This all felt so unreal to me. I literally hadn't stepped outside my door for years. This was unthinkable, and I felt useless.

Stan

10 September 2018, 9 p.m.

Stan and Alice had more in common than it would seem at first glance. At twenty-six, Stan still lived at home under the care of his formidable but very nurturing mother. Like Alice, Stan was abandoned by a parent. In his case, it was his father, who, according to his mother, had baby mommas scattered around South East London like seeds in the wind. Despite appearances, Stan had also found it hard to fit in. He was too white for the big bad gangs that roamed his vast estate like wild animals, his big blue eyes and light coffee colour skin excluding him automatically, and yet, ironically, he was too black for the packs of chavs and Eastern Europeans that made up the rest of the demographic.

What Stan had was bucket loads of charm. His mother always joked that he could charm his way out of a paper bag. This meant that, although he was not welcomed into any group with open arms, he could flit seamlessly between them, never quite lifting his head above the parapet to get himself into trouble. Stan had realised early on that this gift of charm could get him far, particularly with women. Teachers with reputations of bulldogs turned putty-like when he shined his little spotlight on him. Forgotten homework was forgiven and detentions magically disappeared.

Despite showing some promise at school, Stan had never settled on a particular job, instead relying on a portfolio career. He sold a bit of dope, enough to keep some of the chavs gently stoned but not enough to tread on any of the gang's toes. His charm made him a natural salesman, so he was often the 'go-to' man when bent goods came onto the estate. He never actually had to get his hands dirty, but he was happy to re-distribute the goods, setting up an office in the playground amongst the broken swings and used condoms. Because of this, he had become the man who knew how to get what you wanted. From frying pans to PlayStations, he always knew how to get his hands on stuff.

By far his biggest money spinner to date, however, had happened purely by accident. Stan had never been short of female admirers, but he found himself bored easily. It was all about the chase with him, and he soon won the reputation as a heartbreaker. This was why the online world suited him so well. There was lots of female attention with little commitment or even actual contact. He had progressed steadily from schoolyard sexting to full-on webcam sex over the years, and he found that this, along with the occasional dalliance, was enough to keep him sated. He wasn't greedy, after all. But then he had discovered that he could also make a few quid out of these women. The combination of hot girls and money making was almost too perfect for Stan.

It was mainly in Europe that Stan sold his goods. He was amazed that people were still prepared to pay for crotch shots and fuzzy amateur masturbation films. Stan was yet to sell any actual penetration shots, but he was thinking about making his own film with one of his women. He quite liked the idea of being a porn star. Gone was the highly polished, fake porn of his youth with corny storylines and flattering camera angles. It was all about reality these days, as though the public appetite for watching supposed real-life shows about posh people or drunken Welsh youths had spilled over into porn. No longer was it about the beautiful yet untouchable woman with the bald cunt and perfect orgasm face, people wanted real hair, at least down there, and hints of cellulite. With reality came the need for evermore risky material, and it was rare for Stan to see a porn film without the woman being raped or at the very least enduring a penis or other objects up her bum. It didn't float his boat, but as a true entrepreneur, he could see this was where the market was.

Stan did have principles and never went for girls below thirteen. He knew there was a definite market for junior porn, but he didn't want to cross that line. He only ever went after girls he would consider sleeping with himself. Sometimes the younger teenagers were the most provocative. He never told them that the pictures or films were for anything other than personal use, and he hoped that by selling them abroad, he would avoid the girls coming across their images saved for prosperity.

Occasionally he would come across one that was a hard nut to crack. It amazed him how easy it was to persuade girls to send him the most intimate pictures of themselves. However, Alice was a work in progress. She was totally not his usual target. For a start, she was older than he usually went for and seemed to have a successful career and social life. However, there was something very vulnerable that he could see in her, and this was what appealed to him. Usually, he went for girls who looked like they were lacking in attention—girls in care were generally the easiest, as they would do anything for some affection—but Alice fascinated him, despite her unwillingness to strip off and bend over metaphorically. He realised that he was quite enjoying the chase for once and checked Facebook often just to see what she was up to.

She had sent him some shots that were supposed to be her in her panties, but being the seasoned pro he was, he knew they were lifted straight from Google; after all, some skin colours were different, and one girl even had a tiny belly button stud. Rather than making him angry, this made him want her more.

He didn't know why she was hiding from him. She was actually out of his league. Her profile pictures showed a stunning brunette with blue eyes framed by those ridiculous giraffe-like fake eyelashes and big, pumped up lips which made all girls look like porn stars these days. She was always in some nice hotel or out on the town, and he wondered when she had time to actually work.

He knew if he pressed enough, he would eventually get what

he wanted; after all, his mother had always told him he was a charming man.

Alice

9 September 2018, 3 p.m.

I always loved Tuesdays as it was the day that Granny went food shopping. She would come home in a taxi from Tesco's, her arms full of bags bursting at the seams with all kinds of delights. Granny would always make the taxi driver help with her bags as though he was some kind of doorman and she a lady that lunches. I loved to help put things away, filling the cupboards and freezer with my treats for the week.

Bang on the dot of three, I heard a key in the lock and heard my granny gently berating the driver who was weighed down with at least six bags in each hand. Once all the bags were in, I began my weekly dive into the treasure trove. I heard my gran sigh and settle on her place on the sofa, marked with a deep indentation that fit her little bum perfectly.

'Bring me my fags through, will you, darling? And a cuppa. I'm gasping!'

I put the kettle on and rooted around in all the bags until she found Granny's B&H. She took them through with an ashtray and lighter, promising the tea as soon as it was done.

'Wow, I'm done in after all that today. You wouldn't believe the queues at the tills.'

I noticed that my gran looked tired and a bit pale. 'You know you don't need to go shopping. We could do it all online.'

'Oh yes, and then we could pay someone to pick out all the bruised fruit or sausages right near their sell-by date,' said Granny, lighting her cigarette and taking a greedy puff. 'And besides, I like to go to the supermarket. It's almost a social occasion for me, as I always bump into people I know.'

I left it; I knew my gran would moan if she went and moan if she didn't. Also, I often felt guilty that my gran didn't have many friends. She had given up so much to look after me while all her friends were going on world cruises or taking up bridge, and she seemed to have been left behind. I had tried to tell her she should go out and play Bingo or even visit the local pub occasionally, but Granny said she didn't like leaving me in the evening. I was secretly pleased about this as I found the house even scarier when I was alone at night time.

I heard the kettle click and went back in to make the tea. As I took it through, I noticed my gran's favourite game show was on: *Deal or No Deal*. This was one that always got her excited, screaming out advice to the contestants on stage. I was surprised when my gran kept quiet. I sat next to her on the sofa.

'I bet that stupid man will lose it all! Ah well, serves him right,' I said, knowing my gran loved it when I had an opinion about the TV. But this time she didn't bite. Instead, she turned down the volume and lit another cigarette.

'I've got a headache,' my gran explained, sipping the hot tea and putting it back on its saucer immediately like she always did. I was worried my gran didn't look well, and I wasn't sure what to do. It had always been Granny playing the nursemaid, not the other way round. As she always said, she was as tough as old boots and rarely got even a sniffle. I vowed that I would make her as many cups of tea as she wanted today and even cook the meal that evening.

Leaving Granny watching quietly, I went back to the kitchen to put away the shopping. I updated my audience telling them I was 'All shopped out', hoping this sounded like I had just been to splurge in the boutiques of Nice rather than the blue and white carrier bags that now littered the kitchen. I was pleased when Stan commented.

'Wud love to see you try some of them tings on, how about a photo?'

I liked his comment and set my iPhone to wait three minutes.

'Sorry heading straight out to the gym maybe I will do you a fashion show later?'

Almost immediately I could see that he was messaging me.

'Hey beautiful girl, how's about you give me a bit of a private show later?'

'I'm not really keen on live action but I can send some pictures?' I told him. I didn't want to be too dismissive in case he lost interest.

'That wud be mighty fine don't suppose you bought yourself some new panties as well?'

I paused to think. There was only so much airbrushing I could do on my photos.

'Let's see if you get lucky hey?' I replied, thinking this sounded elusive but also hopeful for him. I figured I had at least a two-hour window to work my magic.

I had been so flattered when I had started getting messages from Stan; after all, he was way out of my league and so different to the boys I remembered from my school days. While not traditionally handsome, I liked his cropped hair and neck tattoo, as it gave him an edge of danger. My favourite part about him was his bright blue eyes, as they softened his look immensely.

Stan was exactly the type of man that people would call 'my bit of rough'. I wasn't sure about his job, but I knew he spent a lot of time in his car (his pride and joy, judging by the number of pictures he posted up). I knew he lived in South London, somewhere called Peckham, and I also knew he went out clubbing most weekends with his crew. Everything about him was exciting and edgy, different to the foreign lotharios and airline pilots I was supposedly leaping into bed with every five minutes.

Once all my goodies were in their rightful place, I made another pot of tea and went through to sit with my gran. The TV was by now showing some Real Housewives somewhere in America. I couldn't quite tell where, just that they all had tumbling blonde locks and bodies hard like Barbie dolls. I passed the time by tweeting my thoughts all about the blonde bimbos in front of me, then sprinkling in a few comments about being in the gym in case any of my Facebook friends also followed me on Twitter. As the credits rolled, I heaved myself out of my chair, taking the tray back in the kitchen and headed up to my room.

I realised early on that I didn't really have any nice underwear—well, at least none that would excite Stan—and I really wanted to keep him happy. My gran bought my knickers from the supermarket, and the only ones that fit me were the giant belly warmers in a variety of pastel shades. Instead, I Googled pantie shots and was rewarded with pages of knickers being worn of all varieties. Feeling a fraud, I took one shot of my underwear close-up so you couldn't see much detail, and then copied and pasted a few more into a message. I titled the message 'fashion show' and then quickly hit send to Stan before I lost my nerve.

I wanted to check on my gran again, so I lumbered down the stairs. My gran had finished my cup of tea, so I took it away for her.

'Can I get you anything else? Do you want a painkiller or something?' I asked.

'No, I'm fine, darling. Don't you worry your pretty little head over me. It would take more than a headache to get the better of me!'

'What's next up on the box?'

'I've got my Aussie soaps double bill and then *Come Dine with Me.* You know me, I'm happy as Larry with my little wonder-box here.'

I almost laughed at the description of the TV as 'little', as it was so huge it took over most of the wall of the living room, dominating the eyelines and conversations of anyone who sat in there.

I sat next to my gran and kept an eye on my phone. Minutes later, just as the opening credits were starting on *Neighbours,* my phone pinged with a new message from Stan.

'Man dem photos were sick, you sure know how to treat a man. You are so beautiful. Can't wait to see what's underneath.'

I blushed bright red, closing my phone down quickly in case my myopic gran had looked all the way across the room at the X-rated message. My breathing was returning to normal when my phone lit up with a new text message, also from Stan. At first, I couldn't make out what it was—it was poorly lit and at a strange angle—but as I looked closer, I gasped in shock when I realised it was a man's penis. Stan had texted to go with his photo. **'I've shown you mine now you show me yours.'** This was well beyond the realms of my knowledge or experience, so I quickly deleted the message and went to my room.

My room hadn't been decorated for many years, and it was as if it was frozen in time, a museum of my life as a thirteen-year-old. Uncle Tom had still been around in my early teens and had indulged my love-bordering-on-obsession of boyband One Direction. This was reflected in the duvet cover, lampshade and posters all featuring the boys smiling out at me. It all looked bedraggled now, much like the boys themselves when I saw them on chat shows, the years of rock and roll now showing on their twenty-something faces and bloated bodies. My curtains had been there even longer; you could probably call them vintage.

Lying on my bed half thrilled and half horrified, I messaged Stan back trying to sound casual and breezy. 'Wow, aren't I such a lucky girl! You will get your treat soon.' I hoped this was enough to keep him interested for now.

Tom
7 September 2018, 8 p.m.

Tom was bored. Tom was often bored, but even he thought he shouldn't feel this way in the middle of a gallery opening. It was as though he had been to this show a million times before, despite it opening that day. The room was full of the same people: the art groupies, the stick-thin models and of course the artists themselves. Same arseholes, different shows. When Tom had first moved to New York, it had been so shiny and new, excitement was on every corner. As a small-town boy who had lived in the closet for many years, New York and its liberal gay scene had literally blown him away. He could reinvent himself as a terribly intelligent and stylish Brit, working hard and playing hard in the Big Apple.

Now ten years on, Tom was finding the dream fraying around the edges. What was the point in being part of a power couple (him, the hot young lawyer, and his partner, Will, big in the art dealing world) if you didn't constantly remind the world of how fab you both were? This meant dinners were always out; in fact, he had only used the oven in his tiny kitchen a handful of times and knew many people who used theirs as extra storage in the tiny New York apartments they all called home.

Amazingly, what Tom now craved was domestic slobbery. He longed for a weekend spent at home with his phone switched off, watching the box sets they always bought each other for Christmas and birthdays and then never got round to watching, eating takeaway and not leaving the apartment. Instead, his and Will's weekends were fully booked now until well into the next year with parties, lunches and weekends visiting friend's 'darling' little vacation homes dotted around the East coast. Tom felt exhausted thinking about it. It was times like this when Tom found himself strangely homesick, reminiscing about the smell of home cooking (well, microwave cooking in reality) and the well-worn sofa that his mum had moulded a permanent dent into.

Sadly this scene of domestic bliss through heavily tinted rose-coloured spectacles was no longer part of his life, and he had not seen his mother or his beloved niece Alice for many years, although he felt like he had watched Alice grow up through her social media files.

He had thought his mother had known he was gay for many years. There had been a couple of illicit kisses in his younger years, and he was sure she must have come across his rather extreme choice of porn when cleaning his teenage bedroom. To him, he guessed, he must have always seemed gay. He didn't mind admitting that he was always the more feminine one in his relationships, and this hadn't come on suddenly. He had even thought his mum might be proud of him when he came out to her officially, but he could still remember the look of absolute horror and disgust in her eyes when he had turned up with his then-boyfriend to stay for a weekend. Before she told him to get out of her house, she informed him she was glad his father had left so he wouldn't have to see what his sick son had become.

Tom tried to get back to focussing on the art back in the room, but it wasn't enough to captivate him, and his mind kept drifting back. He avoided getting into a conversation with two old queens who he knew vaguely from the scene, and he tried to catch Will's eye, but he was deep in conversation with the artist, no doubt stroking his already monstrous ego. Will was the kind of man that Tom had always thought he should end up with. In his late fifties, he was balding and had a paunch because of all those dinners and glasses of wine. Tom was relieved he had finally started using a personal trainer. What he lacked in appearance, he more than made up for in personality and stature. When he walked into a room, people sat up and took notice. It was hard to resist the lure of success either. Will was a well-respected art dealer, and this brought with it many benefits, including an apartment only a couple of blocks away from Central Park with a real-life doorman and the pre-requisite house share in the Hamptons, which they rarely had time to visit but still made them feel as though they had a sanctuary.

Tom finally caught Will's eye and pointed to his watch, the agreed signal it was time to go. Annoyingly, Will ignored him and grabbed another drink from a passing waiter. Tom guessed the conversation he was having was turning out to be potentially lucrative. Ignoring his two-drink maximum rule on a weekday, Tom also grabbed another drink and walked over to gatecrash the queen's conversation. At least if he was going to be bored, he may as well be bored by someone else.

Alice

7 Sept 2018, 9 a.m.

My gran always liked to make sure I started the day with a good breakfast. She often told me she had always sent her own kids off to school with a hot meal inside them. Most of the other food of the day travelled between freezer and microwave, so breakfast was the only one that Granny cooked, if you could call putting a load of ingredients into a deep fat fryer actually cooking.

Funnily enough, Granny and I were obsessed with cooking programmes, well before *The Great British Bake Off* came along and everyone became an armchair foodie. We loved sitting enchanted as chefs with varying degrees of cheer beat and cajoled the ordinary ingredients into something that looked enticing. It was unlikely we would ever try it ourselves.

I could hear the TV on loud in the living room and recognised the noises of the morning chat show Gran watched religiously. She watched most programmes religiously, as there wasn't much gatekeeping involved. It was an unwritten rule, but the kitchen was my domain during the day, while Granny usually stayed in the living room plugged into her TV at all hours. Sometimes there was a crossover, like when Granny was cooking or if she wanted me to watch a show with her, but most of the time the two of us lived a happy existence side by side, both enclosed in our own little worlds.

Although my gran definitely looked like a granny should with a blue rinse and hair put in rollers every night, she was actually the only mother I had ever known. This wasn't really talked about in our house, but then nothing important ever really was. It was only when Granny had one too many sherries that she might talk about her role as the saviour. She had single-handedly rescued me from the care system where a life awaited me of resentful foster parents and faceless institutions. I was incredibly grateful for the rescue, but Granny wasn't to know it had been an out-of-the-frying-pan-into-the-fire situation for me. She never knew what she exposed me to by bringing me back here. It wasn't her fault, and I repaid her by being the best granddaughter I could ever be.

Unlike most of the girls I had known at school, my only vice was food. I loved everything about food: the smell, the texture and the comforting feeling I felt after I had eaten everything on my plate. It was as though I was filling a gap, or more like a deep hole. Whenever I was feeling low, food would appear and magically take the misery away, for a while at least. It didn't matter if it was savoury or sweet. I would dream of sugary doughnuts and big creamy pasta shapes. Granny always said that I was a growing girl and should eat well, and over the years, I had indeed grown.

I sometimes saw Granny watching programmes about fat people as a form of entertainment and would feel a little uncomfortable. Gran would laugh and point along with the voiceover, and I would feel as though she was actually poking fun at me. I tried to laugh along too, like I had done at school.

None of this really mattered, because I was a different person where it counted: online. Online Alice was beautiful and slim because of the incredible apps you could use these days on your phone. Online Alice had an interesting job as an air hostess and would fly all over the world. Online Alice liked to drink wine with her friends in the latest bars and go on dates with handsome young doctors. Online Alice lived in Bournemouth in her very own flat. Online Alice had an air of mystery.

The intrigue hadn't been intentional in the beginning. I guess to some people, I must have disappeared from the world the day I decided that the outside world was no longer something I wanted to experience, with my body punishing me with panic and living nightmares.

I hadn't returned to sixth form as had been expected of me, and then I found out that there were hilarious rumours circulating that I had run off to London amid some kind of scandal involving a teacher. I had always been an awkward, lonesome student, and so I was surprised when I suddenly started receiving friend requests from some of the most popular girls at school. The mystery had given me a chance to reinvent myself.

As Online Alice, I could lead the kind of fantasy life I would have chosen had my life been different. I could choose a career, a home, even a dress size. No one had any idea of the reality, which was me sitting in my kitchen in my pyjamas, thighs splaying across the chairs, never having been kissed and never having worked an honest day in my life.

I made elevenses, one of Granny's favourite rituals, and carried the tray into the living room. She didn't take her eyes off Jeremy Kyle on the screen as she grabbed a biscuit and I poured milk in her flowery cup.

'He accused her of shagging his best mate, but it turns out it was him doing the dirty,' she said, pointing at the pimply skinhead on screen.

I made all the right noises. I knew how much Granny loved this show and revered Saint Jeremy who, in her eyes, was the saviour to a nation of council-house-dwelling scroungers (I never pointed out the fact that neither of us had ever worked either).

Granny continued. 'Only the person he was doing it with was his best mate. He's just admitted it to her and in front of all those people too! It's the kids I feel sorry for. It's not natural, is it?'

I didn't really think there was anything wrong with being gay but knew only too well her views on the subject, so I simply nodded in agreement. Her view was so entrenched that she had even kicked Uncle Tom out. I remember when she found out, seeing her go through denial (it's only a phase!), grief (my only son!), and then eventually anger that led to her cutting him off. I knew that Granny would be furious if she knew that I was still in touch with him.

I shoved another bourbon in my mouth and poured the tea. The pimply skinhead was angry now and was screaming at a woman dressed in a tracksuit who had long greasy hair with her roots showing.

'Do you think he is going to try and hit someone, Gran?' I asked, knowing that Granny loved it when I got involved.

'If he tries, then I'm sure the lovely Jeremy will calm him right down.'

The crowd by now was baying for blood as pimply skinhead's best mate was telling him he loved him more than the greasy-haired girlfriend. Looking at the clock on my phone, I knew it would all be wrapped up in the next four minutes. Some-one would be offered counselling with Graham, there would be tears and Jeremy would congratulate someone, likely to be the best friend in this case for being so honest. That's what her gran liked about the programme; no matter how complicated things seemed, everything could be sorted out in an allotted twenty-minute slot.

I finished my tea and a couple more biscuits just in time for the end credits. Granny quickly snatched up the remote and switched channels.

'I always like to snatch the end of this auction show. You never know what treasures might come up, and you know I will empty my loft one day and make my fortune. I may even get that lovely suntanned chap to come round and have a look for me or the nice news lady from the antiques show.'

'Got buried treasure hidden up there, have you, Gran? Maybe we should go up there and sort it one day.'

'Yes, we should. Have to wait for a day when we are not busy though; maybe next week?'

I knew this was strictly hypothetical as Granny had been talk-ing about clearing out the loft for as long as I could remember. I had never been up there but liked to imagine boxes dripping with jewels.

I cleared away the tea things and left Granny trying to guess how much a battered old suitcase would make for the thin, mousy-looking woman on screen. I updated my status. I had left my audience with a cliffhanger last night when I had told them that Andy was about to call me to have the 'make or break' chat. This was a pilot I had been sleeping with—in my online world—for many months. I hadn't realised how many of my online friends were happily married, and when I had faced a backlash earlier in the story, I had to backtrack and say his wife had left him, rather than me being painted as the homewrecker.

I decided that Andy had run his course and told everyone that we had broken up because of our clashing schedules. My feed was flooded with hearts, inspiration and gifs. They loved me when I was dating but loved me even more when I was breaking hearts. It was like being at the centre of my own soap opera, one where I was totally in control.

I suddenly remembered that I had mentioned I was away for work. Realising I had already posted breakfast and therefore couldn't claim to be anywhere that required a noticeable time difference, I settled on France, quickly Googling beach view photos of Nice. Finding a suitably amateur one with a glimpse of a curtain for added authenticity, I posted it and told everyone it was the view from my hotel that morning. Minutes ticked by and no one said a word. The online silence was so deafening, I couldn't even concentrate on what other people were up to. Finally, I could stand it no more and changed my update again.

'I woke up with another fine view this morning, not quite sure of his name though and he only seems to speak French... whoops #toomanybellinis!'

Almost instantly, I was rewarded for my sluttiness with a barrage of likes and comments. I felt a surge of happiness that everyone was so interested in what I got up to.

I heard Gran come into the kitchen, and I quickly minimised my browser. It wasn't that Granny ever took any interest in what I did on my laptop, but I didn't want her finding out that her Alice was not the innocent girl she thought she was.

Granny was doing her coat up. 'I'm going into town to go to the post office and the bank. Shall I get you a little treat while I am out? Some of your favourite sweeties maybe?'

'You know you don't have to spoil me. You have already given me my pocket money this week!'

'Yes, but you have been such a good girl this week that I think you deserve a little something.' Granny laughed, tickling me under my chin as though I was eleven, not ten years older.

I didn't like to admit it to anyone, but I was always a little scared being left in the house by myself. I found the silence without the TV blaring very uncomfortable and put some music on to try and ease the discomfort.

My world had always had sound and distractions. Even when my mother had left me at home alone when I was barely walking, I remember having TVs, radios and even pets for company. Stints in foster homes had always been really noisy with scores of children vying for attention by seeing who could scream the loudest, and then my gran's house had its comforting TV and domestic sounds, the gentle whirr of the dishwasher or growl of the hoover. This is what home sounded like.

PART 3

DAY 1 AGAIN

Rachel
8 November 2018, 6.30 p.m.

It had felt like hours, but finally Rachel could see the family liaison officer talking to the men in white and then heading over to relay the information to them. The noise and the crowd had increased, and the police had set up a white tent outside the home. She realised this must be something to do with the body, or whatever it was they had found.

Rachel held her breath in terror as the officer approached them, a serious look on his face. She knew he would be giving them bad news, the news that every parent dreads, even if they have had no contact with their child for many years. It was strange how, for many years, being apart from Alice had been a faint pain, like a hangnail—always there but not bad enough to do anything about it. Alice could well have been dead for years, and Rachel would have been none the wiser. But being here in this situation and facing the horrific thought of her daughter's body rotting away in that horrible house was unbearable.

The officer was now in front of her and Tom.

'They can't see anyone alive or dead in there, and they have checked most of the house. However, they say there are signs of life. There is a small gas stove set up in the kitchen and some dirty plates on the counter, but it's impossible to say how long they have been there. They have also said there are towers of books all over the place. Were either of them big readers?'

Rachel almost choked. 'I don't remember Mum reading anything unless it was a trashy TV magazine. I don't know about Alice. Tom, do you know if she was a big reader?' Rachel felt so bad that she didn't even know this basic fact about her daughter.

'I don't think she read, unless it was through her iPad. She was pretty addicted to social media, like most young people these days I guess,' Tom answered.

Rachel noticed that they both were already talking about her in the past tense.

The officer continued. 'OK, I guess that could show that someone else was living in the house. You thought maybe there were squatters or something?'

'Yes, but you said yourself that it was impossible to get in,' Rachel responded.

'Now, yes, but for all we know the windows could have been left open or this person or persons may have been invited in. It might have been them who locked it all up so securely.'

Rachel immediately thought of that horrible man in custody who they now knew had been in the house. Again, he didn't seem the type to curl up with a good book or play at boy scouts.

There was another crackle of the radio and the officer stepped away for a moment before returning to impart his latest information.

'We can confirm that we have found Alice's phone, iPad and laptop. They are all completely out of charge, but we will take them out as evidence and see what we can find on them.'

This was serious. Nobody these days goes anywhere without their lifelines, and the phone is probably more important than a wallet or passport. From what Tom had said and from what she knew of kids she looked after, it was unlikely that Alice would have gone anywhere, willingly, without at least one of her devices.

The whole of the front lawn was more like a railway station now, with people running around in organised chaos. Suddenly, out of the corner of her eye, she noticed something strange at the front door. This person wasn't dressed in any kind of uniform and didn't look busy at all; in fact, she looked perplexed by it all, standing there in her strange '80's jeans and sweatshirt. For there, standing at the front door, trying to leave her house for the first time in half a decade, was Alice Carmichael.

Alice

I knew it was her immediately, but I was still surprised to see her standing there and even more shocked when she came running towards me. It was one thing knowing someone on social media but quite another seeing them in real life. More than most, I knew if I had bumped into any of my so-called friends in real life, we probably wouldn't stop and have a conversation. In fact, they probably wouldn't recognise me. I don't know if it was because she was my mum and not just some random contact, but as soon as I saw her, I was flooded with emotion.

For a while I stood frozen at the front door, looking around at the chaos outside and trying to work out what was happening. I presumed that I was being rescued from the war I had seen online before I lost all power, and I was pleased to see there were others left. I had no way of knowing if anyone else had survived. When I had first heard the sirens and the rising noise outside my house, I thought it must have been the enemy coming to get me. I had panicked when I heard them break the door down, and I had run up to my favourite hiding place in the loft. However, when I had heard voices interspersed with the heavy footsteps below me, they were talking as though they were there to rescue me, and so, after gathering myself, I let myself be known.

Even with all this going on around me, it was still a struggle actually leaving my sanctuary, but I guess it wasn't such a retreat anymore. My entire body was in fight-or-flight mode, and I wanted to stay put, but I knew I couldn't live like this anymore. I wasn't really living; I was barely surviving. I thought if I could control my breathing and make those first few steps out, then maybe I could escape. I had thought that what was out there, life and all its problems, was something I never wanted to step into again, but my wish for survival had finally kicked in. I wanted to live.

Cautiously, I tried to ignore the noise and the lights and took a step outside.

Rachel ran to me immediately and enveloped me in a huge hug, tears running down her face. I didn't quite know what to do.

'What are you doing here?' I asked her in a stupor. Then I noticed Uncle Tom was following behind her. I knew the situation with the war must have been bad over here and I must have been in a lot of danger for him to fly over.

'Oh, let me look at you, my darling. Are you OK? Has anyone hurt you?' She was staring at me intently, just as Tom got to us.

'Oh, thank god. We thought when they mentioned a body that something really terrible had happened to you!'

'What do you mean they found a body?' I asked, now worried what else had been going on.

'They found human remains somewhere in the house, and we were not sure who they belonged to.'

The penny suddenly dropped. Poor old Granny in the freezer. It's funny, but I hadn't really thought of her as a body or as remains, but I guessed by now with the electricity gone that she probably wasn't in a great state.

'Oh, that was Granny. Don't worry, nothing bad happened. As far as I can work out, she died of natural causes.'

They both looked at me, evidently shocked at my unemotional response. I was about to explain, but I was suddenly whisked away by a paramedic. The man seemed very nice. He reminded me of the nurse from *Casualty*, the one who had been in it since before I was born.

I could see Rachel and Tom hanging around outside the ambulance as the man laid me down, and they were joined by two police officers.

'Can you tell me your name, love?' the paramedic asked gently.

'Of course, it's Alice Carmichael.'

'And do you know what day or year it is?'

'I'm afraid I have totally lost track of the days, but I am pretty sure it is still 2018. I am so reliant on my phone that as soon as the war started and we lost power, I had no idea what the date was.'

He looked at me strangely as I said this. 'Can you tell me if you are hurt in any way?'

'Not as far as I know.'

'I'm just going to look at all your vitals,' he said as he put an armband around me and shone a torch in my eyes. He seemed satisfied, and I was pleased that I had passed his tests. Then he seemed to nod at one of the policewomen who swapped places with him and sat on a little chair opposite me.

'Hi, Alice, my name is Detective Chief Inspector Kingsley. I want to find out a bit more about what has happened here. I know you may not be in a great state to tell us much at the moment, but do you mind answering a few questions?'

I was trying to focus on her words, but I was transfixed by her hair. I instantly renamed her the Scarlet Detective.

'Of course not, but I really know little; after all, I have been stuck in the house all this time.'

'Can you tell me why you have been stuck in the house? Was someone holding you there? Did anyone hurt you?'

'The problem obviously wasn't inside the house; I was just stay-ing there to stay safe,' I told her, not explaining about the issues I had been experiencing before the war started as it hardly seemed important now.

'What were you staying safe from, Alice?'

'The war, of course.'

The woman looked perplexed and spoke slowly as though I was a child. 'What do you mean by *war*, Alice?'

'The world war I read about. I couldn't find out more because the house lost power.'

She gave her colleague a strange look. 'Do you want to tell us more about this war?'

'That's just it. It was breaking news, and I was so scared because it looked like the whole country was under attack after what happened in Bournemouth, but then I guess the power was cut for some reason. I thought the best thing for me to do was to stay put and wait for help.'

The officers exchanged another look which I couldn't read.

She spoke gently. 'Alice, we also found some remains in the house. Do you know who they belong to?'

This was the moment I had been dreading. What I had done at the time had seemed like the right thing to do, but now with all these police cars and ambulances, I had no idea how to explain this.

'I know who it is. It's my granny.'

No one looked surprised at this news.

The Scarlet Detective was a bit more forceful this time. 'OK, can you tell me what happened to her? Did someone hurt her? Did anyone hurt you?'

I blushed thinking back on what had happened with Stan. He had hurt me, but I didn't think that's what they were talking about. I really wanted to give them the right answers. I wanted to do well.

'I don't think so, not unless someone hurt her when she was out shopping. She actually died in the house, and it was just me there.'

I paused, realising how this sounded.

'I mean, I didn't actually see her die. I found her that way.'

As soon as I said this, I knew I must have sounded uncaring and that I would possibly get into trouble for not telling anyone what had happened. I could see sympathy soon turn to something else—possibly disgust—on the faces around me.

'I am pretty sure she died from natural causes—probably her heart or something in her brain. She went pretty quickly and didn't seem to be in any pain.' I hoped that made them feel better. I also hoped Rachel and Tom weren't listening in. After all, it had taken me a while to grieve and become used to the fact that Gran was dead.

The woman spoke again. She was kind but more forceful this time. 'Can you tell me why we found your grandmother's remains in the basement freezer? Why isn't she buried in the churchyard as I'm sure she would have wanted to be?'

This, I couldn't really answer. It had felt like the best option at the time, but now it seemed silly that I hadn't wanted to let anyone know.

'I don't know, I was terrified of being taken away, I guess.'

The Scarlet Detective looked annoyed or perplexed and stepped outside the ambulance. I could see her speaking to her colleague as Tom stepped in.

'Can we leave any further questions until she is feeling better? She has clearly had a terrible time with whatever has happened. We need to allow her some time and then hopefully we can make sense of what has happened here.'

The two officers ignored him and walked away, chatting before they appeared back in the door of the ambulance. The Scarlet Detective looked different this time, harder somehow.

'Alice Carmichael, we are arresting you for the suspected manslaughter of Josie Carmichael. We would like you to come to the station and answer a few questions so we can establish what exactly has happened.'

This didn't feel real. I had never been in trouble, not even at school. The male officer helped me down and held my arm as he steered me across to the waiting police car. I suddenly noticed that we had an audience and flashbulbs were going crazy. I even noticed a couple of big news vans. I guess they say everyone has their fifteen minutes of fame, and this was to be mine.

Tom was trying to talk to the officer.

'You can't take her away like this. God knows what has gone on in that house. Me and my sister can testify to what terrible people our parents were, so even if she has killed her, it would have likely been in defence.'

I was relieved that someone seemed to take control of the situation but annoyed that even Tom thought I might be capable of killing Granny.

'Mr Carmichael, you know this needs to be done at the station. You are welcome to join us there. I understand you are a lawyer? She might be better off with you by her side rather than some of the poor sods that get drafted in for evening custody. We know nothing at the moment, and we need to uncover the facts of what has happened here.'

Tom grabbed Rachel and they headed off towards a crappy blue car, which I guessed was the 'rustbucket' Rachel and I had joked about on Facebook. I thought how surprised she would be when she found out we had been in touch. I could reveal myself as Tania and we could laugh about it. That was if I wasn't locked up with the key thrown away. From one prison to another.

Alice

I felt almost relieved when we arrived at the police station and I was led to a cell. I guess for some people, being locked up in a small room would fill them with dread, but for me, it was the big, bad world that had always been the problem. The chaos and noise that had greeted me when I left the prison of my making had left me feeling very shaken. There had been the lovely fact of seeing Rachel and Uncle Tom again after so long, but it was hardly the moment for a reunion or even a catch-up.

The police officers who had booked me in were very nice and had treated me well. No one wanted to talk about the war that had been going on, but I guessed there would be time for that. For now, it was almost a relief that other people were taking care of me again. Since I had arrived, I had eaten a hot meal, albeit straight out of a microwave, but it was tasty nonetheless. I had improvised with tins out of the basement cooked on a campfire for the previous few weeks.

Not so long ago, the idea of sitting with nothing to do would have freaked me out, but over time, I had learnt to sit quietly in the house with nothing but my thoughts. I was amazed by the world that had been opened by the books I had discovered in the attic. I had always thought my phone was the key to the universe, but reading had given me back my imagination. I found that the worlds I had read about would keep me going for hours after I had put the book down.

It wasn't easy at first; in fact, I had felt myself almost go through a physical withdrawal of the constant noise and interaction from my technology. It had felt as though there was something always missing in my life without being able to reach for my phone, but not knowing what was happening out in the world had eventually become a relief. It had felt like I had been living like that for years when actually it must have only been a matter of weeks.

I had been in the cell for around an hour when an officer arrived to take me through for questioning.

'How are you feeling, my love? It must be scary being in here all alone,' he said, leading me to a table in a room. I was relieved to see that Tom was in there already, and I wanted to run up and hug him but thought it might be inappropriate in the circumstances.

'Actually, it was quite a relief after all the chaos at the house,' I admitted taking a seat. They offered me a cup of tea, which I gratefully accepted. It was stewed and too sweet, but it was also my first cup of white tea in months, so it was bliss.

They left us in the room alone, and Tom reached over to hug me. It felt like he was a stranger, which I guess in many ways he was. We hadn't actually seen each other for years. I was surprised at how old he looked.

'Oh my god, Alice, how are you doing? Have they been treating you OK?'

'Actually, it has been great! I haven't had a meal cooked for me for ages, and everyone has been really nice.' I tried to put a brave face on; after all, Tom was clearly facing a difficult situation. But there was some truth in what I said.

'You know why you are here though, right? They will question you about the body they found today. I would love to run through your account first, but we don't have time. I just want to say for now that you can tell them "no comment" at every stage.'

I couldn't understand why he would want me to do this when I had done nothing wrong. The sooner they heard what had happened, the sooner they could let me go again.

'I don't mind answering their questions if it means this gets sorted out quicker. How is Rachel? Why is she here? Why are you both here?'

'As you can imagine, this has all been a lot for her to take in. I mean, I haven't seen her since we were kids, but the last time she saw you was when you are still in nappies. It says a lot she is here though.'

'Do you think she will stay around until I'm out?' I asked timidly, fully expecting her to head back to her real life as soon as she could.

'Yes, don't worry, she is waiting back at the hotel for me. She will probably have to head back to London soon, though, as she has two young girls.'

'Oh yes, I know. Kylie and Jess. They look like gorgeous kids,' I said, forgetting for a moment that I had this information by dubious means. I hesitated. 'Has she told them about me?'

He looked puzzled and a little embarrassed. 'I think she is planning to when we get you out.'

We were interrupted from any more catching up when two serious-looking people entered the room. The whole atmosphere changed, and Tom immediately became official and polite.

'We met at the scene,' the female officer said. 'I am DCI Kingsley, and this is my colleague DI Barnes.' The woman pointed to her colleague who looked grey and non-descript next to her. I was surprised that neither were wearing a uniform, which I guessed meant they were high up. The male officer switched on what looked like a tape recorder. I only knew about these from retro pictures on Insta.

'We have brought you in to chat about the discovery of a body at 34 Doncaster Avenue. You have already indicated that the remains may belong to a Mrs Josie Carmichael. Are you able to tell us why you think this is her body?'

'If you are talking about my granny, I know it's her because I put her there.' I answered truthfully, noticing how Tom looked shocked and annoyed at this disclosure.

'Can you clarify when you say you put her there? Are you admitting that you had a part in her death?' Kingsley asked.

I almost laughed, but she looked deadly serious. 'Of course not. She died on the sofa one day. I told you before I think she died from natural causes.'

I almost told them about the mess and the new sofa but realised that might sound even more strange that I was thinking of soft furnishings with a corpse next to me.

The man spoke. He sounded kind. 'Can you tell us what happened to her, in your own words?'

'It was nothing dramatic really. Gran had been out shopping, and when she came home, she said she had a headache. I left her with a cup of tea and a ciggie, and she seemed fine.'

'Go on.'

'But then when I walked back in the room, she wasn't. Wasn't fine, I mean. She wasn't really . . . there anymore.'

I had been through this so many times in my head, but somehow saying it out loud made it real, and I realised that I had a horrific memory of her. Flashes of her grotesque dead face penetrated my brain, and I could smell a horrific mixture of cigarette smoke, tea and shit.

For a few moments it felt like I was right back there in the room with her, and I felt helpless.

The Scarlet Detective clearly didn't notice anything, which made me relieved that no one else could see how crazy I was feeling.

'So, at this stage, we are assuming that poor Mrs Carmichael had indeed passed away. Did you check her vital signs? Administer any first aid?'

'Yes, I did, actually. I even Googled how to give the kiss of life, but nothing worked.'

I could suddenly feel Gran's rapidly cooling, dry, papery skin as though I was still touching her, trying to figure out how to wake her up. It had felt like I was on autopilot at the time.

'So, Ms Carmichael, tell me something: are you a doctor or have you had any medical training at any time?'

Tom cut in. 'Come on, you know she hasn't.'

'I wanted to check, as it appears you somehow decided that you had the skills and knowledge to decide that your grandmother had passed away and that there was nothing anyone could do. Most people leave that kind of decision to a doctor, or at least a paramedic.' It felt as though she was mocking me.

I knew how stupid it sounded. It was like Granny thinking she was some kind of high court judge just because she had an obsession with the Judge Rinder show. Granny considered herself an expert on lots of things.

'OK, so if we accept your account that she died suddenly on the sofa, presumably in the living room, can you explain why the remains we found were in the basement downstairs?' The Scarlet Detective was back, and she was mean.

I rushed to get my explanation out. 'As I explained, she was a mess and the whole house began to smell, so I moved her down to the freezer, which was actually a pretty good place for her until the power went.'

This was the bit I couldn't really explain. It seemed like such a normal thing to do at the time, but to an outsider it must have seemed like a strange thing to do. I don't really remember much about actually doing it. The detective took my silence as her cue to carry on accusations, and she reminded me of Jeremy Kyle when he used to get heated, knowing he wasn't getting the truth out of his guests.

'Until we have carried out tests, we can neither prove this is Josie Carmichael or know how she died. So for now, this is very much your word. Now I would like to show you some pictures from the crime scene. For the benefits of the tape, I am now showing Ms Carmichael and Mr Tom Carmichael pictures one to five of the Doncaster Road crime scene.'

As he lay them out in front of us, I could see Uncle Tom wince as he saw the black bags spilling out in the freezer. There was clearly human flesh and liquid seeping out of the bags. Although it had been me who had put them there, seeing them laid out like this in front of me, like a crime scene, suddenly seemed so gory. How had I ever felt that this was the way to deal with a body?

I felt the familiar quickening of breath as the room swam. Within moments, I felt like I was having a full-blown heart attack. Tom obviously didn't know what was happening, and he started to panic. I also could see the look of disgust in his eyes.

'Christ, can someone call a doctor? Alice is clearly not well,' Tom barked at the room.

By this stage, I no longer felt like I was in the room. I sat glued to the spot, taking in the chaos, and eventually a younger officer, who was obviously the first aider, came running in with some kind of high vis vest on to show his role. He crouched down in front of me.

'OK, Alice, what I want you to do is hold your breath. That's right, hold it for as long as you can and then try to let it out very gently.'

This seemed impossible, and I was worried that if I held my breath then I would stop breathing, but he kept on speaking and counting which gave me something else to focus on. Eventually, after what felt like hours, I felt fully conscious again. We had been given time to get ourselves together, and someone bought me another hot cup of tea.

While we were alone, Tom spoke quietly but with force. 'I know they will try to make you confess everything, but I need to know: why did you do that to my mother? Why on earth didn't you call the doctor or the police or whoever needed to know so she could be taken away and her body treated with dignity? Not left to rot like this.' He sounded angry, and I had never seen this side of him before.

'I don't know; I panicked, I guess. I was so reliant on Gran, and when she was gone, I didn't know what to do. I was scared they would take me away.'

He paused for a long time, looking torn. I noticed the clock in the room showed it was quarter past five, but I had no idea if that was morning or evening. This room had no windows.

'But, Alice, you are not a child. I mean, you weren't even living there, were you? I am probably most hurt about the fact you lied to me. I asked you directly how my mum was, and you told me she was down in the basement when actually that was your opportunity to tell me everything.'

'I didn't think you would care. I mean, you hadn't seen her for years. I hadn't seen Rachel since I was a toddler and you since I was a teenager, so it felt like I was completely alone.'

I shivered remembering how empty the house felt without Gran.

'I know it sounds stupid, Uncle Tom, but it didn't even feel like it was me doing it. I actually only remembered what had happened when we were sitting here. It was almost as if it was a dream.'

He didn't look like he believed me, but he had calmed down. I clearly hadn't done this because I was evil; I was just stupid.

'But what about your friends? I mean, you have hundreds. You even went through the whole pretence of a funeral, right? So why bother pretending when you should have been doing that in real life?'

I was mortified that he had seen my funeral show. It had seemed like the right thing to do at the time, but thinking that finding the exact right outfit and tweeting about it was somehow normal now seemed like the biggest crime. I really wish I had been able to give her a funeral. I started to cry.

'Please tell me if you are still covering up for that piece of scum who they arrested. I mean, that would make sense. We know what he did to you.'

I was horrified that Tom and possibly Rachel knew about my relationship with Stan and wondered how they found out. No wonder he was so disgusted with me, with what Stan had made me do. Just then the officers arrived back in and switched on the tape. The woman started the questioning again.

'Alice, I hope you are feeling better now. It was obviously a shock to you seeing those pictures. Can you clarify that your grandmother died with only you in the house and that it was you alone?'

'Yes, it was me.'

'OK, but can you confirm that you were visited in the home by a Mr Stan Crane? Are you able to tell us if this was before or after your grandmother had passed away?'

So, it wasn't just Tom who knew about Stan. They had obviously been doing some real digging.

'No, Granny was dead and in that situation before Stan came to the house. In fact, I invited him there because I had run out of money and was beginning to run out of food.'

Tom and the officers all looked disappointed.

'OK,' the Scarlett Detective said, 'let's go back to the beginning and see if we can find out exactly what went on.'

'OK, but can we do it without photos please?' I asked timidly.

'Why is that, because they make you feel guilty?' said the male cop. Tom glared at him.

And so, I told them in my own words how my granny was my world and the rest of my life was a fantasy. How I found her dead one day but didn't really believe it until she started to decompose.

I told them I was worried I would be taken away by someone official and so I dealt with the problem myself. Then, I told them how when I ran out of money, I had to reach out to my then-boyfriend to step in and free up some cash.

They listened intently and seemed to nod and ahh in the right places.

'But why did you not want to tell anyone official? I mean, it makes little sense. You seem like a clever girl, and surely you know when someone dies you have to go through the proper channels.' The Scarlet Detective showed a glimmer of sympathy underneath her perfect makeup.

'I guess in the beginning, I didn't really want to believe it was true. And then I wanted no one else to intrude. It had been just me and Gran for years. The last time social services got involved, it ended badly.'

The officer looked towards Tom for an explanation.

'Alice was taken out of her mother's care when she was a young child because of child protection issues. She spent time in the care system, before being placed with my parents.'

'Yes, and it was when I got taken away from my mum that *it* all started.'

'Can you elaborate on what you mean by that Alice?' she asked quickly.

I looked at the floor. I really didn't want to open this can of worms. I have never shared this with anyone, but I needed understanding right now.

'The horrible stuff, the touching and the kissing. Well, I guess you would call it abuse.'

'Who did that to you, Alice?'

'I don't even remember his name, just that he was in the second foster home I was placed in. I wasn't there for long. I mean, I wasn't anywhere for long.'

I hadn't let myself think about this for years, but sure enough, as soon as I opened the door, all the memories came flooding back. The smell of their washing powder. The incessant yapping of the dog they kept tied up in the yard. But most of all the heavy feel of him.

'He was meant to be my big brother, and at first, I thought he was being nice to me. I had never had another person to play with, so it was fun at first, but then he started touching me.'

'So, to clarify, you are making allegations that you were a victim of abuse while in a foster care placement, and that this made you wary of outside intervention, even as an adult?'

'I guess so, yes. I know it is not an excuse, and I can't really explain it.'

The male officer leant forward and put a hand on my arm. It was so rare for me to be touched that I flinched. Even Granny hadn't really touched me for years.

'I am really sorry to hear that, Alice, and we will look into this for you. Child abuse is never acceptable. It must have been a relief when your grandparents took you in,' he said with kindness.

I must have gone white at this thought, and Tom noticed.

'Alice, please tell me you were safe living with Granny and Grandad and that nothing else happened while you were there?'

But I couldn't. I looked over, and Tom knew. I wonder if it happened to him too. I thought I was always Granddad's special little girl, but I know now that this is rarely the case.

'It didn't start immediately. In fact, he waited until I was about nine before he turned his attention on me. '

'Who are you talking about, Alice? A member of your family?' The Scarlet Detective was clearly angry but no longer at me.

Tom broke in, knowing exactly who I was talking about. 'Why didn't you tell someone, get away?' Tom asked slowly, looking devastated.

'Actually, I tried. Do you remember the train crash?'

'Of course I do. I was so scared for you when that happened.'

The officers clearly looked confused, so Tom explained it to them.

'Do you remember the fatal train crash in 2008 near Poole?'

They nodded. It had, after all, been national, even international news. A train went through a red light at a crossing not only destroying a car that had been taking their newborn back from hospital but also killing five and leaving life-changing injuries for the others. I had been the only one in my carriage—the one that bore the brunt of the impact—to actually walk away. I had always known how unfair this was and that it should have been me that died that day rather than the innocent families who lay broken beside me.

I went on to explain this. 'What I told no one was that things had become so bad, I was running away. I had a crazy idea I would track Rachel down in Bournemouth. I must have only been about ten. I had only ever been on a train once before. But look what happened there. Me trying to do that ended up in people dying.'

'You had nothing to do with that train crash! It was a driver fault, they proved that,' Tom pleaded with me.

'Maybe, but I know that it was God's or whoever's way of trying to punish me. They just got the wrong people.'

Just then, someone popped in with a note. The tape recorder was switched off, and the male officer talked gently. It felt like I had gone from perpetrator to victim. I didn't know which was harder to deal with.

'Alice, it sounds like you have had a lot of trauma in your life. I am so sorry that you were abused. You know we need to investigate what has happened here, but I also want to make sure you get the support you so obviously need. I will arrange for one of our doctors to come in here and talk to you after we have finished this interview, and then I will arrange for you to come back in and report the crimes against you.'

He was being so nice that I burst into tears. It was probably the first man who had ever shown me kindness, apart from Uncle Tom. Somehow, I felt a bit lighter. I had always thought if I told anyone else my world would collapse—that nobody would believe me, or even worse, they'd blame me—but it was actually a relief to get it out in the open. Tom was holding my hand now. I was worried he would run a mile when he found out what had happened.

Even though I was in tears, I was so relieved that I would hopefully be out of here soon to see Rachel and maybe even start putting my life back together. All thoughts of a future were then smashed when the Scarlet Detective swept back into the room with a triumphant look, and I was switched back to being possible criminal again.

'It seems they have found other remains in the home that don't appear to be connected to this case; it's more of a historical crime. Alice, I think there may be a few things you are not telling us.'

Alice

I had never told her, and, of course, she never asked me—that wasn't the kind of family we were—but I knew that she knew. I think she knew that if she did probe me, then she would be forced to confront the truth, with no Jeremy Kyle around to sort us out.

She had almost caught him at it once. He was tucking me into bed, even though I was quite capable of putting myself to bed; in fact, I often begged to go myself. Often, I was allowed, but on Fridays, usually after Grandad had been at the pub, he would insist on putting me to bed after my Friday treat, which was usually a packet of Scampi Fries. They had been my favourite for a while but now even the smell turned my stomach. I managed to hide all the unopened packets in the bin each week. I didn't want to appear ungrateful.

One time, my fish and chips dinner was sitting heavy in my stomach, and I was feeling a bit sick knowing what was to come. I had told both him and Granny that I had a funny tummy hoping it might put him off, but he still made a big show of getting me dressed in front of the electric fire.

He had a routine. He would like to get me dressed in my clean pyjamas and carry me upstairs over his shoulder. He would make me say my prayers like a good girl, and then as soon as I was in bed, he would turn out the sidelight and tell me to pull down my pyjamas. I often wondered why he was so interested in them going on if all he was going to do was take them off again. Then he would climb in next to me and would touch me there and make me touch him there. It was always the smell that was the most powerful. It was a mixture of whisky and sweat that made me gag.

This whole thing would never last more than a few minutes. He would never say a word when it was going on—it was all just action —but as soon as he was done, he would cuddle me and call me his special girl. The rest of the time, he was a fairly cold, unapproachable man, and in some ways, although I knew that what he was doing was wrong, I somehow craved this affection. I knew if I gave him what he wanted then he would give me what I wanted.

That night, while he was doing this to me, I realised that I could magically leave my body when this happened. This meant although I was definitely in the room, it didn't feel like this was happening to me. Suddenly my gran walked in and turned on the big light. Both of us jumped up guiltily. It was all done under the covers, so she wouldn't have been able to see clearly what was going on.

She stood there for a few minutes, and then she spoke. 'Frank, leave Alice to sleep and come down; your cup of tea is getting cold.'

This was when I realised that quite often a cup of tea could cure anything.

Alice

Far from being over, this news meant that the interview was back on. Scarlet the superhero—or supervillain, I wasn't sure which right now—had obviously reapplied her lipstick. She looked more powerful than ever, and I knew I needed her on my side.

The nice officer switched the tape recorder back on, and he looked confused. Scarlet Detective didn't know whether to pity me or hate me right now.

'So, Ms Carmichael, it appears there is a theme arising. The theme being dead bodies turning up in the home you have now told us you have lived in all your life. Are you able to tell us any more about these remains or do we need to wait for some identification?'

I didn't have to lie this time. I actually didn't officially know about this body, but I knew—I had known for years. Just like Granny had known what he had done, I had known what she had done, and of course I had protected her. She had only done it because of me.

'I'm afraid I can't help you with that. I have told you everything about what happened with my granny, but I have no idea about this.'

'Do they have any idea how old the remains are?' Tom asked, switching back to lawyer mode. 'Can you tell me where they were found?'

'I'm afraid we can't tell you any more, and actually, because of the location of these remains and the fact that you, sir, were also a previous occupant of this house, it means that you may need to be questioned about this, alongside your sister. Rachel, is it?'

I couldn't bear the thought of Rachel and Tom being questioned over this, but I equally wanted no one to find out what Granny had done, or what I thought she had done and why, so I kept quiet.

The two officers left the room again, and Tom turned to me in horror. 'Alice, what the fuck has happened in that house? Is this going to turn out to be some kind of Fred West situation?'

I didn't actually know what he was talking about but assured him I knew nothing. 'I know it is hard to believe, but Granny died naturally. And, OK, I was stupid to try and hide this, but do you now know why I didn't want other people getting involved?'

'I know what you have told me, and you have to know that I am so sorry about what happened to you. I believe you fully, and I only wish I had known. You know I would have had you out of there and him in prison as soon as possible, right?'

He stopped to fiddle with his watch. I had noticed him doing this a lot during this interview. I wonder if it meant he was nervous.

'But now I am becoming concerned that the reason you wanted no one in the house was because you were hiding something else. You know you can tell me; whatever you tell me is confidential. Were there others like Stan? No one would blame you if you had done something. I mean, there was clear provocation.'

I was about to tell him my theory when the uniformed policeman who had put me in my cell earlier came in again. He was still kind and spoke to us nicely. They obviously hadn't told him what they thought I had done.

'They have decided to release you on bail for now while we investigate the situation further. We will need you to hand in your passport and report to us regularly, and we will need to continue to speak to you about this situation. I understand it has become more complicated in the last hour or so.'

He must know; he obviously just has a nice manner.

'I don't have a passport; in fact, I really have nothing now. I guess my phone and computers have been taken away as well, right?'

'Yes, they have, love, but as soon as we have taken what we need from them, you can have them back for your surfing or what-ever it is you youngsters do these days.'

Strangely, the idea of allowing social media back into my life was a scary one.

Tom looked at me. 'So I guess that whole story about being an air hostess and flying all over the place was a lie too?'

'Afraid so. Before today, I hadn't left the house for years.'

'It feels like you really are someone completely different to who I thought. But then again, nothing is what I thought it was. My entire world feels like it has been turned upside down.'

After Tom posted bail for me, we left the station and arrived at the hotel where Tom and Rachel were staying. He had obviously texted ahead as Rachel was waiting outside for us. I needed to get inside to the safety of a room somewhere. I was amazed that my heart hadn't stopped when I had walked out of the door, but my body was buzzing with adrenaline just being out in the world.

I was looking for signs of a war, and still nobody had told me anything. I guessed I would get the chance to ask more now. Rachel ran up to hug me, but I was so focussed on getting to safety, I couldn't really speak to her. I noticed everyone looking at us. I guess news travels fast when you have a mobile phone. I was close to collapse again as Tom got me in the lift.

'Let's get away from all these prying eyes.'

We went up to the fourth floor, and Tom used a card to unlock what was apparently my room. Rachel and I followed him in.

I had never been in a hotel room before, despite my social media pages being littered with views from hotel rooms across the globe. This wasn't a fancy one, but I still loved walking around the room, delighting at the sachets of coffee and the mini bot-tles of shampoo. The room didn't have a sofa or anything, so we all kind of stood around awkwardly.

'You must be starving; shall I order something up for you or would you prefer to go out and eat?' Rachel asked.

Tom looked like he was about to unveil the sad human I had become, but I didn't want my own mum to think of me a failure, so I quickly grabbed the room service menu. The silence was so deafening that Tom picked up the remote and put the telly on. It was on some news channel and the headlines screamed out to me.

'House of Horror!'

I was amazed to see that the channel was live from outside my home. It looked different on the TV—scruffy, unkempt, invaded. I could see the text on the page was providing updates on the 'situation', telling the audience that two bodies had been found and that a suspect had been released on police bail. I was relieved when Tom turned it over to some kind of programme about finding homes abroad.

He could obviously not handle the stress in here and made some excuse to go to his room. I felt relieved we all seemed to have our own rooms. After he left, the atmosphere was even more strained. After all, I hadn't been in the same room as Rachel for nearly twenty years.

'So, Tom tells me you are an air hostess. I would have loved to have done something like that, just taking off to different countries each week.' Rachel sounded like she was interviewing me for a job. I didn't want to disappoint her, but I was also sick of lying.

'Well, actually, no. This is something I would love to do, but I have been stuck at home looking after Gran for so long that all my plans were put on hold for a while. I guess I kind of embellished the truth here and there. I actually never even moved out.'

Rachel had probably seen my social media profiles since this had all happened and so must have known it wasn't just Tom I was lying to. I couldn't tell if she was disappointed in me.

'Uncle Tom says you have two little girls?' I acted dumb. I didn't want her to know I had been stalking her on Facebook and knew everything about her happy little life.

She came alive at this, in the same way Stan had come alive when he talked about his car. She got her phone out and showed me pictures of the girls, many of which I had seen before. I felt sad. I had been expecting more. I thought maybe we would instantly click and she would fall in love with me again, but she still seemed to be completely caught up with her youngest children.

We were interrupted by a knock as the room service arrived. I had ordered a burger and chips, something I had been dreaming of for several months. Now that it was in front of me, it had lost some of its allure and looked like a greasy pile.

'So what kind of music are you into then?' Rachel asked. This made me so angry. I was reunited with my mother, who had abandoned me as a child, according to my grandmother. We had met for the first time in all those years after I spent the night in a police cell, and she was still asking me the questions you reserve for a distant family friend.

'Listen, I think I am going to finish this and then have a sleep, if that's OK. I didn't get much sleep last night.'

She jumped up. 'Oh god, yes, of course. I'm so sorry. You must be exhausted, and this must all be overwhelming for you. Can I get you anything before I go? Shall I leave you with my number? Oh, no, you don't have your phone, do you? Well, you can always use the hotel phone to call either the reception or one of us. Mind you, my kids haven't got a clue how to use an actual phone!'

'I'm sure I will be fine.' I bristled at the mention of *her* kids, as though I was excluded from this label. I added silently that I had looked after myself for the last twenty years without her help.

'OK, I will take one of the cards and pop back in an hour or so to check that you are alright.'

I nodded, and she reached over as if to give me a kiss, but that felt way too strange at this time, so I turned my face and she got a mouthful of hair.

I let out a big sigh of relief when I was finally alone again. This was the moment I had been waiting for almost all of my life. I had dreamed that I would run into my mother's arms and be welcomed into her life, but it had all been such a letdown.

I put my untouched dinner onto the side table and switched back to the news again. They had moved on, not too far away, to the terror attack in Bournemouth. The local news outlets must think it was Christmas with all the top news happening in their county.

Apparently, someone had been arrested in Birmingham in connection with the killer. As the reporter talked through these latest developments, the image of a row of houses turned into one of a young man laughing into the camera. This was apparently him, the one who had shot all those people in the middle of the town. He looked so normal, so nice, the kind of boy I would have probably had a crush on.

He was clearly dead now the way people were talking, and I wonder if this was what he was thinking of when he recorded the carefree video image, messing round with his mates one day. The teenager in this film looked like a world away from the boy dressed in black who had a beard and was forever immortalised because he decided to cause carnage in the middle of a town centre full of shoppers.

The story moved again onto something about Brexit. Grey men in suits were talking about how we would divorce ourselves from our nearest neighbours. I watched for the full hour, but there was no mention of the war I had been so scared about, the war that had kept me petrified that my home was about to be bombed or that I would be captured by some strange foreigners with a grudge.

I slowly came to the realisation that maybe the war was also a figment of my imagination. No one else had talked about it, and now that I thought about it, I had only seen a couple of mentions on social media that made me build the story myself.

Of course, it wasn't just the fear of war that had kept me inside for so long. That was simply the latest in a long line of excuses my mind had offered up.

There was irony in the fact that, despite some of the worst parts of my life taking place in the home that I later found impossible to leave, it was the world outside my door that scared me. My body had now left the physical prison, the house I locked myself up in for so many years, but I was beginning to realise it wasn't going to be as easy for my head to break free.

Tom

Tom was in his room trying to answer some work emails when Rachel knocked on his door.

'She is having a sleep, so I wondered if you wanted to grab something to eat and drink downstairs.'

'Sure, I guess we need to keep doing normal things like that. Wait there, I will just nip to the loo.'

As Tom looked at himself in the mirror, he knew he looked terrible. Just a few days of crap food, no exercise and minimal sleep had aged him by ten years. In some ways, he longed to go back to his uncomplicated life in New York. Never again would he complain about having to go to dinner with boring people or staying late to finish a case. Getting away from all this emotional shit would be enough for him. He would have to keep his shrink on retainer with the amount of crap he would have to offload and process on his return.

Yet, there was another side of him that had never felt so alive. He had forgotten how infuriating yet almost wonderful it was like to be in a family. Not that he had ever had a chance to really live a normal family life. These people were growing on him.

They found a table in the corner of the hotel bar, and Tom went to order drinks, picking up a bottle of wine and some fizzy water without even asking what Rachel wanted. He was surprised that she went for the water first. He had no such restraint and poured himself a large glass.

'So, you haven't really told me what went on at the police station,' Rachel said. 'You mentioned on the phone they had found another set of remains. Jesus, what the hell happened in that house?'

Tom couldn't look at her. 'Alice is insistent that she has no idea about this new set of bones. She was very honest about Mum's body; she says Mum died of natural causes and she panicked so she moved the body down to the chest freezer.'

'Oh gosh, I remember that chest freezer, always full to the brim of specials from Iceland. I used to sneak down there to see if there was any ice cream hidden below the onion rings and oven chips.'

'I don't think now is the time to get all nostalgic, especially considering that this was where they found her rotten and putrid remains.'

Rachel went white, and Tom was worried she was going to be sick. He knew it was mean to spring that on her, but he was also sick of shouldering the burden alone. This was as much her mess as his, and she should have to deal with it too.

'My god, what did Alice do to her? And why?'

'I don't know exactly, but it seems like she didn't really know what to do when Mum died, and so when she started stinking out the house, Alice moved her down to the basement to store the body. That would have been fine apart from the fact that the house lost its power a couple of months ago so poor old mum started to rot. Oh, and Alice keeps mentioning some kind of war, which is what she blamed for the lack of electricity. I hate to say it, Rach, but she is pretty crazy. Some of the stuff she was coming out with was insane. I am really annoyed I didn't notice what was wrong before.'

'But why didn't she call the doctor or the police or something?'

'She claims she hasn't left the house for years. I mean, there was me, oh, and the rest of her social media world, thinking she was living the life of Riley, flying round the world and living in her own swanky flat when actually it was all just a fantasy.'

'The Alice that came out of the house was definitely not the Alice she portrayed online. I had no idea she was so big and awkward. She is almost like a child rather than a sophisticated young woman.'

Tom stared at her. 'I think Alice's BMI is the least of our concerns at the moment.'

'I don't mean that. I mean it was such a shock to see how different her real life was to the one we had been reading about.'

Tom softened. 'I know, and she even said in there that she literally had no one she felt she could tell. I always thought I was being a great uncle by liking her Facebook posts and sending her money, but really, I abandoned her as much as everyone else did.'

'That is so sad. My poor little girl. There must have been some terrible reason she was locked away all alone for so long.'

'Actually, there is more.' Tom stopped and took a big sip of his drink. 'Alice disclosed to us that, after she was taken into care, she was abused.'

'By one of the foster families?' Rachel looked horrified but also relieved.

'Yes, by one of the other children in care, but then the abuse continued when she was returned to Mum and Dad's house.'

'You mean *he* hurt her?'

'Yes, it looks that way, sadly.'

The change in Rachel was immediate. Gone was the weeping mother. She was furious and immediately grabbed the wine from the table.

'You mean that bitch, after knowing what that man did to me, allowed exactly the same thing to happen to her beloved granddaughter? What kind of a fucked-up woman allows that to happen?'

Rachel was standing by now, and Tom could see people looking at her.

'If she was alive right now, I would tear her apart myself. All those fucking social workers telling me they knew what was best for my baby, and actually all they did was put her in far more danger than she was when I looked after her. OK, I wasn't the world's best mother, but at least she was loved. And god forbid, if anyone would have tried to hurt her, I would have killed them.'

'Rach, I know you are upset, but you need to calm down. We don't want to draw any more attention to ourselves. We are already the freaks from the house of horror.'

'So, who the hell is the other body in that house then?'

'They have no idea. I guess things will be moved through pretty quickly.'

'Poor Alice, it must have been a shock to her to hear this news. She seemed so calm when she talked about Mum. I guess she had a few weeks to digest what happened. Having no one else judging her actions, she must have felt as though it was a plausible option.'

'They have told me we are all "people of interest" considering the fact we all lived in that house, but I have every faith in science. They should be able to identify both remains from dental records and date them. Hopefully they should be able to ascertain that Mum died from natural causes also. If you had seen Alice in that room, you would have seen that she is one messed-up girl. She needs a lot of help and support. There is no way they will charge her with anything, even if the forensics are unclear. We need to be there for her now. We need to ride out this storm and make sure that she is kept safe.'

Rachel

Rachel managed to stop at one glass, although she longed for oblivion. She knew she had to be the grown-up here, the mother to an adult who still bore all the hallmarks of a teenager. She knew she shouldn't be drinking at all with a child inside her, but she had no idea how to deal with what she was feeling. It was very hard to think about bringing another child into the world when the one she had was upstairs falling apart.

She was feeling completely wrung out and had passed through almost every stage of grief in the space of a few hours—well, at least denial, anger, and depression. The acceptance was still a long way off. She no longer knew what she was actually grieving for, her dead mother whose mangled body lay in a morgue or her poor daughter who she now knew had suffered more in her short lifetime than most people ever deal with.

Rachel hadn't allowed herself to get really drunk for years. She had lost so much of her life being completely out of it that her drinking had become a very controlled affair. It involved a carefully measured calculation of units combined with a longing that never went away. As a respectable mum of two (well, three), her past had been kept hidden away as she sipped her one or two glasses of wine.

She found it hilarious how so many of the mums groups on Facebook posted funny little memes about wine and gin fuelling motherhood. All those funny little chats about 'Wine O'Clock'. For all she knew, those mums were lying in a pool of their own vomit by ten o'clock every night, but it was all dressed up in such a fun way, almost a rite of motherhood. How many of them were like her, always craving, always controlling, never really enjoying a social occasion because all they could think about was the next top-up.

Both Tom and Rachel had been to check on Alice almost hourly, but she hadn't stirred.

Tom settled back down with some crisps and more water, but

neither could think about eating.

Rachel started to give him advice. 'I know I was telling you before that you should have kids, but I have actually changed my mind. You think all the hard stuff is babies, but actually when they are that small you can protect them. Not that I did a good job with Alice, I know, but knowing she went through all this and that my other girls are at a similar risk makes me want to give up.'

'Oh, come on, Rachel. I know this has been a horrific few days, but you have had a second chance. Your kids are great, and you are clearly a good mum—this time round.'

This set Rachel off and she started sobbing. 'That's the thing, I'm really not. How can I be when I have messed up with Alice so much and when I have a child growing inside of me right now, one that I really don't want.'

Tom was shocked into silence and looked at her as though she was a monster.

'See, I knew you would look like that, and for good reason. I am the evil bitch that Mum talked about all those years ago. I always thought I would be such a strong woman and that I would protect my kids no matter what, but I seem to be repeating history.'

'What do you mean?'

'I don't know for sure. This is something I have always wanted with Dave—I mean, we always talked about having our own—but now I am petrified that he is like the rest of them. How on earth can I even think about bringing another child into this fucked-up world?'

'Come on, Rachel, you are just being stupid now. Not every man is an abuser. Why are you even thinking this?'

'I don't know, it's just a feeling. Do you remember after Jimmy Saville when suddenly all these paedophiles were popping out of the woodwork? It seemed like everyone was at it. As you can imagine, this triggered a lot of feelings for me. I mean, it was all over the news every day, and I did a lot of reading about it. It was then I started noticing things, like how Dave would always want to give the kids a bath or how he called Jess his "special princess".'

'Have either of them ever told you anything or shown any signs?'

'Well, no, not really. I mean they really love Dave. He is really the only dad they have ever known, but they could be trying to protect him. I did with my dad for a while. I thought no one would believe me, and when I told, I was proved right. I have tried to approach the subject a couple of times, but I don't want to put words in their mouth either in case I'm not right.'

'Rach, you do have to trust your instinct, and I can understand why you would be so worried, but not everyone in the world is evil. And no matter what you think of yourself, I know you are a brilliant mum. We need to focus on Alice right now, and then we can think about what to do about this.'

By *this*, she guessed he meant the tiny blob of life currently being assaulted by red wine and cortisol inside her body.

She couldn't escape the feeling of hatred she had for herself. She should never have become involved with Alice again. She was bound to bring more pain into her life.

Alice

It was around two in the morning when I felt someone get into bed next to me. My immediate reaction was to freeze and panic. I had seen lots of men walking around the hotel earlier; was it one of them coming to get what all men seemed to want? I realised almost immediately that this wasn't a man; the body was lighter and softer. As a hand stroked my hair, I breathed in the scent of Rachel, my mum. Funny how the smell of her was so familiar. She was sobbing quietly as she cuddled up to me. I wondered if I needed to comfort her, but I found it was just so wonderful lying there with her. I didn't want to scare her off. I wanted to drink in every moment.

I had wanted to stay awake all night just to experience the closeness of my mum, but I must have fallen asleep at some stage as the next thing I knew the light was streaming in through the window. At first, I didn't understand where I was. I had woken up in the same room for most of my life, so being somewhere different was a new experience for me. I was alone in the bed. I wondered if Mum had gone for a shower or even if she had gone to fetch me some breakfast. I wandered over to the kettle and switched it on, loving the little wrapped up teabag I plunged into the cup. I was flicking through morning TV when I heard a knock at the door. Thinking it was Mum, I opened it with a huge smile, but it was Tom who stood there, looking very crumpled as though he hadn't slept at all. He looked angry and stressed, so I offered him a cup of tea.

'The police called. They have had developments which means they want you back at the station for some questions. Let's get downstairs to get some breakfast and then we can head straight there. I am not allowed to represent you anymore, so I have put a call into one of the local law firms. We don't want to end up with some work experience boy.'

'Have they said what the development was?'

'Yes, actually.' He couldn't look at me, so I knew it was bad.

'They have done some initial analysis on the bones they found, and they have concluded that they are that of a man in his sixties. Alice, you will really have to talk now. What the fuck happened?'

I don't know why I felt so calm. I guess because I knew; I had always known. 'My guess is that it is Grandad, and that Granny finally gave him what he deserved.'

Alice

He disappeared maybe a month after Granny had found us together. The official story, and one I heard her tell all her friends during loud phone calls, was that he had left her for some tart from the local betting shop and run off to Malaga.

On my eleventh birthday, Granny had gone all out, putting up balloons, making my favourite food, even inviting Tom and some neighbours over. This was before Tom had been banished, of course, before I had lost my only real lifeline to the outside world.

It had been a jolly party where Granny had knocked back a few glasses of sherry. She had been strange for a few weeks, and I had noticed her crying silently by herself when she thought I wasn't aware, but then at other times she was cheerful, almost too happy.

Tom didn't like coming to the house when Granddad was around, but I heard Granny reassure him that Grandad wasn't here and wasn't coming back. As she put on a display of joy and celebration for my birthday, he wasn't mentioned. Him being gone was added to the list of things never to be mentioned again in this house. It was locked away with the rest of the secrets.

It was only when the cake had been eaten and the neighbours were practically pushed out the door that Granny sat down, suddenly looking exhausted with the strain of trying to play the happy family.

She was clearly drunk by that stage. I had never seen her drink more than a glass or two at Christmas. Tom had made us all a pot of tea.

She had saved one last present for me. Tom had, of course, spoiled me as always, buying me some amazing trainers that would be wasted being worn around the house.

Her present to me was beautifully wrapped, and I wondered if she had asked one of the store ladies to do it. Granny wasn't the type for ribbon and bows.

I gasped as I opened in. It was the most beautiful jewellery box I had ever seen, one with a ballet dancer that moved around as you opened it. It was something I had wanted for years as a child.

'There you go, my darling. I wanted you to have something lovely to put in your room. I know it hasn't always been the happiest space for you, but I hope now every time you look at that you will think nice thoughts and any nightmares will be well gone.'

I now know that this was her way of trying to recapture my childhood. She was trying to bring back the innocence by ridding the evil in the house.

Alice

Tom stared at me. 'Why do you think that?'

I explained about the birthday and what I thought Granny was trying to tell me. 'Don't you think it's strange that he was never mentioned again, that he never turned up? He literally disappeared, and I know Granny always said he had made a new life in Spain, but there was never any proof of it. Then again, I guess none of us ever went looking.'

'I always thought that she supported him in whatever he did. I mean, she never intervened. He used to hit me, you know? I always knew he was an evil bastard, but it wasn't until what Rachel told me that I realised what he was capable of. I am so sorry.'

I realised he had mentioned Rachel's name.

'What do you mean, what Rachel said? How did she know what had happened to me?'

'I didn't mean to you. Oh, I think it should really be something she tells you herself. Listen to me. I will make sure we get justice for what happened to you, but we really need to tell the police everything, and this includes what your gran may have done. At the moment, we are going in there voluntarily, and if you tell them what you told me, then we can hopefully make this whole nightmare go away.'

Tom left me to have a shower and get dressed. He had left a bag of clothes on the bed from the local supermarket. They looked like they were designed for a teenager. My t-shirt had an amazing rainbow made of sequins that changed colour when I stroked it. I had seen similar ones on Instagram, and although it probably wasn't designed for an overweight twenty-two-year-old, I still loved it. I was worried I wouldn't fit into the jeans he had bought me, but to my surprise, I was able to get them up my legs. I couldn't do the button up, but luckily the t-shirt covered my fat. I guess I must have lost weight. Funnily enough,

I had never tried to lose weight before, despite being exposed to clean eating Instagram and perfect bodies. My way had always been to reach for the filter rather than the salad. It wasn't as if anyone ever saw me, and actually the fat had been almost like a protective layer for me—not to keep me warm, although it had definitely been a bonus, but the more unattractive I felt, the safer I felt.

After the food had run out and the power had gone in the house, I had begun to discover that food didn't just come from the freezer. I had kind of expected the army to drop off food parcels or something, but I guess that is because for most of my life I had just waited around for people to look after me. At that point, I was still sitting most days listening for sounds of life outside the door. I had heard signs of life a few times, but no one had come and knocked, which made me both pleased that I was safe from the enemy and sad that I was yet to be rescued. I had taken extra precautions during the first few days, so the windows were all locked and I had even managed to seal the letter box in case there was some kind of gas attack.

There had been a day when I had actual hunger pains, which was not something I had really experienced in my life. I remember seeing adverts on TV for starving children in Africa as I was growing up, and my gran was always telling me I should finish everything on my plate. Because I had never even really been hungry, I had no idea of what they were going through. As I had been wondering what to do about my impending starvation, I had suddenly remembered something that Uncle Tom had said the last time they had spoken, something about Gran stockpiling food. For years I had ignored it when Gran took a bag or two of shopping down the basement 'just in case', but now I realised that this could be my salvation.

At the time, I hadn't been down to the basement for quite some time because of the electricity situation, and the smell hit me as soon as I opened the basement door. There was a very small window in the room, and I had noticed an object on the shelf next to the useless light switch. A torch! I had grabbed it and was gratified to find that the beam it threw out was strong and bright. This didn't do anything for the smell, unfortunately. I had gone upstairs and found a jumper to tie around my face to block out some of the smell.

With the smell having at least a positive effect on my desire for food, I had poked around in the basement and was rewarded when I opened a big cupboard in the corner and found it stuffed full of food. I had grabbed a bag and filled it full of the first things in line before almost sprinting back up the stairs. When I got to the kitchen to examine my haul, I was disappointed to find that apart from a few tins of beans, I had things that I didn't know what to do with, like flour, egg powder and a couple of tins of vegetables. I knew that beggars couldn't be choosers, but this wasn't going to be able to feed me for long.

After that I was a regular visitor to the basement. I even got used to the dark and the smell until it became a normal part of my weekly shopping 'haul'. I had also made a discovery that improved the whole situation. Fire! I had discovered a little camping gas stove. It was new in a box, and I guessed that Gran had kept it there 'just in case'. It wasn't as though we were a family who ever went camping. It took me a few goes in the kitchen, but I finally had heat! After what seemed like weeks of eating cold food out of cans like a dog, a warm meal in a bowl was heaven. I even ate some of the tinned peas I had found, which by now tasted as good as a cream puffs. This little discovery filled me with joy and a feeling of hope that had been absent for a good few weeks.

I went to knock on Tom's door when I was clean and dressed. Even walking three doors down by myself felt surreal, and I had to stop and breathe slowly for a few minutes before I knocked. At least at this point we were still inside a building. I know I must still look a bit strange in my outfit, as my hair was long and ragged and my skin had an ugly pallor—I guess because of the lack of sunlight. I had actually found the world too bright, and being outdoors had burned my eyes, adding to the general discomfort that leaving my prison was causing me. Tom was looking a bit better. I think he had shaved, but he couldn't hide the sorrow and pity in his eyes.

'I have spoken to the police, and they are expecting us down there in about twenty minutes. Let's grab Rachel on the way and I will pick us up a couple of bacon baps to have on the drive.'

Although we had shared for most of the night, Rachel, well, Mum's room was across the corridor, and Tom rapped on it, joking that he was room service. We stood for a few seconds, listening for any signs of life, but it was clear there was no one in there.

'She must have snuck downstairs. I know Rachel is a sucker for a breakfast buffet. Let's go and catch her at it.'

The idea of walking into a packed breakfast room filled me with dread, so as soon as we were out of the lift and all the prying eyes were on us, I made an excuse and went and hid in the toilet. Tom was still alone when I got out, but the pity had been replaced with anger.

'I can't believe she has fucking done this again,' he shouted, kicking the wall.

I had no idea what he meant.

'Alice, I'm really sorry, but your mother has decided to abandon us again. It must have all gotten a bit much for her. I checked in at reception and they told me she checked out early this morning. I really hope she didn't get stopped in her car, as she must have been well over the limit. The receptionist asked me to give this to you.'

He handed me a folded piece of hotel paper. It had one word on it: *Sorry.*

I thought I was too hardened to pain to feel anything, but tears started flooding my eyes as Tom called a taxi and led me to it. I was crying so hard that I hardly noticed the flashbulbs and the people screaming my name as he pulled me from the hotel doors to the waiting taxi. The taxi driver looked horrified yet thrilled to be driving us. He looked like he was about to start a conversation, but Tom shut him down by barking out our destination, just in case he was in any doubt who we were.

Tom

Tom was relieved that the questioning this time round was not done under caution. He wasn't allowed in with Alice and was horrified to see her led into a windowless room like a lamb to the slaughter. At least he had managed to get a decent enough solicitor. The man was in his fifties and probably had kids Alice's age. Tom was a complete mess emotionally. The roller-coaster of emotions he had been feeling over the last few weeks had veered between anger, disgust and just plain sadness. Right now, it was the anger driving him, better than any caffeine. He could not believe that his sister had done this to him again. He really thought they had managed to bond over the previous few weeks. They were a completely fucked-up family, but at least in some way they were battling this together. This really wasn't his mess, but somehow, she had landed him in it again.

Tom was finishing his fourth cup of dishwater coffee when he was called through for questioning. Again, they were not questioning him under any caution, and he was actually looking forward to getting some facts across. He only hoped that Alice was being truthful. There had been far too much lying and deceit over the years, and he for one had every faith in the law. He had been offered a solicitor too but laughed this off as he sat down with the now-familiar DSI Kingsley. She had been joined by a male officer who was clearly in awe of his boss.

'So, Mr Carmichael, as we mentioned on the phone this morning, we have had some breakthroughs with both sets of remains that we found. We have identified the second set as an adult male and have had a bit of a guess at how long they have been lying around, which we believe to be about a decade, give or take a year or two. Now I know you and your family have been through the mill here, but we do have to ask: when did you move out of the home? For the tape, I mean the Carmichael family home, the scene of the investigation.'

That was an easy one. Like his sister, Tom had fled as soon as he could. When he got a space to study at university in Durham, he had jumped at the chance to escape and never return to live with his parents.

'I moved out around 1996 to go to university.'

'I'm guessing you returned home for holidays?'

'No, not really. As you have probably gathered from speaking to us, we didn't have the best upbringing, so I actually never went home unless it couldn't be avoided. It was the occasional quick trip down at Christmas—well, only for the first few years of course.'

'So, you were estranged from your parents then?' she asked without judgement.

'My dad, yes, definitely. I actually hated him for many reasons, but now I can add child abuser to that list. I guess my instincts were pretty spot on. I actually had a fairly good relationship with my mother until I disclosed my sexuality, and then in her mind, I was dead to her.'

Tom noticed the younger officer give him a look of understanding and he wondered if the man had dealt with a similar situation at home.

'OK, so I guess we can formally remove you from our people of interest then.'

This was of no great relief to Tom. He had always known he wasn't the suspect here.

DSI Kingsley looked at her colleague, giving him the silent nod to carry on the interview.

'Sir, we would love to have your help with this inquiry. I understand you were not present in family life when the incident occurred, but can you tell us, do you have any idea who the bones belong to and why he was found buried in the garden of the property?'

Tom had no hesitation in retelling the version of events he had earlier heard from Alice. He managed to keep his voice even and his delivery factual. 'Well, yes, as a family, we would like to offer you as much help as we can give. Following a conversation I had this morning, I have reason to believe that the remains are of my father. I have no idea what happened to him, but it could be concluded that my mother sought her own justice.'

'Are you saying that your mother killed her husband? Do you have any motive?' DCI Kingsley was back in there with this juicy morsel.

'I think it is quite clear, really, not that I would ever condone murder, but she clearly realised that her husband was a rapist and serial child abuser. But I guess we will never know for sure.'

'You said "serial child abuser". Do you know of other victims?'

Tom paused. It really wasn't his place to say, but if he was going to strengthen Alice's case, then another victim would be really useful.

'Yes, Alice's mother, Rachel.' Tom hesitated. He really didn't want to say this out loud. It was so horrific and unthinkable. 'We haven't been close for years, really. Well, that is an understatement. I really hated her for how she abandoned Alice. I always felt like I was left to pick up the pieces. Of course, now I know I did a pretty crap job at that!'

Tom felt close to tears. He tried to focus on the coffee cup in front of him.

'The truth is that Rachel told me recently that she had been abused by him, by our father, when she was a child.'

It was too much for Tom as tears started falling from his eyes, and he struggled to get the last few lines out through his tears. 'Rachel believes, well, *knows* that her daughter was actually a product of rape.'

He was broken. The confession had taken everything out of him. The horror he had not yet processed himself was now served up in front of two relative strangers. Someone handed him a tissue, and he allowed his whole body to sob, crying openly for the stolen childhoods and ruined lives at the hands of his father.

There were a few minutes of silence when Tom was given the chance to take a breather, but he just wanted it done. DCI Kingsley spoke gently, almost as though he was the victim here.

'Are you suggesting that he was also Alice's father?'

'Yes, I'm afraid so.'

'I am so sorry for all of you. What a horrible situation. It would be really useful to speak to Rachel to validate the story. Would it be OK to call her into the station? We can obviously set her up with some trauma counselling. This is still an active investigation, but we will do what we can in these circumstances to ensure that all questioning is done with care.'

Tom wanted to hug the officer. He had been so intent on hating everything about his country of birth, including the policing, but he seriously doubted if hardened New York cops would show so much empathy when it mattered. He tried to hide his frustration that Rachel had done a runner again.

'Rachel has had to travel back to London where she has a young family. I think we will all be heading back up there when the questioning has finished, so maybe one of your colleagues at the Met can speak to her? As you can imagine, this has all been quite traumatic for her—well, all of us.'

'Yes, of course, Tom.'

It was the first time she had called him that, and he thought they could have probably been friends in real life. Indeed, if he was sitting here as a lawyer rather than a witness, or victim, or whatever he was now, then they probably would have been. He went out for drinks with his friends on the force all the time back home. But this wasn't real life and he wasn't just retelling a story to fit procedure. He was living it.

When Tom saw Alice emerge a couple of hours later, she looked lighter and brighter, more like the child she should have been for all those years.

Kingsley took him to one side. 'Alice has been fully compliant with us. The post mortem on your mother has come back showing that she died from a heart attack. Of course, we could charge Alice with preventing lawful burial of a body, but I think given the circumstances it would be in no one's interest to take that to court. The complication is, of course, with the other body. However, given Alice's age at the alleged time of death, we have concluded that she is unlikely to have been complicit.

'Of course, if either of your parents were still alive, we would be arresting them immediately, and if Alice wants to, we can open an investigation into the abuse that she alleges took place in foster care, but if she is not keen, then we are happy to close the case.'

'OK, thanks. I think that will come as a huge relief for Alice and the rest of us.'

'I am no expert, but I would say that Alice is a deeply traumatised young woman who probably has at least one mental health diagnosis. I would recommend that you seek some proper help for her as soon as possible. The fact that she stayed locked up in that house for so long says a lot about her mental state.'

Tom nodded and shook her hand before he went to find Alice.

He was halfway down the corridor when Kingsley called out to him. 'Oh, and one last thing, Tom.'

He turned around, worried that yet another horror was going to be revealed.

'If you ever decide to return to our terribly boring little island to practice law, look me up. I really like your manner, and there are people I can introduce you to. Just tell them that Sophie Kingsley sent you.'

He smiled in thanks. He had never had her down as a Sophie. Somehow the name made her human for the first time.

When Tom reached Alice, he found that the nice solicitor was showing pictures on his phone of his daughter running round with the dog. This young girl was full of promise, probably back from university holidays with stories of nights out and unsuitable young men chasing her. What a contrast to Alice, who had only lived that life through her social media. He vowed right then to put things right.

Stan

Stan had never been so relieved to find out about one of his conquests. When he had been told that Alice was OK, well, alive at least, he could have kissed her, but he guessed that that was what had got him into all this trouble in the first place. Stan had his swagger back as he went into the interview room for what felt like the hundredth time, but this was short-lived. He was no longer facing a murder charge, but he would be likely spending just as long in prison.

The police delighted in telling him that he was going to be one of the first people charged under a new law around pornography that involved filming someone clearly under duress and without consent. Ironically, this was getting a lot of press attention already; he would be famous for his filmmaking after all. But Alice's footage was just the first bit of material he was going to be charged with, and he had been told he would be getting at least ten years for this.

They had brought in a woman to formally charge him, DCI something or other. Right old battle-axe, pushing fifty with ridiculous bright red hair. He was always open to more mature women, and he wondered if there was a good market for it. But this one was scary. Looked like she hadn't had a good shag for a long time. She was probably a bitter feminist, and she seemed to take great joy in charging him.

As well as the footage with Alice, which he was told was likely to be tried as rape, there were the separate charges for fraud and theft, and of course the number of other rapes on camera, many of whom turned about to be technically still children.

It wasn't fair; he knew that there was far nastier stuff going on out there in the name of entertainment. He was just a small-time crook with a nice car. He really felt like he was taking the flak for mankind, not just him. He would have been alright if it had been dealing or theft, as that would have pushed him high up the pecking order in there. It could have even improved his business model. But he knew the fate of men in prison who were suspected of hurting women or children. One of his mates had told him about the fate of his cellmate during his latest stint inside. It involved a blade and genitals.

He wasn't a rapist or a kiddy fiddler, but that is what would be on his sentence. For the first time in his life, he felt like he had lost. The worst thing was that the police had seized all his assets and were talking about compensating victims. So not only was he not able to give his mum the comfort she deserved, but he would also be poor when he finally came out of prison. That is, if he ever came out.

Alice

It is hard to believe how much my life has changed over the last year. At first, I was almost upset when Tom told me I wouldn't be going to prison. The big, bad world was a scary place, and I had strangely enjoyed the prospect of someone else locking me away, taking away my choices and decisions. But now I am here. I am beginning to learn how to live, and to my surprise, it isn't as bad as I thought it would be.

We managed to sell the house for a ridiculous sum. I was worried that nobody would want to go near it, but it seems that people are pretty sick, and it got all sorts of writeups in the press when we put it up for sale. I think it was sold to a developer who was going to knock it down and build a load of flats on the big plot. I hoped they didn't come across any more surprises as they dug up the foundations.

I am currently renting the kind of place that 'Online Alice' may have happily lived in. It was near the seafront, although not in Bournemouth, which had too many possible triggers and bad memories. Tom encouraged me to try out Kent, as he heard that Margate was similar to what Brighton had felt like all those years ago, which he said was the last time he had felt footloose and fancy-free. When this all happened, I would have been horrified at the idea of living alone with no one to look after me, but actually I have realised I can cope. I am stronger than I thought.

Tom had helped me move in and had actually decided he wanted to move back to boring old England for a while. I couldn't understand why he would give up his amazing life in New York, but it seems that, like all of us, he had been living a bit of a lie. He loved bacon sandwiches and shit British TV even more than he had Manhattan sushi and plays off-Broadway.

He even has a job for a local charity helping refugees who arrive on our shores running away from unbearable horrors. For us as a family, we didn't need to flee war or persecution, but we still had to flee our own demons.

Apparently, his job pays a fraction of what he used to get as a big corporate lawyer, but he seems happy. He says that this whole situation has made him re-evaluate his life and stop running away. He also has a new boyfriend, not that he calls him that, but I always tease him. Evan is young and very homely. He has a *real* job as a plumber. I love going round for dinner to the flat that Tom claims he doesn't live in (but spends most of his time at). There are always various friends and family members popping by, and they officially adopted us as one of them, offering up a different version of a family to what we have been used to.

I have been having a lot of therapy which Tom thankfully has been paying for after we were told of the waiting lists. At first, I was horrified when I heard the term 'mental health'. I had only ever come across these 'nutters', as Gran called them, on reality TV shows or Jeremy Kyle. Of course, there were a few social media campaigns that I had joined blindly without ever really knowing what I was supposed to be supporting. I am working with a wonderful team who have gently been picking apart what happened to me and then trying to build me back up again.

I have managed to talk properly for the first time about the train crash without ending up in the midst of a panic attack. We have talked through how the Bournemouth terror attack may have triggered some really horrific memories, even though I was never actually there. Seeing what was happening, secondary trauma was enough to make me feel as though I was in the middle of it.

It sounds ridiculous and it is certainly not something I can see being embraced as a psychological model, but I think the whole healing process actually started when I was alone in the house. For so long, I had allowed my brain to be busy, always stimulated with technology. Even when I was watching TV, I would be tweeting or snapchatting or surfing at the same time. It was only when I was forced to sit alone with myself and my feelings that it began to come back to me. So much of my life, I had closed off, forgotten about. Being without anything to distract me started something really strange. I began to think. At first, it scared me. I thought I was hearing voices or something, but I realised it was my imagination that had sat dormant for so long. When I started reading, I began to experience all these wonderful worlds in my head. The irony was that I had been living a fantasy life for so long, but not for me, for everyone else. Real fantasy worlds and daydreams are fantastic.

To think I would have been happy to spend the rest of my life locked away with no one around me seems so strange now. I still find it hard to go out, and most of the time, I need to have someone with me. It tends to be Tom or one of Evan's family. But I am also making my own friends. I deleted my dormant social media accounts, and I didn't even look. I'm sure they were full of people speculating about what happened to me, people who would never have wanted to actually meet me for a coffee but who loved to know everything about my life online.

We were eventually able to hold proper funerals for my grandparents, although they were both starkly different. Granny's was done publicly as a cremation, just as she had always wanted. She would have been pleased with the turnout, although I think it may have been bolstered tremendously with the press coverage. Today is the day we have decided to scatter her ashes.

My grandfather was also cremated, but as far as I know, it was only a formality. None of us actually attended, and there was no ceremony. The sad possibility is that knowing what I know now about abuse, it was highly likely that he was abused himself. No one is born a monster, and as much as I hate what both he and Stan did to me—and I am so glad they got punished, one above and one below the law—you probably don't have to look far into their history to see possible causes.

Just as I am boiling the kettle, the doorbell goes. Rachel is there, looking windswept with my new little half-brother, Alfie, in the pram. We still don't really know what we should do to greet each other, so I focus on Alfie instead.

'Sorry I am so late. The traffic was murder. Oh, I guess I shouldn't really say that anymore, should I?'

She looks awkward, so I try and laugh it off. 'At least you didn't say the traffic was crazy, then I would have been really offended! I was just making a cuppa. Do you want one here or shall we go straight out and grab a drink on the seafront?'

'Well, this one has been cooped up in my rustbucket for hours, so let's go and get some fresh air.'

As we walk, the conversation is a bit stilted, as it always is when we first get together. The last time she was down here, she brought her kids, my sisters Jess and Kylie, which was amazing. They had so many questions for me, and it was hard for them to get their heads around the idea that they were my sisters when I didn't live with them.

In a way, I think it was a nice way for my mum to get to know me as well, although until now, there really wasn't much to tell. When I was at home, I had no life, really, so trying to describe a life that wasn't really lived doesn't take long. During that visit, Rachel had spoken to me about her relationship with Dave. When she had gone home in the middle of the whole house-of-horror scandal, she had immediately moved his things out of the house, accusing him of all sorts. It was only when she agreed to some family counselling that she realised he hadn't been hurting the kids; in fact, it was quite the opposite. Unlike our father, Dave was a good man. Apparently, it is quite common for women who have been abused to never trust men in their lives.

As the fresh air is on our faces and the watery sun warms our bones, we both start to thaw out.

'So how is the therapy going? What do they do, shine lights into your eyes or something?' she asks, looking sceptical.

'Some do use a light, but mine uses her finger. I know it sounds really strange, but it does seem to be helping.'

And it's true, it is helping. I do still have bad days where I want to scream uncontrollably and throw plates at the floor. I still have dark nightmares that torture me during my sleep, and I still have panic attacks at the mere thought of leaving the house most days, but I guess if you dredge up a lot of crap, you are going to have to deal with it. It doesn't just go away. I am also now having OK days. Not jumping-round-the-room, happy-to-be-alive days, but days where I get through.

'How is yours going?' Tom had joked that we should be having double therapy sessions and claim a two-for-one offer. It is good that he hasn't lost his humour through all this, or it might just show that he is really tight!

'Well, I'm glad I am not having to look at someone's finger, but having to sit and talk to some stranger about all my innermost thoughts really isn't my idea of fun. In some ways, though, it is the only time of the week that I get to have an hour to myself, so I do enjoy that!'

'And how is the course going?' Rachel decided to go back to university to do an access course so she can get a degree, something I am really proud of and may even follow her in the future. She had a surprise windfall in Granny's will, and Dave found another job, so she is putting herself first for the first time in many years.

'I am surrounded by people young enough to be my children. I think most of them are your age! But it is really good to be using my brain again. My brother had better watch out or he will no longer be the only intelligent one in the family! How is all your stuff going?'

All my stuff is me learning to have a life again. I am doing some voluntary work for a small, local charity. I'm running their social media channels, of all things. Tom was worried when I first started doing this that I would get sucked in again or trolled, but I am keeping it strictly business.

'I am actually really enjoying it. It is really amazing to hear stories from people who work for the charity or have been helped. It gives me a bit of a sense of purpose. I hope one day I will actually be able to work somewhere like there.'

'Give yourself a break; you have your whole life ahead of you to worry about working for a living. For now, you just focus on yourself.'

I notice she is wearing a little pin, and I admire it.

'It is to mark a year. You know, I didn't do all that AA stuff— I tried, and it wasn't for me—but I found a really great group on Facebook, of all places. Apparently being sober is now quite fashionable!'

At first, I don't know what she is talking about, but then I realise: the day she gave up booze for the second time was also the day after I emerged from the house. Maybe I need to give myself a new birthday—the day I started my life again.

Tom arrives with Evan twenty minutes later. Much to Tom's annoyance, Evan and Mum get on like a house on fire, and he sweeps her up in a hug before turning to Alfie.

'Oh gosh, every time I see this little bugger, it is as though my sperm swims up and talks to me, "Please make one of these Evan, please . . .".'

I see him glance over at Tom fondly, and I do really hope that they decide to start a family somehow. Given how our family has been created, there would be no judgement, whichever route they decide to go down.

Tom changes the subject, and they start talking about Rachel's upcoming holiday. It is her first in years thanks to the little windfall from the sale of Gran's house. I think about sharing the news I read online this morning, but I don't want to ruin the mood.

The story, which would have been easily missed, was about a man who was found with life-threatening injuries in a prison.

He was identified as Stan Crane. There were no witnesses, but the attack bore all the hallmarks of a vigilante gang who targeted known child abusers.

The news doesn't make me happy as such. It took me a long time to put Stan in the same category as my other abusers. After all, he wasn't much older than me, and I invited him into my home. He would probably even say I encouraged the sex. But I see now that he was an attacker just like my grandfather or my foster brother. In a way, Stan being attacked is a sense of justice, I guess. Not just for me but for the dozens of other girls he abused on camera, many who were young, lost and flattered by the attention, and also for the thousands of girls who live with the horror of abuse every day.

We walk along the seafront just behind the gallery. This has become one of my new hobbies, wandering round the Turner and taking part in workshops there. I have even been looking into doing some volunteering here. It turns out I quite like being creative.

I find the right spot, looking out to sea at my favourite piece of art: the cast-iron man looking out to sea. I don't know the tides yet, so it is always a nice surprise not knowing if I will see him, or at least how much of him I will see. He reminds me a bit of myself when I was in the house, hiding in plain sight and yet immersed.

'This is the spot,' I declare to our gang.

Tom smiles. 'You know how much Mum would have hated that statue. Bloody modern art or whatever crap they are throwing money at this week. Remember the outrage of the pickled shark?'

Rachel laughs and joins in. 'Remember how she always said she was going to draw a few dots on a page and try and flog it for a million pounds? That along with all the treasures she was going to sell from the attic!'

The mood around Granny has softened, and it is really good to hear them both talking about her with some fond memories. For most families, having someone commit murder would drive an even bigger wedge between them, but for us and what happened to us, it has elevated her to a woman who finally took charge.

She was also a woman who showed some need for forgiveness. Rachel was right, there was nothing of value in the loft, but I did find my beloved jewellery box, the one with the twirling ballerina that Granny had given me on my birthday.

I have no idea what it was doing tucked away up there, and I can only presume it was moved out when One Direction moved in. It was only when I rediscovered it that I realised it had another layer to it, a hidden one. Tucked into this space was a short and badly written note from Granny.

I waited until this moment to read it. I was worried that it might incriminate her or, even worse, that it was just a shopping list. As I get the surprisingly heavy urn with the ashes out from Alfie's pushchair, I hand Rachel the note. After we scoff at her terrible writing, Rachel reads it out loud.

Dear Rachel, Tom and Alice,

I know this is too little too late, but I have lived with regrets for most of my life, and I guess I may never get the chance to put them right.

I am a stupid, weak woman, blinded by some kind of loyalty towards my husband when I realise now that he was actually a total pig. He was always keen with his fists, but I just thought that's what men did. My old man was the same.

Rachel, I didn't believe what he did to you because I didn't want to believe it. I was so disgusted, and it was easier to write you off as a naughty teenager.

It was only when I realised that he was fiddling with Alice that I knew you had been telling the truth. I could always see him in Alice, the family resemblance doubled by his part in her creation, I guess.

I got rid of him in the end, and I wish I had been a brave enough person to tell you I was sorry, but I was too embarrassed.

Alice, my baby, I have always loved you as though you were my own. I always lived my life trying to keep you safe and protected as I should have in the first place.

I know I am a coward by writing this, hoping I will be long gone by the time it is read, which is why I am not sending this. Instead, I am hiding it away where it may never be discovered.

I hope you both have long, happy lives. You will have probably all been surprised to see that I threw a few quid your way in the will. Enjoy it. Just don't go spending it on crack pipes or rent boys or whatever it is you two do these days.

Tom, finding out you were a poofter was one of the hardest moments of my life. But I have missed you, my little boy. I was so scared that your dad might have caused this by interfering with you too, and I couldn't deal with that on top of everything.

Once I had driven you both away, it was so much harder to even think about welcoming you back, and so I took the easy option.

I don't want or expect forgiveness. I will be facing my judgement up or even down there by God, but I wanted to try and explain why I did what I did.

Love Mum/Granny. x

I look across at Rachel and Tom. Both have tears in their eyes. This does not in any way excuse how she treated either of them, but I hope it makes both of them realise that they were loved in a strange way by their mum, and that none of this was their fault.

No words are needed after that, so I take the urn and tip it out into the sea to be swept away and become a part of the big world. Some of it blows back towards us, and Tom makes a face.

'Urghh, she is trying to have the last word even from beyond the grave,' he says, trying to spit out the crunchy dust that has landed in his face.

After the ashes are spread, we decide to order a late lunch. Tom orders a bottle of wine, and I am proud to see Mum stick to her water. I ask for a cider. I have no worries about following that particular path as the taste of most booze makes me wince, but I do like feeling like the grown-up that I am with something fizzy and sweet in front of me. As I look around the table, Tom is playing with Alfie. He is again the devoted uncle he was with me, and he is so pleased there is another boy in the family to even things out. Evan and Mum are talking about some reality show they are both hooked on, and I am just enjoying sitting there taking it all in. I reach for my phone to take a picture of the scene, but then I realise I don't need to. This is now my life, and I am living it.

AFTERWORD

I first started to write this book twelve years ago. It is some-thing I have abandoned and come back to many times. When I first started writing social media was still in its infancy, and I was fascinated by the effects this may have on lives and self-image. Clearly, many other platforms have become popular, and it was just a mild FaceBook obsession, but Alice had to take on Instagram and Twitter in the last couple of years. Many have noted that Alice is somewhat childlike and this was inten-tional. Her fear of leaving the house and over-reliance on grand-mother and social media has left her unable to do many things adults rely on to function in society.

 I watch my friend's daughters' hitting puberty and becoming more addicted to smartphones. I worry we are raising a gen-eration who seek constant reassurance and who fail to form knowledge and personal opinions as well as a group who may find it unusual to socialise in real life.

However, as I sit and write this in the middle of the Covid-19 crisis I can also see the freedom social media and the internet have offered us. My child who would usually be in school has a world of learning at her fingertips, friends available to play with via a screen and I have managed to co-ordinate a huge response to the crisis in my area via Facebook and Whatsapp. I have also managed to 'meet' an incredible group of lockdown friends. All local who share my interests and passions but who I may have never encountered if it were not for social media.

We had a power cut just the other day and I momentarily felt a little like my character. It was late at night and as my wifi was also down I had no access to the stream of news I usually rely on to update me on what is happening. My world was literally plunged into darkness and in this time of heightened anxiety, I was a little worried that something had gone seriously wrong. I sat, alone in the dark and didn't know what to do with myself before I eventually gave in and went to bed!

I have realised that my writing always turns dark at some point and in this book we have abuse, death, addiction and mental health problems. However, I wanted to end on a positive note. Issues like those Alice has faced are far too common and her recovery would take years, however, when the truth has been revealed and there is a family reunion of sorts, there is a way back. I hope you have enjoyed reading this as much as I have enjoyed writing it.

Please stay in touch by taking a look at my website and signing up to my mailing list.

jenniregan.co.uk

ACKNOWLEDGEMENT

I would like to thank my late father for my love of writing. He was a tabloid journalist who also wrote books about royalty and celebrities.

We were both very different journalists. He spent time in India with the Beatles and broke the first scandal about Charles and Diana before being sued by John Major. I used to write news about business and finance.

However, he instilled in me a love of storytelling. He could make even the most dull everyday experience into a gripping drama. He would rarely make things up entirely but was a master of embellishment.

In his twilight years he had a gathering most days in a Wetherspoons in Camden which he would call 'The Kindergarden.' A group of local characters and Fleet Street survivers would sit around and listen to him talk. I am pretty sure the same stories were wheeled out every day but he still had a captive audience. Cheers Dad.

ABOUT THE AUTHOR

Jenni Regan

 Jenni spent many years working as a journalist at the BBC before turning her hand to fiction and charity work. She lives in London with her daughter Stella, husband Joe and a house full of animals.

PRAISE FOR AUTHOR

I'm not going to go into too much detail so as not to spoil it but he twists are superb. You question your feelings about some of the characters and then bam! You're realising they're questioning themselves too. An emotional, sometimes dark, but ultimately hopeful book

- AMAZON CUSTOMER

This was one of those books I simply couldn't put down. The plot, which is set during the financial crisis of 2007-8, has so many nuances, from personal identity, self-worth, addiction and, ultimately, hope. This may be a novel about women, but is by no means 'chick-lit'. Jenni's characterisation has relevance to both men and women alike, covering the twists, turns, insecurities and dreams that many of us face, especially as we get to the 'I'm really am meant to be a grown up' part of life. Highly recommended.

- AMAZON CUSTOMER

As someone who reads approximately 2/3 books a week, and all of this genre, I consider myself a 'minor expert!' in the field. I LOVED this book and did not see the twist coming. Interesting and real characters with enough questions about whether they were 'goodies' or 'baddies' to keep my interest all the way through. Underneath all the tight and accurate 'thriller-ish' narrative are also some serious issues that will resonate with many. These were honest and realistic and added another layer to the novel. This author deserves massive success - this is a bloody great, un-putdownable novel that contributed to me nearly missing a work deadline. Loved the London setting; all true and accurate..... I NEED the next one

- AMAZON CUSTOMER

I love this genre and so was eager to read The Girl who just Wanted to Have Fun. I found that the author as the ability to engross you in the story so that it makes you not want to put the book down. The plot twists and turns at every level and at a nice pace to keep you entertained. I liked how the characters gradually grew. All of them having real depth and are presented really well. I liked how the chapters were divided by each character so you were only concentrating on one particularly person at any one time. I certainly look forward to more books by this author. All in all, highly recommended and certainly worth a read.

- AMAZON CUSTOMER

Omg this book is hard to put down. Have not read a good thriller like this for sometime. After the first few pages of the first chapter you realise you will not be able to put this book down. Some delicious twists and layers of psychological distress await you in this book. Love the three women characters and their flaws come to life. Great setting and the end was classic! Fab! Go buy and lock yourself away

- AMAZON CUSTOMER

BOOKS BY THIS AUTHOR

The Girl Who Just Wanted To Have Fun

Three stories. Three women. One life in ruins.
Watch out for the unexpected twist.
Liz is a career woman who is desperately trying to break through the glass ceiling in the world of finance, Betsy is the motherly figure with more than enough on her plate, while Ellie is a wild party girl, hooked on having a good time. As the lives of the three become increasingly interwoven, the sudden financial crisis creates a different set of problems for each one, as they battle to maintain their individual lifestyles. And as it deepens they find that the pressure of life becomes almost unbearable, as Liz loses her job, Betsy's mother dies and Ellie is assaulted while out one night. As lives begin to unravel, Liz suffers a crisis as her increasingly bizarre behaviour spirals out of control and she suddenly finds herself shunned by the people she knows. Rescued by friends, life begins to look a little brighter and there is yet one last surprise for her. The question is, will Liz be able to regain control, or is it already too late for her?

You can find out more and be first in line for news and freebies by signing up to my book club www.jenniregan.com

>>> Dark and Gripping
Set against the run-up to the global financial meltdown of 2008-2009, this is the story of another meltdown, much more personal and, in some ways, far more destructive

>>> I LOVED this book and did not see the twist coming
Underneath all the tight and accurate 'thriller-ish' narrative are also some serious issues that will resonate with many. These were honest and realistic and added another layer to the novel.

>>> Sheer Brilliance
What a rollicking good read! Gripped from the first page - the characters of the three women unravelled from the outset leaving the reader wanting more and more. Wonderful descriptions of London which made me feel as if I was there

>>> Surprised me...
I found that the author as the ability to engross you in the story so that it makes you not want to put the book down. The plot twists and turns at every level and at a nice pace to keep you entertained.

>>> This book, I would literally MAKE TIME for
A bit like 'Girl on the Train' which I also got sucked into - but better. I avoided thrillers, etc. for ages, probably due to a snobbish hangover from studying English Literature. But this book is proper literature - and exciting, well-written literature at that. It's also so much more than a thriller, but an interesting portrayal of three-women. Actual three-dimensional, you'd-meet-them-in-your-life women. I don't often write reviews - had to for this book. Read it. Now.

Printed in Great Britain
by Amazon